The Irish Convict

A Jayne Sinclair Genealogical Mystery

M. J. Lee

ABOUT M. J. LEE

Martin Lee is the author of contemporary and historical crime novels. *The Irish Convict* is the tenth book featuring genealogical investigator, Jayne Sinclair.

The Jayne Sinclair Series

The Irish Inheritance

The Somme Legacy

The American Candidate

The Vanished Child

The Lost Christmas

The Sinclair Betrayal

The Merchant's Daughter

The Christmas Carol

The Missing Father

The Inspector Danilov Series

Death in Shanghai

City of Shadows

The Murder Game

The Killing Time

The Inspector Thomas Ridpath thrillers

Where the Truth Lies

Where the Dead Fall

Where the Silence Calls

Where the Innocent Die

When the Past Kills

When the Evil Waits

When the Guilty Cry

When the Night Ends

What the Shadows Hide

Other Fiction

Samuel Pepys and the Stolen Diary

This book is a work of fiction. Names, characters, organisations, places and events are either a product of the author's imagination or used fictitiously.

Any resemblance to actual persons, living or dead, events or locales is entirely coincidental.

Copyright © M J Lee 2023

Look for more great books at writermjlee.com

In the end, we'll all become stories.

Margaret Atwood

CHAPTER ONE

October 07, 1836
Kilkenny Assizes, Ireland

The smoke hung over the crowded courtroom like a shroud. The bailiff banged his gavel forcefully on the desk in front of him, making an even deeper indentation in the false oak.

'The court will come to order. Order. Order. ORDER,' he shouted, producing little effect on the crowd gathered to see the petty sessions.

As usual, the gentry were in the best seats in front of the witness stand, to better see the anguish of the prisoners. The gentlemen of the press were arrayed to the left of the judge, to catch the words of his sentencing and ensure his *bon mots* were preserved for posterity. The prosecuting and defence barristers were sitting nearby, directly beneath his podium. His Honour was famous for being extremely short-sighted, once sentencing one of the court sergeants to be hanged instead of the prisoner.

The rest of the hoi-polloi were scattered around the court, eating, smoking and drinking, waiting for the afternoon's entertainment to begin.

8

His Honour, Mr Justice McLaglen took a long gulp of claret from the glass in front of him, indicating to his attendant to fill it once again. He belched loudly and then drawled in a bored, distracted voice, 'Bring in the next prisoner.'

The bailiff shouted once more. 'Order in the court. Bring in the next prisoner.'

The hubble and bubble of the court died down for a few seconds as the crowd examined the latest miscreant to appear in the witness box, her arm held firmly by the sergeant-at-arms.

The bailiff read from a charge sheet held up before him. 'Annie Kelly, you are charged with stealing three baskets of apples, the property of Lord Ashbrook. How do you plead?'

The defendant tried to stand taller in the dock but failed. Her short size meant she could only just see over the wooden rail in front of her.

'I plead not guilty, your honour,' she whispered.

'What? What did the woman say?' His Honour asked the question directly of the bailiff.

'She said she pleads not guilty, your honour.'

Mr Justice McLaglen's eyes flared red. 'Not guilty? Does she not realise she has been charged by the constabulary for this heinous act?'

'I think she does, your honour.'

'And she still wastes the court's time by pleading not guilty?'

'She does, your honour.'

With a loud harrumph, the judge took a long swallow of claret before saying, 'Bring in the first witness.'

The bailiff repeated the words and a small, mouse-like man was led sheepishly to the witness box.

The prosecuting barrister adjusted his wig as the judge finished his second glass of claret and indicated that the glass be filled up once more.

'Is your name Michael O'Flaherty?'

'It is, your honour,' the man whispered, all the time looking down at his old-fashioned hat held in his dirt-rimmed fingers. It was a tricorn, a hat that had fallen out of favour well before the king's reign and was now worn by only the very worst of Irishmen.

The judge cupped his ear. 'What? What did he say?'

'He agreed that his name was Michael O'Flaherty, your honour,' said the bailiff.

'Tell him to speak up. I will not have silence in my court.'

The prosecuting barrister asked another question. 'And are you the owner of the premises on 7 George Street in the town of Durrow in Queen's County?'

'No, sir.'

The prosecutor frowned.

'I'm the tenant of that place, not the owner. The owner is Lord Ashbrook, I pay him rent every half-yearn May and November.

The prosecutor's eyes rose as he looked to the ornate ceiling of the court and sighed loudly. 'Do you know the woman who is in the witness stand?'

'Of course, she is the daughter of the healer, Liam Kelly.'

Annie glanced at her father and mother, sitting amongst the rest of the crowd in the gallery. Neither of them looked at her.

'She's my neighbour and often helps her father in the making of his balms, elixirs and lotions. Very good they are too, my mother swears by them. Despite being so young and a woman, she can write. Letters, poems, anything she puts her mind to.'

The man said this almost in awe at the prodigious ability to put pen to paper.

'On September twenty-third in the sixth year of His Majesty's reign, did you see the woman at present standing in the dock in her garden?'

'I did, your honour.'

'And what was she doing?'

'She was carrying the baskets of apples to her outhouse, your honour.'

'And did you recognise these apples?'

'I did.'

The prosecutor sighed, asking the next question slowly. 'Tell me, how did you recognise them?'

'Very easily, your honour.'

'But how, man? Tell the court how,' the prosecutor snapped.

The man fiddled with his hat. 'Well, they were round and green with just a blush of red. They were definitely apples, your honour.'

The prosecutor glared at the witness. 'I know what an apple looks like. Who did they belong to?'

'They were Lord Ashbrook's.'

'And how did you know this?'

'They had his mark on the baskets. His orchard man, Mr Mungovan, always marks his baskets as he fills them with the crop of the year.'

'This mark was what?'

'A blue circle, your honour. Everybody knows Lord Ashbrook's mark.'

'Thank you, Mr O'Flaherty.' The prosecutor sat down.

'Next witness,' said the judge.

The bailiff leant in and whispered in his ear, 'There is no legal representation for the defence, your honour, they haven't the money.'

'Good, it will save time and all that bleating from barristers.'

'But she must be allowed to cross-examine this witness.'

'Must she? I suppose she must. Miss Kelly, do you have any questions for this witness?'

Annie's head came up for the first time. 'I have just a few questions, your honour. Mr O'Flaherty, did you fall out with my father over the supply of balms for your mother's consumption?'

'Falling out is a strong term, miss. Your father refused to supply my mother with the medicines she needed. He said she was past help and the only person she should look to was the Good Lord.'

'So you had an argument with him?'

'Young lady,' the judge interrupted, 'whether or not your father and this man argued has no relevance to the charge of theft of three baskets of apples. Please keep your questions relevant.'

Annie looked down as she was admonished by the judge.

'Do you understand?' he added.

She nodded.

'Have you any more questions?'

'Just the one, your honour. Did the witness see me steal Lord Ashbrook's apples?'

'I saw them in your garden and you were hiding them,' O'Flaherty said.

'I was not. I was putting them in an outdoor shed to keep them safe. It was raining heavily that day and I didn't want them to rot.'

'The jury will ignore that last remark from the prisoner as it was not a question to the witness. Next.'

Mr O'Flaherty shuffled out of the witness box, glanced up once at Annie's father in the gallery and smiled.

A police sergeant took his place, swearing on the bible to tell the truth and nothing but the truth.

The prosecutor stood up, adjusting his wig once more. 'You are Sergeant Miles of the Royal Irish Constabulary.'

'I have that honour, sir.'

'Can you tell us what happened on the afternoon of September twenty-third?'

'I was called by Mr O'Flaherty to go to the house of the defendant's father.'

'Liam Kelly?'

'That is correct.'

'And how did you know where this house could be found?'

'Everybody knows Mr Kelly's house. It's next to the schoolroom. He's well known in the area, proper trouble-maker he is, teaching the children about Ireland and the Irish language and Brehon Law.'

'Not the law of our most gracious sovereign, the King?' asked the judge.

'No, your honour. He says the old laws of Ireland were better and fairer.'

'Does he? And is he one of the Whiteboys?'

'I am not,' shouted Liam Kelly from the gallery. 'I am a healer, nothing more, nothing less.'

The bailiff rapped his gavel on the wooden desk. 'Silence in the court.'

The judge stared up at Annie's father. 'One more outburst like that and I will have you arrested and thrown into gaol for contempt of this court. Please continue giving evidence, Sergeant Miles.'

'Like I said, on receipt of this intelligence from Mr O'Flaherty, I proceeded immediately to the Kelly house, where I found three baskets of apples hidden in an outhouse.'

'And who did these apples belong to?'

'They had the mark of Lord Ashbrook on them.'

'So you arrested this young woman for theft. Why did you not arrest the owner of the house, Liam Kelly?'

'Because he was not there, sir, the rest of the family had gone to the fair in Abbeyleix. This woman was the only person in the house.'

'So she was the only person who could have stolen the apples?'

'That is correct, sir. On further investigation, I discovered that Mr Mungovan had left the apples in the baskets for collection on the road outside his cottage.'

'What time did he leave them out?'

'At seven o'clock in the morning, sir.'

'And does Miss Kelly live close to this man's cottage?'

'She does, your honour, less than one hundred yards away.'

'How did she move the apples?'

'She used a donkey and cart, sir.'

'Mr Mungovan didn't stop her?'

'He was at the fair in Abbeyleix too, sir. In fact, he gave Liam Kelly, his wife and their other children a lift to the fair.'

A buzz of excitement ran through the courtroom, which was swiftly stopped by the bailiff banging his gavel.

'So the defendant knew that Mr Mungovan wasn't at home?'

The policeman glanced at Annie standing in the dock. 'She did, sir.'

The prosecutor sat down, smiling, confident he had proven his case.

Annie asked the next question.

'Did I not explain to you, Sergeant Miles, that nobody had collected the apples by noon so I took them to my house for safekeeping? The rain had come in the afternoon and they would rot if I didn't.'

'You did.'

'But you did not believe me?'

'I did not.'

'Why?'

The man looked extremely flustered, his lips flapping open and closed without making a sound.

'It was because the woman had made no attempt to inform Lord Ashcroft's agent or Mr Mungovan that the apples were with her. Isn't that true, sergeant?' said the judge helpfully.

'It is, your honour. Plus, I found she had already taken some apples and was cooking them on her stove when I went into the house.'

'That is not true, I already had those apples. I was cooking them with mint and thyme to make a stew to feed young children. It is one of my father's herbal recipes. They weren't the apples belonging to Lord Ashbrook.'

The judge banged the table in front of him. 'I have heard enough. Thank you, Sergeant Miles.'

'Am I not allowed to argue the case for my defence?' asked Annie.

'Not in my court, no. You may question the witness but this is a Court of Law, not a debating chamber.'

Annie stood there for a few moments before turning to the witness. 'Have you seen me before, Sergeant Miles?'

'I have.'

'On what occasion?'

'At the Easter celebrations.'

'And did I not turn down your advances on that day? Advances that were as unwelcome to me as they were unbecoming of you.'

The judge banged his gavel. 'You will not impugn the character of this witness, Miss Kelly. You are excused, Sergeant Miles.'

'But I have not finished cross-examining him.'

'But I have finished listening to you, Miss Kelly. Prosecutor, sum up and make it brief. I have five more cases to get through today and this one has taken far too much time already.'

The prosecutor stood up. 'I will be very brief, m'lud. You have heard the witnesses who said they saw the defendant, Miss Kelly, hiding the baskets of apples belonging to Lord Ashbrook with intent to keep them. She is guilty of theft.'

The man sat down again, adjusting his wig as he did.

'Very brief, Mr Boone, and very convincing. Miss Kelly, it's now your turn but let us not hear any of your Irish speechifying, I am late for my lunch.'

'I am not guilty of theft. I took the apples to keep them safe, otherwise they would have rotted in the rain. I was merely looking after them until Mr Mungovan returned. I had no intention of stealing them.'

'But that's what you did, Miss Kelly, when you placed them out of sight in your outhouse. And you convicted yourself out of your own mouth when you used the word "took".'

'It was just to keep them safe, your honour, until Mr Mungovan returned.'

The bailiff's gavel banged loudly.

'Enough, enough, Miss Kelly,' said the judge. 'You have gone on too long. Has nobody ever told you Irish that brevity is the soul of any argument? Anyway, I am ready to give my judgement.'

'But I have not finished speaking in my defence.'

'You have, Miss Kelly. Gentlemen of the jury, have you reached your verdict?'

The jury talked amongst themselves for twenty seconds. The foreman stood up, announcing, 'We have, your honour.'

'And what is that verdict?'

'Guilty as charged, your honour.'

A buzz of excitement ran through the court. In the gallery, Annie's mother was weeping openly and loudly.

The bailiff banged his gavel for the last time and continued until the court quietened down again.

'Annie Kelly, you have been found guilty of the charge. However, thanks to the swift action of the authorities, the apples were returned to their rightful owner, Lord Ashbrook. Given these extenuating circumstances, I am prepared to be lenient this time.'

19

Annie Kelly held her breath, hoping for a light sentence.

'The sentence is transportation for seven years to the colony of Australia. As for your family and particularly your father, he should not be in charge of healing sick people if he has a daughter who is a felon. Bailiff, make my views known to the relevant authorities.'

'I will, my lord.'

'What is my next case?'

'A trial for sedition, my lord, a Mr Isaac Devereux.'

'We will see to him after I have partaken of luncheon.'

Annie stood in the dock, silent and unmoving. A large hand grasped her around the top of her arm. 'This way…'

The officer pulled her down the steps and into the cells beneath the assizes.

As she went down, she took a last look at her parents sitting all alone in the emptying courtroom.

Her mother was crying and her father had his face buried in his hands.

She didn't know it then, but she would never see them again.

CHAPTER TWO

Monday, September 14, 2020
Perth, Australia

Jayne Sinclair took off her sunglasses and stared over the still waters of the swimming pool.

At the far end, tropical palms stretched their long green arms to the blue sky. Beside them, a lemon tree, its branches festooned with fruit, provided shade and a delicious scent. A gentle breeze wafted from the coast, brushing against her suntan-oiled skin.

The only noise was the slurp of the little machine that swam along the top of the water removing dead leaves and other bits of twig that had been blown into the swimming pool by the breeze.

What was the machine's name? She would have to google it later.

She smiled to herself.

There was no need to google the name of the little machine that cleans a swimming pool in Manchester. Firstly, she didn't have a pool at her house in Didsbury, and secondly, in most years the weather never really became warm enough to sunbathe outside.

21

But this was Perth, Western Australia. It was September, and the hottest day so far had been recorded – 27°C.

She had been in Australia for a little over six months now. A lot had happened in the world as she lay by the pool doing very little and doing it extremely well.

In fact, she could get used to this life very easily.

They were staying at Harry Duckworth's house in the suburb of Dalkeith, just a short drive from the centre of the city. Jayne was alone in the house. Robert and Vera had gone for their usual constitutional along the Esplanade to Otto Point Reserve.

Jayne thought it was too hot to go out today, but neither of them would be dissuaded from going out.

'Robert needs his walk after lunch, it helps settle his stomach. And, of course, I have to go with him,' Vera had said.

'And Vera is the grumpiest old thing in the world unless she gets a bit of exercise, aren't you, dear?'

'Anybody would be grumpy if they had to listen to your snoring every night, Robert Cartwright.'

The truth was that both loved being together, any moment when they could just luxuriate in each other's company, no necessity to talk, just being there with one another.

Jayne had watched them leave the house once. Within five yards, Vera had hooked her arm through Robert's and off they went, slowly and carefully navigating the area's tree-lined streets.

Harry, Vera's long-lost brother, was at his place in the country where he spent most of his time these days.

'I can't abide the city any more, Jayne. Too much noise, too much shouting, too many galahs wandering the streets.'

'Galahs?'

'You know, rowdy people, like noisy birds. I much prefer the quiet of the bush, not a soul to be seen. Suits me best.'

Harry had been one of the migrant children expatriated by the Catholic Church from England in the 1950s when he was very young. Placed in the hell that was Bindoon School, along with many others, the children lived together in austere dormitories. He had survived by being tougher and smarter than the rest. After a few years of restlessness and wandering through Australia after leaving the school, he had founded Duckworth Tyres and Auto, becoming one of the biggest franchise operations in Australia. Selling the business had given him the opportunity to indulge each and every one of his whims.

He had visited Vera in England, travelled the world, eaten at the finest restaurants, even gone back to the area near Oldham where he was born years ago but, in the end, he found he just wanted to spend more and more time in the bush, on his own.

'I think it's because of growing up in one of those schools, always surrounded by other kids and the awful monks. Never a moment to myself or to be alone. One bloke who went through something similar said "every childhood lasts a lifetime". He was right. I think the years I spent at Bindoon as a kid conditioned me for life.'

He came back often, though, to spend time with Vera, talking about what could have been if he had stayed in England, talks that went on long through the night. It was like he was trying to find out about an alternate life for himself, one surrounded by family that might have happened but never did.

He was a gracious host, giving them free rein throughout his property in the city and an open invitation to visit the farm in the bush whenever they wanted. Jayne found the other place a little bleak, even though Harry obviously loved it and was happiest there.

'Sometimes I feel like we're taking advantage of you, Harry, staying in your house while you're out there.''

He'd laughed loudly. 'You're family, Jayne. You and Robert and my sister Vera, you're all I've got. I've never had family before and it's lovely to have you here. It makes me feel less lonely even if I'm on my own, if that makes any sense.'

Originally they had intended to stay just six weeks in Perth before heading back to England. But the arrival of the pandemic and the subsequent lockdowns had scuppered those plans. Western Australia had called a state of emergency on March 15, not long after they had arrived. The restrictions were only in place until the end of April, when schools were opened again and life basically returned to normal with cafés and restaurants opening in mid-May.

By June, most of the restrictions were removed completely and even sporting events were allowed, albeit with a distancing rule applied stringently.

The news out of England was less good, though, with the lockdown being tougher and strictly enforced from March 23.

As soon as the restrictions had been announced, they had sat down together and had a family discussion. Harry recommended they move out to the country.

'No people there, can't spread any disease. You obviously can't go back to England now, so you can stay here as long as you like.'

'We couldn't impose on you like that, Harry, we don't know when it will end. I think we should go back,' said Vera.

'You saw the news yesterday. A thousand people have died in the UK already and, knowing how all governments are economical with the truth, it's probably a lot more than that. We'll just have to extend your visas. I'll get in touch with a mate who'll help us.'

Jayne, Vera and Robert looked at each other.

'Well, I've got nothing to go back to right now,' said Jayne.

'And we've paid for the Residential Home already, so let's stay here.'

'It's decided then. You can stay here as long as you want, until this disease goes away. We've got the bush property and the place in Dalkeith. We'll make them our little boltholes and ride out this storm together. Agreed.'

And so they had stayed in Perth. Within weeks, news from Robert and Vera's residential home in Buxton showed the correctness of that decision. Two of their good friends had already died of the virus, despite the Home taking steps to protect and shield the residents.

'Just think, Jayne. If we'd been there, what would we have done? Robert would have hated being cooped up, day in and day out,' said Vera.

They watched the news from England religiously, and it saddened them to see the distressing scenes from hospitals around the country.

'Imagine knowing your mum or dad was dying but not being able to say goodbye to them,' said Vera one night as they were watching a news report from near Huddersfield.

'I couldn't imagine not saying goodbye to you and Vera,' said Jayne.

'And not being able to attend the funeral? You have to be able to say goodbye, don't you? It's part of grieving.'

'Apparently not any more. I'm glad we stayed in Australia.'

'We'll have to go back soon, though,' said Robert.

That was four weeks ago now. Jayne recognised the regret in Robert's voice. He missed England more than any of them, having a deep attachment to the place. For Jayne it was less strong. She missed some parts; the countryside, the people, the cheese and, of course, Mr Smith, her cat. But she didn't miss the shoddiness of the place, the fact that nothing seemed to work any more and the awfulness and incompetence of the media, which had even affected the once reliable BBC.

She looked out over the pool and thought they would go back, but not just yet.

Jayne sat up from the lounger and finished her fresh orange juice. She checked the time – 1.25 p.m.

She had a phone call with Ronald Welsh at 1.30 concerning a client. Ronald was a researcher she had worked with before, in particular on a case involving a first edition of Charles Dickens' *A Christmas Carol*. He was the best, the most assiduous in the business and he was a great asset to her when she wasn't actually in Manchester.

She went into the house and logged on to her laptop. She had deliberately cut back on her genealogical work in the last six months, partly because of the pandemic and partly because she was a little tired and burnt out. A rest was needed and, after her last case involving a soldier who went missing during the Fall of Singapore, a rest was what she had taken.

Recently, however, she had got back in the genealogical saddle again, offering her services to a few of the migrant children who had come from the UK in the fifties and sixties, now much older, who were looking for their ancestors. People who had contacted her because they knew Harry from Bindoon.

Unfortunately, many of the direct relatives, mothers and fathers of these young children – the so-called 'orphans' – were no longer alive, but there were siblings and cousins who could be found.

She logged into Zoom and waited for Ronald to join the meeting. She always found it amazing, and one of the wonders of modern technology, that here she was in a suburb of Perth, Western Australia, talking in real time to Ronald in Crumpsall, a suburb of Manchester. In the old days, simply sailing to Australia would have taken more than three months.

Ronald's face appeared on the screen, looking fresh and lively despite it being early morning in England. 'Hiya, Jayne, how's it going?'

'Can't complain, Ronald, how are you?'

'A lot better now I can go back to libraries. House sales are still few and far between but there are book auctions online. I hate buying stuff I can't pick up and feel with my own hands.'

28

Ronald had a lucrative sideline in finding first editions for collectors. He was particularly good at picking them up from old house sales, buying boxes of books knowing that in one was a hidden gem.

'How did you manage during lockdown?'

'Well, I had my baked beans and I got in a whole chunk of Lancashire cheese and a hundredweight of spuds. I've never eaten so well in my life.'

Ronald's limited food repertoire always amazed Jayne. At least he had expanded it since they had first met, adding cheese and potatoes to his usual diet of baked beans.

'But I did miss my auctions, and when the libraries closed, that was the end for me. How can you close a library? But they did…'

'How is it now?'

'Getting better, but I still can't do my primary research. You know how it is, Jayne, I like to get down and dirty with the documents, not work online.'

'How'd you go on my project?'

'Tracking down the relatives of Henry Whittaker? That was pretty easy. I worked with the family tree you created. Luckily, your client remembered the name of his mother, Margaret Whittaker, and where he lived when he was a child.'

'He was sent across as a six-year-old, but I guess some things stay with you for life.'

'So true, Jayne. I discovered that after her husband, Charles Whittaker, died in Essex—'

'That was when their son Henry was placed in the children's home.'

'Right, and then shipped out to Australia in 1954. Anyway, after he was placed in residential care, I found Henry's mother Margaret in a psychiatric home. For some reason, she was admitted under her maiden name of Harris. I haven't been able to get to the original files, but I'm sure I can find them just as soon as this pandemic is over.'

'She was in a hospital?'

'She was admitted in April 1954 and released in July 1956. Shortly afterwards she married again, a Thomas Gatesby, taking his surname and moving to Wolverhampton.'

'They told six-year-old Henry his mother had died and that's why they were shipping him off to Australia.'

'She was definitely still alive at that time. I've found the death certificate for Margaret Gatesby and she didn't die until 1995.'

Jayne's heart sank. All this time her client had believed his mother was dead, when she was actually still alive. If only he had started his quest to search for her much earlier.

'But the good news is,' Ronald continued, 'Margaret and Thomas Gatesby had two children together, Evelyn in 1958 and Charles in 1960. Your client has a half-brother and half-sister. They are both alive and still living in Wolverhampton.'

'My client will be over the moon. Do you have their addresses, Ronald?'

'I'll send them across with a family tree I've created for Margaret's second marriage. I can see if I can get telephone numbers from the White Pages if you want?'

'Not yet, Ronald. I want to take it easy with Henry, he's going to be shocked to discover his mother didn't die in 1954. Let him decide if he wants to take this further.

'No worries, Jayne, I'll wait for your instructions.'

'Can you send me your bill, Ronald?'

'Will do, but it won't be very much, this was only a few hours' work and, honestly, I loved getting back in the groove. Anything else for me, Jayne?'

'Not at the moment. I'm taking it easy on the genealogy front, just working for Harry's friends.'

'Right-oh. Anyway, I'll be off. There's a programme on the telly I want to watch all about first editions. I sure they'll make so many mistakes I'll have to write to the Beeb to correct them. I like writing to the BBC, they always send me a letter in response.'

'Thanks for everything, Ronald.'

The picture on her computer screen went blank. No long goodbyes from Ronald, he wasn't the best person at social niceties.

31

She would ring Henry after lunch and ask for a meeting. She always found delivering such heart-breaking news was better done in person rather than over the phone.

How would he handle the knowledge that his mother had been alive for forty-one years after his arrival in Australia?

Jayne never knew. All people handled it differently.

Every childhood lasted a lifetime.

CHAPTER THREE

March 28, 1837
Grangegorman Gaol, Dublin

'Haven't seen you before, when did you get here?' the thin woman sitting next to Annie Kelly whispered out of the side of her mouth, lest the Matron heard.

'Two months ago. I've been working with another group, they've all been sent away.'

The woman looked at Annie's work and then at her own. 'You're good at the sewing, I haven't the fingers or the patience for it.'

'I picked it up since I've been here. Never sewed an inch before.'

'What you in for?'

'Stealing three baskets of apples.'

The woman glanced up from her needlework as the Matron patrolled the top of the table in the main wing.

'What'd you get?'

'Seven years.'

'In here?'

'Here' was Grangegorman Gaol in Dublin, remodelled only a year ago to house female prisoners.

A stark, austere building, it had previously been Richmond Penitentiary and then converted into the first gaol for all-female prisoners. Following the ideas of Elizabeth Fry, it was supposed to be one of the most progressive jails in the whole of the United Kingdom. But none of the inmates could see it. For them, it was just gaol.

'Seven years' transportation,' Annie Kelly emphasised.

'You don't say. For three baskets of apples?'

'They were left out in the rain, so I put them in an outhouse for safekeeping.'

'Seems a likely story.'

'That's what the old spalpeen of a judge said, McLaglen was his name. He didn't believe me either, but it's the whole truth, so help me God. So now I'm waiting to be transported to Australia.'

'He likes the transportation, does that old fart. Saves the cost of keeping a body in gaol.'

'Be quiet down there,' shouted the portly Matron, swishing the end of her cane. 'No talking when you are working.'

Annie concentrated on her needlework, sewing the quilt together and focusing her eyes to make sure the stitches were perfect. Yesterday, she had received a reprimand from the edge of Matron's cane when the old harridan thought the stitching wasn't neat enough.

After a few minutes, the woman next to her spoke again.

'The name's Honorah Duffy, but everybody calls me Norah.'

'Mine's Annie Kelly. What are you in for?'

'Nothing.'

'You can't have done nothing.'

'Well, that's the point, I was going to do something, but the man I was with turned out to be a scuffer. Nabbed me there and then, and we hadn't done a thing yet. At least, that's what I told the judge. He didn't believe me, they never do.'

'What'd you get?'

'Nine months. For nothing.' She glanced towards the Matron, who had her back turned. 'Mind you, I'd been caught a few times before, so it was time to go down for a while. At least we get two meals a day here and the oatmeal stirabout ain't that bad. Most days, I eat better here than at home.'

Annie Kelly remained quiet. She was a country girl from Queen's County and had never been to Dublin before. The city looked a grand place. Well, what she'd seen of the buildings and the people through the barred window of the Black Maria that had brought her here three months ago.

'When are you leaving?'

Annie shrugged her shoulders.

'Must be soon. Two new lots came in this week. You're supposed to be here for three months to learn the sewing or the knitting, far better than doing the laundry or cleaning the jakes.'

'Two lots?'

'Donegal came in on Monday, and another lot from Antrim yesterday. Maybe they have a ship waiting for you in Kingstown Harbour?'

'If I hear you speaking again, Honorah Duffy,' the Matron boomed, 'you'll be in solitary on bread and water for the rest of the week.'

'Sorry, Matron Rawlins. It's this chest of mine, it makes an awful wheezing, it does.'

'It speaks to the girl next to you too, does it?'

'This poor culchie? She wouldn't say boo to a goose at Easter.'

Annie kept her head down, not letting on that she had heard anything.

'That's enough, Duffy, I don't want to hear another word out of you for the rest of the day.'

'Sure enough, your honour, I won't say another word even if my life depended on it.'

Annie lifted her eyes to see the Matron marching towards them with her cane raised.

'Are you going to say anything else, Duffy?'

There was silence for a moment, then Norah Duffy said, 'Didn't I promise I would not speak any more today, and now you're asking me questions which I have to answer? I wish you'd make up your mind, Matron Rawlins.'

36

The cane swished down in a perfect arc, striking Norah on the left temple. She dropped to the floor like one of the sacks that held the fabric remnants they sewed together to make quilts.

'You two, take her to solitary. She's on a week's bread and water.'

Two of the Matron's trusted prisoners rushed over and grabbed Norah by the hands and feet, carrying her roughly back to the cells. As she passed Annie, she winked and smiled broadly.

CHAPTER FOUR

June 29, 1837
Grangegorman Gaol, Dublin

In the months after their first meeting, Annie Kelly and Norah Duffy became the firmest of friends.

It was Annie who was waiting for Norah when she came out of solitary looking thinner and paler.

'I had a grand old time of it on my own. Nobody to bother me or get into an argument with. Except myself, of course, I do like an argument with myself.'

Annie passed over half a bowl of oatmeal stirabout she had saved from breakfast.

'I missed the food, though. After a couple of days, the water and the bread lost all their attraction. I used to lie there in that small cell dreaming of a steaming pile of taters with butter oozing all over them, a dollop of the greenest cabbage heaven can grow on the side, and a nice lump of fatty bacon lying on top. Not that I've ever eaten anything as good as that, but I saw it once.'

'Where?'

'At the Overseer's house. Myself and my sister were staring through the window with our mouths open and the drool staining our chins. Of course, he chased us off when he saw us, but that picture and the smell stayed with me in the cell. I ate that meal every night in my dreams – after I'd finished the bread and water, of course.' She scratched her behind. 'How were things without me?'

'The same, I suppose. Matron Rawlins has been waiting for you to return. She's hoping you've repented for your sins.'

'Repented for my sins? Rejoiced in them, more like. It was only the sweet memories of the fellas I've known that kept me alive. That sour old harridan could curdle milk just by looking at it.'

'Be careful with her, Norah.'

'Oh, I will, but it won't stop me having a wee bit of fun with the woman, just for the craic of it.'

In the last couple of months, Annie had become quite good at sewing, picking up the skill quickly, learning the different stitches; running, baste, back, invisible, catch, whip and blanket. She even graduated to making clothes for some of the warders in the latest styles. They provided the materials, patterns and thread, while Annie used her new-found skills to sew them together. It was work she found interesting and pleasing, while the warders gained a free dress or shirt. It helped that they paid her with extra food and special privileges, little extras that made living in Grangegorman just about bearable.

However, she still had to do the more mundane tasks, like stitching quilts together under the watchful eyes of Matron Rawlins. All her other work had to be done late at night or early in the morning.

That afternoon, they were sewing the quilts once again in the Great Hall when the Matron approached them.

'I hope you have learnt your lesson this time, Duffy.'

'I have, Matron. In the week in solitary, I repented and regretted my sins. I have led a wicked life but I will change.'

The Matron smiled like a cat who had just swallowed a canary. 'That is good to hear, Duffy, a sinner can always repent for their sins and they will be forgiven.'

'Yes, Matron, I repented and regretted my sins. I thought about it long and hard, and I realised the problem with sin is that it is so enjoyable.'

'That is the devil, Duffy, he always makes sin pleasurable.'

'It is, Matron. I spent every day and every night thinking on my past life and sins. And do you know what I decided, Matron?'

The old woman smiled again. 'Pray tell me, Duffy.'

'When I was in solitary, I finally realised I hadn't done enough sinning, I haven't had enough pleasure in my life. When I get out, I'm going to sin and sin and sin. And when I've stopped sinning, I'm going to sin some more. Just for the pleasure of it.'

The Matron's face darkened and glowered. 'For those words, you will receive one more week on bread and water in solitary.'

She called over two of the burliest warders.

'Take her to solitary. Make sure she doesn't eat tonight.'

'Can I not share a cell with a man? A nice ripe young fella from Galway would go down a treat,' she shouted as she was dragged away to the cells.

She returned a week later, and this time decided to keep her mouth shut. 'I can't do it again, Annie, not on my own. That old harridan Rawlins has me beat. From now on she won't hear a peep out of Honorah Duffy. I'll be as quiet as a church mouse who's lost its squeak.'

'Well then, you'll be pleased to hear that Matron Rawlins was assigned to a different wing of the prison yesterday. We've been given a new Matron, an Englishwoman called Collins. She's much better.'

Norah looked up to the heavens and crossed herself extravagantly. 'Thank all the saints and cherubs in heaven. For once they are looking down on me. Tonight, I'll say seven Hail Marys in my prayers, just to say thank you.'

Two weeks later, Annie and Norah were assigned a cell together, along with six other prisoners.

'How have you pulled this off?' asked Annie.

Norah simply tapped the side of her nose, saying, 'What ye don't know won't hurt ye. But let's just say Matron Collins is after a new dress herself. She has her eye on some Dublin beau and wants to present a pretty picture for him. I don't think her warder's uniform made an impression.'

Annie was told she would be sent out on the next female boat leaving Dublin for New South Wales. For the rest of her time, she learnt more techniques of sewing, even showing Norah how to follow the patterns published in the *Lady's Economical Assistant* given to her by Matron Collins.

'But I can't read or write, the words dance like mice in front of my eyes.'

'Just look at the pictures and the numbers. It's as clear as the nose on your face.'

Very soon Norah was becoming used to the patterns and when Annie taught her the basic words written on each one, she became adept at creating dresses herself. So much so, the warders turned to her as well as Annie to make clothes for their children and themselves.

'You know, when I get out of here I might not go back on the streets. None of them young fellas wants an old harridan like me sharing a drink with them. I think I'll get a job as a seamstress for the girls. There's always the need for a good seamstress, after all, nobody wants to throw away good clothes just because they have a small hole in them, do they?'

'It sounds like a good idea, Norah.'

'Aye, and pigs might dance a jig. I'll have a few jars inside me and then I'll spy some handsome fella from Wicklow across a crowded bar and I'll be banjaxed.'

'You won't, not this time, Norah.'

The woman stroked Annie's hair. 'Ah, you have a lovely way about you, Annie Kelly. I hope the world and Australia doesn't make you change.' Suddenly, Norah's voice became far more serious, losing her usual light-hearted tone. 'Promise me you won't change, Annie Kelly.'

Annie laughed. 'I won't.'

'No, be serious now. There are so many devils in this world and so few angels. Swear on the bones of the saints and the Holy Spirit, you won't change.'

Annie placed her hand on her heart. 'By all that I hold dear, I will not change.'

Inside, she hoped against hope she would be able to keep her promise.

CHAPTER FIVE

Monday, September 14, 2020
Perth, Australia

After her call with Ronald, Jayne was thinking about making herself something to eat when she heard the phone ringing in the hall.

Who could that be? Nobody ever rang them on the home phone. Perhaps something had happened to Robert or Vera on their walk to Otto Point.

She ran down the hallway and grabbed it. 'Hello?'

A female voice came on the line. 'Is that Jayne Sinclair?'

'Speaking?'

'Hello, you don't know me but Harry gave me your number.'

'Harry Duckworth?'

'The one and only. You are the genealogical investigator, right?'

'I do look into people's family history,' Jayne answered slowly, wondering where this was leading, then added, 'but I'm taking a bit of a holiday in Australia.'

'You have been looking into Henry Whittaker's family in England, though, haven't you?'

This woman seemed to know more about Jayne Sinclair's business than she did.

'He was one of the poor orphan children who migrated from England in the 1950s. I'm looking to help him with a possible family reunion.' A long pause. 'How can I help you?'

'Well, that's it, I don't know if you can. You see, I've discovered something about my family history but I don't understand it.'

'So you're not one of the migrant children.'

A short laugh. 'Oh no, my family has been in Australia a long time.'

'I'm sorry I can't help. As I explained, I'm on a sabbatical at the moment.' Jayne thought of Duncan Morgan, who had helped her discover Harry's story. 'I could recommend a very good Australian genealogist if you want some help with discovering your family tree?'

'But I heard you were the best. And my problem isn't about the family in Australia. I'd like to know where we came from. It could be England or, with my name, it could be Ireland. There's a mystery about our origins I just can't work out.'

'Irish genealogy is quite difficult. There are so few records, particularly for Catholics.'

'I understand, that's why I want somebody who knows her way around the archives.'

'I'm sorry, Mrs…?'

'It's Elizabeth Guglietti. But before you start worrying that I'm going to ask you to trace my Italian ancestors, it's my married name. My maiden name is a bit more prosaic: Elizabeth Kelly.'

'I'm sorry, Mrs Guglietti, but as I said, I'm not actually doing any work in Australia.'

'I'm willing to pay you for your time, Ms Sinclair.'

For a second, Jayne was tempted. Despite living rent-free in Harry's house, they had still been spending far more than Jayne had planned.

'I'm sorry, but I would prefer it if you found somebody else to help you.'

'Well, if you change your mind, Ms Sinclair, I'll be at Botanical Café in the park tomorrow morning at nine thirty. I'm there every day, it's my daily routine and the coffee is great.'

'I don't think I'll change my mind, but thank you for the offer.'

Jayne put the phone down and stood in the hall.

Should she have taken the job? The client was very cryptic about the nature of the problem. Why? Perhaps she should have asked her for more details before turning it down.

Just then, the door opened and Robert and Vera returned.

'You're back early, how was the walk?'

Vera helped Robert off with his windbreaker. Despite the heat, he always insisted on wearing one outdoors. 'Call me old-fashioned, but I have to go out with a jacket on, lass. Doesn't feel right without one.'

You can take the man out of Lancashire, but you can't take Lancashire out of the man.

Vera hung the jacket on the hook in the hallway. 'Your dad has been coughing badly, so we came back, Jayne. Now, Robert, you go and sit down while I make you a nice cup of tea.'

'Make it nice and strong, Vera, you know I hate it weak.' He coughed twice and headed off to the living room.

Since a bout with pneumonia a few years ago, Robert's lungs had never really recovered. They still had a weakness and a frailty that worried Jayne.

'Is he okay, Vera?'

Her stepmother frowned. 'I don't know. He's not his usual grumpy self. Something's wrong, I need to keep an eye on him. He's probably picked up a cold or flu from somewhere.'

Vera was an ex-nurse. Jayne trusted her instincts regarding illnesses and knew she would watch over Robert like a lioness guarding her cubs.

Jayne followed her stepfather into the sitting room. He was sitting in his usual chair and had already started on one of the crosswords from the *Guardian* book she had given him.

'I just had a strange call.'

He didn't lift his head from his book. 'Really?'

'From a friend of Harry's. She wanted me to look into a family history problem she's discovered.'

His head finally came up. 'What problem?'

'You know, I didn't ask and she didn't tell me. Not much of an investigator, am I?'

'You should call her back and find out.'

'I didn't get her number.'

'I'm sure Australia has the equivalent of 1471,' he said, referring to the telephone number you called in England to find out who had just rung you.

'It's *10#,' said Vera from the doorway. 'Harry told me.'

'That's okay, I won't bother calling her back.'

'I think you should call her, Jayne,' said Robert, looking up from his crossword.

Jayne was surprised. 'Why?'

'Well, you've been doing nothing for the last six months, just sitting beside the pool all day.'

'I'm on holiday, Dad, remember? And I haven't been doing nothing, I've been helping some of Harry's friends from Bindoon look for their family in the UK.'

'It's time you did something to keep the brain working, Jayne. You're far too young to retire.'

'I haven't retired, Dad, I'm just taking a break. I've been working very hard recently, even in Singapore when we were there.'

Jayne had finally solved the mystery of Alice Taylor's missing father. He wasn't killed during the Fall of Singapore, but had survived, lived through the hell that was the Japanese prisoner-of-war camps and, thinking that his wife and daughter had died in the Manchester bombing, and decided to make a new life for himself in the Far East. It had been an exhaustive and exhausting investigation for Jayne.

'But that was six months ago. I've been watching you, Jayne, you're restless, unsettled. You need something to occupy you, a problem you can sink your teeth into.'

'I hate to say this, but I agree with Robert,' said Vera.

'Thank you, love.'

'There's always a first time for everything,' she muttered under her breath.

Robert coughed again and then repeated, 'You're too young to retire, Jayne, and your business is doing so well.'

'I'm not retiring, I'm taking a break to recharge my batteries and relax.'

Robert harrumphed loudly. 'I don't understand that, me. Taking a break from something you love. We always had to work; it was in our blood and our upbringing. You grafted and then you retired. End of.'

'The world has changed since you were born, Robert,' said Vera.

'Aye, and not for the better either.'

'Don't listen to him, Jayne, he's Mr Grumpy today, not feeling too well. If you want to relax and recuperate for another month, you do exactly what's right for you.'

'Thank you, Vera.'

Her stepdad struggled to his feet. 'Well, I'm off for a lie down, this heat is getting to me.'

Jayne rushed over to help him.

As their heads came close he whispered, 'Sorry, I was a bit grumpy. You do what's right for you, don't listen to me. But don't tell Vera what I said.'

'I can hear every word, Robert Cartwright. My eyes might be going, but my hearing is sound.'

'She's got ears like a hawk, that one,' he whispered before talking directly to Vera. 'Come on and have a lie down with me.'

She took his arm. 'Come on, Mr Grumpy. Perhaps we shouldn't be going for our afternoon walks if it makes you this tired.'

'You try to stop me, Vera Cartwright.'

Vera winked at Jayne as she led Robert to the bedroom. 'Perhaps we should just walk around the garden instead.'

'You walk around the garden, I'm going to the Point.'

They wandered into the bedroom, arm in arm, still discussing the necessity of an afternoon walk.

Jayne was left on her own in the living room. Perhaps Robert was right, and she should go back to work. There must be lots of people in Australia who needed help researching their families in the UK. Investigating Elizabeth Guglietti's case could be a new start for her and for her business. It wouldn't be too difficult finding just one ancestor, would it? And besides, having a bit of extra money couldn't hurt.

She decided to sleep on it and decide in the morning. Meanwhile, her lounger – and perhaps an afternoon pina colada beside the pool – was calling her name.

She could very easily get used to not working.

CHAPTER SIX

July 07, 1837
Grangegorman Gaol, Dublin

One day, Annie received a letter from her father.

Dearest Annie,
This is just a short note to tell you we have received a final confirmation from the Chief Secretary in Dublin Castle.
He has turned down your request for a retrial and stated strongly that there can be no more grounds for leniency regarding your sentence of transportation.
You must prepare yourself, for I believe they will put you on board a ship to Australia in the near future. We have requested to see you in the prison but that has been refused too.
I am so sorry, my dearest Annie, your problems are the result of my foolishness. We have now been thrown out of our house in Durrow and will be moving to Kilkenny to look for a new place in that city. I will write to you when I have more information and a more settled situation.

I am so sorry, Annie, but at least it is only seven years. We will see you again when you return from that desperate place. Please write after the voyage and let us know how you are.

Your loving father,

Liam

PS. Your mother, brother and sister send their love. Your mother has cried a river of despair since you have been gone. She misses you terribly, as do I.

When Annie had finished drying her tears, she was approached by Norah.

'A letter from home?'

Annie nodded.

'I'm lucky, I never get any. Nobody can write in my family and I can't read them anyway. See, I told you them words were bad for you.'

'It looks like all the appeals have been rejected. I am to serve my sentence.'

'What did you expect from the English? Justice, fairness and a pat on the back? You'd get more from one of the dogs on the street.' She checked over her shoulder that there was nobody watching and whispered, 'I have something for you.'

From beneath the straw mattress in the corner of the cell, Norah produced a sheet of paper, a pen and a small bottle of ink.

'How did you get these?'

'The warder, the ugly one, Mrs Ward, needed a new dress for her even uglier daughter. I bartered these for it.'

'But you could have asked for food for yourself.'

'What do I need food for?'

Annie smiled. 'Thank you, Norah.'

'Don't waste time thanking me. Write to your parents and let them know you are well. Quickly now, before old mother Ward returns and takes back the ink.'

As Annie took up the pen and began to write, she could hear the screams, shouts and calls of the other prisoners echoing through the walls, their voices revealing all the different accents of Ireland.

Dearest Father,

Do not worry about me, I will be fine in Australia. Seven years is but a short time to be away from you and Mother.

I am told that if you work hard and well, often the sentence is reduced and a ticket-of-leave can be obtained. I will do my utmost to come back home to you and to Ireland.

In my absence, you must concentrate on attaining a new position for yourself in Kilkenny. I have heard it is a fine city, perfect for yourself and the family, a city that will appreciate your balms and elixirs more than the country folk of Durrow.

As soon as I arrive in Australia, I will write to you letting you know all about the voyage and the new country.

You always taught me to treat every setback as an exciting new adventure. I will make sure this is one that I will enjoy and relish.

Please send my love to Mother and ask her to dry her tears. Nothing can be gained from being sad, the only way forward is to make the best of what has happened.

Please do not come to say goodbye to me. I do not think I could bear the sadness of such a parting. Rather, wish me well and godspeed, for I will come back.

I send my love and my kisses to my brother and sister, John and Sarah. They may be grown by the time I return. I will sorely miss watching them grow into fine young men and women of Ireland.

I remain respectfully your own daughter,

Annie

A tear appeared in the corner of her eye and dripped slowly on to the page, landing on the ink and smudging her name.

She laid her pen down, wiping her eyes with the edge of the rough sleeve of the prison uniform. Taking a deep breath to calm herself, she folded the letter carefully, giving it to Norah.

'I'll make sure Mrs Ward posts it for you. She wants another dress in the same pattern for her youngest.'

* * *

A week later, after she had spent six months in Grangegorman, Annie was finally told that the transportees would be taken out to their ship the following morning.

'You'll be grand. You're a fine sewer now, at least you can make your living at that in the New World. It's only seven years, you'll soon be back,' whispered Norah.

They were both sitting in the Reform Room next to each other, their heads close together and their lips barely moving in case the Matron saw them talking.

'I'll miss you.'

'You'll miss me like you'll miss O'Reilly's donkey. And I'll be out myself soon, back to Aungier Street in Dublin's fair city, plying my trade.'

'You're not going back on the streets, are you?'

She laughed. 'I'm too old for that and I have a new trade now.' She held up the sewing in her hands. The stitches were neat and tidy, the purple thread creating a wonderfully elegant border for the quilt. 'What will you do in Australia?'

'Be quiet, Duffy, or it's bread and water for you again,' shouted Matron Rawlins, who had returned to be their warder.

Norah was about to reply, but Annie nudged her in the ribs. There was no point kicking against a system that could grind you down to dust. The only way was to work the system to your advantage. Make it work for you. If she had learnt one thing in her time in Grangegorman, this was it.

For the next three hours, they sewed together in silence, creating the quilts from scraps of material placed in front of them.

Annie Kelly left the following day without saying goodbye. She was marched out of the prison and placed in a Black Maria and taken to a ship lying at anchor in Kingstown Harbour.

As she was being rowed out to the vessel with the other female convicts, she remembered Norah's ruddy face, seeing it smiling broadly in front of her. She knew her friend would survive whatever Dublin threw at her.

Would she survive Australia?

CHAPTER SEVEN

Tuesday, September 15, 2020

Perth, Australia

Jayne walked into the Botanical Café in the centre of Kings Park right on the dot of 9.30 a.m.

In the middle of the night she had finally decided she was going to meet with this mysterious woman, waking up to find Robert's words haunting her dreams.

We always had to work; it was in our blood and our upbringing. You grafted and then you retired. End of.

She'd had a chat with him and Vera over breakfast that morning.

'I've decided to go and meet this woman.'

'Good for you, lass.' He coughed twice, sucking in air as if he couldn't breathe.

'Are you okay, Robert?'

'I'll be fine, lass, must have caught a cold on the walk.'

'I told you we should have come home earlier,' said Vera.

Robert looked sheepish, coughing again.

'I decided the least I can do is find out what she has to say. It doesn't hurt to know what the job is. I can always turn it down if it seems too much of a palaver or is going to stress me out.'

'It never hurts to find out, does it?' said Robert breathlessly.

'At least by finding out, you'll know if it's right for you. You wouldn't want to regret it later.'

'Exactly my thoughts. So I messaged her this morning. We're meeting at the café she goes to every morning.'

And here Jayne was. She stood at the entrance looking around at the patrons. At the back, a woman with grey waves through her thick black hair waved at her.

Jayne walked over and the woman rose to greet her.

'Jayne Sinclair, I presume?'

'Elizabeth, it's great to meet you.'

'Please call me Liz, all my friends do.'

'How did you know it was me?'

'I'm afraid I did some checking, saw your picture in one of the newsletters with some of the the Bindoon boys.'

The woman put out her hand and Jayne shook it. She was in her late forties but looked incredibly fit and healthy, wearing a bright purple running top and shorts.

'Sorry for the outfit but I go running most mornings and end up here for breakfast. You don't know how good coffee and cake tastes after a 5K run. I always tell myself

I've burnt off the calories and deserve a little treat. That's my excuse, anyway.'

The words came out quickly, as if the woman was nervous. Jayne sat down opposite her.

A waitress approached them quickly with a menu.

'If you're hungry I recommend the Eggs Benedict, they do it wonderfully here.'

'Thanks, I'm not really a morning food person. Just a latte will be fine.'

'No cake?'

Jayne shook her head.

There was a moment's pause as the waitress walked away before Liz continued speaking. 'I bet you're wondering why I asked to see you.'

'You were extremely cryptic over the phone.'

'Harry was very complimentary about you when I spoke to him. Said you were the best genealogist he'd ever met. The Bindoon boys raved about you too.'

'I didn't realise I was so well known or popular.'

'You'd be amazed at how quickly word gets about. Those poor people were treated so badly over such a long time…' She trailed off, not finishing her sentence.

'So you know about the orphans?'

The woman looked up and smiled. 'I met most of them through the Catholic Church. At one time I was fairly devout, a function of my upbringing, I think, but then as the details of their awful treatment of the children leaked out and was revealed fully in the Royal Commission, I was at a loose end and decided to help out, becoming involved in the support group.'

'Loose end?'

'My marriage had just ended. No real reason, we just grew apart and, with the kids grown up and having lives of their own, we simply separated.'

Jayne understood completely. Her own marriage to Paul had suffered in the same way, with both of them going in completely different directions in life. She also understood the need to be busy, it was one of the reasons she had become a genealogist in the first place.

'So that's my life story, what about you?'

Jayne was always uncomfortable talking about herself, particularly with someone she had just met. It was the part of her that was terribly English. She quickly changed the subject.

'You alluded to a mystery in the past...?'

'I did, didn't I?' Liz reached into a small backpack beside her feet. 'My father died one month ago...'

'I am so sorry for your loss.'

Liz paused for a moment, took a deep breath and continued. 'He was a good man, loved his cricket, his lawn bowling, Australia and being Australian. You know, he never left the country. He had the wealth to travel anywhere he wanted and live the high life, but he chose to stay here with his friends.'

'And your mother?'

'She passed away when I was young. Dave – that's my dad – never married again, just brought up two kids on his own with the help of aunties and friends.'

'You must have been close to him.'

'I was. He was more of a friend than a dad, somebody I could talk to about anything and anybody.'

Jayne immediately thought of her relationship with her stepfather, Robert. He was exactly the same; a good friend but a dad when he needed to be. She didn't know how she would have survived her teens without his presence.

Liz took a clear plastic folder out of her bag. Inside, Jayne could see a letter with faded brown ink that would have once been bright blue. 'Anyway, I was going through his things, working out what to throw away and what to keep, when I came across an old family bible. I looked through it and noticed by chance that the cover seemed too soft and springy. Hidden inside I found this.'

Liz handed over the plastic folder. The letter inside was written in a beautiful script that leant heavily to the right.

'I'm sorry, it's quite hard to read.'

'No worries, I'm used to it from looking at old documents.'

Jayne began to read it aloud, working out the copperplate writing as she did.

Fremantle
July 25th, 1852

Dear Annie,

I leave on the high tide this evening and I wanted to send you one more entreaty, one more letter pleading with you and our children to join me.

You know how much I love and care for you, how much I worship the very ground that you walk upon. Ever since we were married all those years ago, back almost before time began, you have been my rock, my strength, when all about me was falling apart.

You were always there guiding me, supporting me, assisting me.

But you know I have to leave now. I made the promise all those years ago to return and now the opportunity has arisen, I cannot let it fall by the wayside as I have done so many others over the years.

There is nothing here for me. There never was and there never will be.

Please join me. Leave this god-forsaken land forever. I hate Australia and all those small-minded felons who live in her barren womb.

After all, isn't it a wifely duty to join her husband? Wasn't that in the vows you made all those years ago; to be by my side in richer, in poorer, in sickness and in health, until death us do part?

We should not part, but remain together for the rest of our lives.

I beg you, please come with me, please join me on this next great adventure.

Your ever loving,
D

'What do you think?' asked Elizabeth, when Jayne had finished reading.

Jayne stared at the letter. 'Well, it's a letter from a husband to his wife asking her to join him as he is leaving the country. They have been married for many years and he obviously still loves her.'

'Do you think the date is correct?'

'July twenty-fifth, 1852? I think so. From the writing I would say this is Victorian; of the queen rather than the Australian state. He's obviously educated by the use of language, and the fact that it was kept in a bible suggests it was important to this woman, Annie. Also, I assume because you found it in your late father's effects, the letter remained in the country, indicating that she never left. She didn't join him.'

'Why do you think it's Victorian?'

'The handwriting. The style is early, suggesting the man learnt to write at the beginning of the nineteenth century. Before then, paper was expensive and quills and nibs were made by hand. After the beginning of the century, nibs and pens were manufactured and paper started to be made by machine. This all led to an explosion in letter writing. Schoolchildren were forced to learn how to write in this style. They used to sit at their desks for hours, copying out account books and excerpts from books to practise. As the century progressed, handwriting became more individual.'

Jayne checked that her client was following her explanation. ' This man has an exceptionally fine hand, an educated hand. My bet is he was a solicitor, a writer, or at least a well-educated clerk. He's just signed it "D", though. Do you know who he is?'

'I was hoping you could tell me. That's the mystery, I have no idea who this mysterious "D" could be.'

'But you do know the woman?'

'I think so. She is one of my ancestors, Annie Kelly. According to the family records she was born in 1830 and died in 1904.'

'So it was written during her life.' Jayne read through the letter again. 'Strange, it says they have been married for years, but Annie would have only been twenty-two when the letter was written. She wouldn't have been married for long at all, even in those days. Also, from the tone and the handwriting, I feel this man is older. The style suggests somebody who was born early in the century, when this copperplate was being taught. Or perhaps it was part of his job to write in this style. An engraver, perhaps, or a journalist? Are you sure this woman is the same person as your ancestor?'

'There was only one Annie in our family as far as we know. She's a bit of a legend in our family history as she was the person who first came to Australia.' Liz paused for a moment. 'But if it is her, it raises another problem. According to what I know, Annie didn't arrive in this country until the early days of Perth's expansion as a city, in 1861. It had been founded in 1829 by Captain James Stirling as the Swan River Colony, but remained a small, sleepy outpost of the empire until it began to expand in the late 1840s and 1850s.'

'Are you sure? This letter was written in Fremantle in 1852, nine years earlier. Could he have been referring to another Annie?'

'Not that I know of. There was just one.' The woman let out a long sigh. 'I should perhaps tell you something about my family.'

Just then the waitress arrived with Jayne's latte. Elizabeth waited until she had left before continuing to speak.

'We come from quite a well-known family in the city. Have you ever heard of place called Kelly's Emporium?'

Jayne sipped her latte and shook her head.

'Back in the day, it was the place to go in Perth for the latest medicines, furniture, fashion trends and merchandise. Annie, the woman who I think received this letter, was the founder. According to family history, she arrived in Australia as a free migrant…'

'A what?'

'Somebody who settled here rather than being sent as a convict.'

'Okay, I understand.'

'Unfortunately, her husband died on the voyage out and she arrived with two young children. Apparently, she had trained as an apothecary and knew medicines and medical balms and elixirs, that sort of thing. She opened her own shop, a chemist, and then followed it a few years later with another shop. This time a haberdashery. She took in sewing at first, mending and repairing the new settlers' clothes. She then had the brilliant idea of combining the two and adding lots of other merchandise, and Kelly's Emporium was born. Of course, the succession of gold rushes in Kimberley, Yilgarn and Cue meant her timing was perfect. The discovery of gold in Kalgoorlie in 1893 brought a vast influx of people into Western Australia, all needing food, clothes, tools, medicines and everything else. Annie served these people, often taking gold as payment instead of money. She also realised the vast, under-served needs of the countryside, setting up a catalogue from which rural folks could order their goods directly.'

'A sort of Australian Sears, Roebuck?'

'Exactly. Eventually, she opened Perth's first department store in the early 1900s and it became an institution in the city.'

Jayne frowned. 'I don't remember seeing the name and I've been shopping in the city a lot.'

'My grandfather sold Kelly's Emporium when he returned from World War Two in 1946. He'd been a POW in Thailand during the war after being captured in the Fall of Singapore.'

Jayne knew all about the heinous acts the Japanese had committed on the unfortunate Allied prisoners who were selected to build the Burma railway.

'By then, it had grown to be Perth's leading department store but he was no longer interested in running the business, preferring to spend his days outdoors sailing rather than stuck inside an office. Now there's a massive shopping mall where the store used to be.'

'World wars often change people's perspective on life.'

'It certainly affected him greatly. I remember him when I was young. It was as if he was always running away from something, never wanting to take responsibility for anyone or anything. The running of the family affairs and its money fell to my grandmother, Louise. A strong woman, she wore the trousers in our house.'

A long pause as Elizabeth obviously remembered her grandmother fondly.

'Anyway, that's the family history. Deeply tied into Perth and its growth as a city. Even today, Kelly's Emporium is remembered fondly by people.'

CHAPTER EIGHT

August 08, 1837

Kingstown Harbour, Dublin

'Will you look at the state of these women?'

The master of the *Sir Charles Forbes* looked across his deck as the female convicts trooped aboard. 'It looks like you will have your hands full ensuring this lot arrive alive in Australia, Mr Clifford.'

The surgeon wrinkled his nose in disgust. 'What is that smell?'

An older woman doubled over as she reached the ship, spewing vomit over the deck. Annie, being the next in line, reached out to help her before she collapsed.

'Belay that woman,' Captain James Leslie bellowed in his broad Scottish accent. 'I can't have my deck soiled by what you have disgorged from your putrid stomach.' He turned to the surgeon and spoke quietly. 'I'll wager this could be your first patient, Doctor, but probably not the last.'

The surgeon signalled a crewman standing off to one side. 'You, man – carry her down to the sick bay. Get that woman to help you.'

Annie pointed at herself and looked around.

'Yes, you, woman. Hurry now.'

'Where is it?' asked Annie.

The surgeon rolled his eyes extravagantly. 'Where it always is, woman, in the cockpit on the orlop deck.'

'I'll show thee,' the sailor said gently.

The two of them carried the older woman past the main deck into a small, foetid area close to the waterline. The cell was no larger than ten feet square, with no natural light or portholes. In the centre, a single lantern threw a grey flickering light.

'Put her down here, I'll string up a hammock for her when I have time.'

Annie helped the woman lie down on top of an army blanket. She knew her from Grangegorman, the woman had been in the cell next to hers.

In the corner, she saw a bucket full of water. She tore a strip of cloth from her skirt and began to gently wipe the woman's forehead to help ease the pain.

'Where does it hurt, Honorah?'

'My st-st-stomach,' the woman gasped. 'Like a hand is gripping my vitals.'

A few minutes later the surgeon joined them in the sick bay. 'What's her name?' he asked in a peremptory tone.

'Brown, sir.'

'What's wrong with her?'

'She was vomiting before we left Grangegorman, sir. She's getting waves of pain from her stomach. It could be gripe or something more serious, perhaps enteritis.'

Surgeon Clifford looked at Annie strangely.

'She should never have been placed with the other transportees.' He pressed down hard on the old woman's stomach. She immediately reacted by convulsing, and threatened to vomit again.

'A case of enteritis. The grim air of the prison has affected her stomach,' he pronounced. He reached behind him into his medical chest, taking one bottle out. Using a dropper, he placed exactly eight drops into a small wooden cup, adding water from a bucket. 'Give her this Chlorodyne and watch over her while I attend to the rest of the prisoners.'

'But, sir…'

'Those are my orders. What is your name?'

'Annie Kelly, sir.'

'You seem to have some knowledge of medical matters.'

'My father was a herbalist, sir, I used to help him.'

The surgeon laughed. 'One of those traditional Irish doctors, all mumbo-jumbo and folk remedies.'

'My father knew how to heal people.'

'Science is how you heal people, my girl. You will stay here with her and give her the medicine.'

'But, sir, I am just a seamstress, I—'

'But me no buts, just do as you are told.' He reached for another empty bucket. 'I don't want my sick bay soiled. If she tries to vomit, make sure she uses the bucket.'

The surgeon left the small cell. Annie raised the old woman's head and let the milky liquid dribble between her lips. 'Just swallow this, it will help.'

The woman did as she was told, lying back on the deck and promptly falling asleep.

Annie was left alone, wondering what to do. Outside, she could hear the shouts of the sailors and the stevedores as they prepared the ship for departure. The timbers of the boat groaned and creaked as the wind filled the sails and she gradually pulled away from the dock.

In the small sick bay, deep in the bowels of the ship, Annie was aware of the rocking of the boat and the creaking of the timbers. Beneath her feet on the deck below, she could hear the rats scuttling, awakened by the rocking movement of the ship.

The surgeon returned three hours later, the stench of drink on his breath, with two women in tow guarded by four large red-coated soldiers.

'Sit down on the deck, over there,' he ordered the women, one of whom was holding a bloodied rag over her eye.

'These two wretches have been fighting over the food in the mess. You there, take that rag from your eye.'

The younger of the two women removed the rag, revealing a deep cut just above the brow. Annie was certain she could see a white sliver of bone through the blood.

'Did you faint, and was there any vomiting?'

The young woman seemed puzzled by the question.

'Answer me quickly.'

The other woman, who had a few scratches about her face, answered for her. 'I put the trollope out to sleep with one punch and she threw up like a dog on the deck,' she said triumphantly.

'Take her to the brig,' he ordered the soldiers.

'But, sir, it was her fault, she stole my oatmeal.'

The surgeon ignored her pleas. 'Take her to the brig, there's nothing wrong with her that a few days on bread and water won't cure.'

The woman was led away by the soldiers, struggling all the time and threatening the evilest slanders against their manhood.

The surgeon leant over, staring at the younger woman's brow injury without touching it. 'Your name, woman.'

This time she answered slowly. 'Bridget, sir. Bridget Ryan from Liscat, County Mayo.'

'And what are you being transported for?'

'Theft, sir, of a shawl.'

He sniffed twice. 'Well, you need your brow stitched up. You, woman,' he said, pointing to Annie. 'You said you were a seamstress. Here's your opportunity to show your skills.'

'Me, sir?'

'Well, I see nobody else. 'Cepting her.' He pointed to the woman lying on the deck. 'And she'll be out for the next twelve hours. Here's the catgut and a needle.'

'But I—'

'But me no more buts, woman. I won't tell you again, simply do as you are told. Sew up her brow. It's just like sewing a garment, only wetter.'

Annie took the needle, staring all the time at Bridget Ryan.

'Don't worry, I won't squeal. I've had it done before.' She lifted her right hand, showing a long scar along the palm. 'Doesn't hurt at all.'

Annie took the rag and wiped the last of the blood from around the wound. She looked back at the doctor, who jerked his head to indicate she should do what she had been told.

Slowly she threaded the catgut through the eye of the thin bone needle. 'Are you sure it won't hurt?'

'It didn't last time. I'll let you know if it does now.' Then Bridget Ryan winked and the flap of skin fell over her right eye.

'Hurry up, woman, my supper is waiting,' the surgeon said.

Cautiously, Annie pushed the skin back in place, pinching it with her fingers to pull both sides of the long gash together. She slowly inserted the bone needle through one side and then the other, watching Bridget Ryan's face for signs of pain all the time.

The woman winked again and smiled broadly.

Annie pulled the catgut through and then looped it over itself and back through the skin again, making each pass close to the last, as if she were hemming a garment.

Within five minutes she had finished, tying off the catgut in a neat, tiny knot at the end of the wound. She sat back, looking at her work. Not the neatest sewing, but at least the wound had stopped bleeding.

The surgeon leant over and examined her work.

'Upon my word, that is the neatest suture I have seen since medical school.'

Bridget Ryan felt the wound with her fingertips. 'See, I told you it wouldn't hurt. Might not even have a scar.'

'Well, young lady, remind me again of your name?'

'Annie Kelly, sir.'

'You now have a job for the rest of this voyage to Australia. You will be my assistant in looking after these women. You may call me Surgeon Clifford.'

Bridget Ryan stared at her. 'I'm sure such an important job will mean extra rations, won't it, sir?' She winked again, this time with the right eye, and winced.

'I'm sure we can get her some extra oatmeal for her work.'

'Thank you, sir.'

'But I insist you bathe before you come to my cabin. You Irish smell so.'

'It's the nightean, sir, for our clothes. We use it to wash them.'

'But it smells like urine.'

'That's what it is, sir. Gets the clothes bright and clean.'

William Clifford sniffed again. 'If you want to work here, don't use it. I'll give you some carbolic soap, Miss…?'

'It's Annie, sir, Annie Kelly,' she repeated.

Another loud sniff. 'You'll sleep here with the patients, not on your deck. I don't want you bringing their dirt and disease in here.'

'And I can bring her food here.'

The surgeon stared at Bridget Ryan, with the large welt and bruising above her eye. 'I'm sure you can.'

'I'll make sure she gets her share, sir, don't you worry.' She flexed her fists.

'Well, I'll leave you here and return to my dinner. We'll start tomorrow at six bells, examining the convicts.'

Annie looked at him quizzically.

'In the morning at first light, you'll hear the ring go six bells. You can count, can't you?'

'Of course, sir, my father was a healer. *A haon, a dó, a trí, a ceathair…*'

'You can count in English too?'

'Of course. One, two, tree…'

'Call me if she begins to vomit. If not, I will return tomorrow. And please wash yourself before then. Unfortunately, you stink of the prison'

He left the small room. Only Annie, Bridget and the snoring Honorah remained.

It was Bridget who spoke first. 'My head is starting to hurt now, feels like there's a whole marching band of English soldiers inside trying to get out.'

Annie looked at the older woman. There was still a small amount of the surgeon's medicine in the wooden cup beside her.

'Try this, it will help you sleep.'

She passed the cup over to Bridget, who drank it down thirstily. 'Any more? I'm feeling better already.' Followed a minute later by, 'I am supposing I should remain too, being your patient and everything. It'll be better to bed down here than with the pox-ridden sows above us.'

Annie unrolled two straw mattresses that were stacked in the corner. Both had blood and sweat stains on the hessian covers. New to them, moth-eaten army blankets were also thrown loosely on the pile.

'I suppose we should use these to keep ourselves warm.'

'Well, they're better than an old coat.' Bridget looked across at Honorah Brown, snoring gently. 'Should we do anything for her?'

'The doctor said she'll sleep until tomorrow.'

'And so should we.' Bridget looked around the small sick bay. 'First time I've ever slept in a place as nice as this.'

She snuggled herself beneath the worn blanket, falling asleep almost instantly.

Annie extinguished the candle in the lantern on the wall with her wet fingertips and lay down next to her, pulling the old blanket up around her ears.

Outside, the sea hissed and gurgled against the bow of the ship. The keel creaked and the wind whistled softly through the cracks in the planking.

Annie lay awake for a while, listening to the sounds of the ship as it raced ever south to find Australia thousands of miles away.

Would she ever see her family again? Or would she die on this ship or in that far-off land?

She didn't know.

Soon her eyes became heavy, and lullabied by the sounds of the ship and the sea, she drifted off into a deep, deep sleep.

CHAPTER NINE

Tuesday, September 15, 2020

Perth, Australia

In the café, Jayne ordered another latte. 'You said this letter was found in a family bible. Was there anything else written in the book?'

'I thought you might ask that.' Elizabeth produced another two photocopies. 'You are wondering if there are any family records at the front of the bible.'

'Exactly. Often these bibles are used to keep a record of the births, and sometimes the dates of death, in the family.'

Elizabeth laid two photocopies in front of Jayne. 'These are the first two pages.'

The first was printed:

This bible belongs to:
Annie Kelly
Given to her on the birth of her first child, John.

'On the next page, there is a list of family names in a variety of different handwriting styles and inks. In our case, it's just the births I'm afraid.'

FAMILY RECORD

John Henry	Dec 8, 1840
Dominic James	Feb 27, 1842
Honorah Bridget	Mar 3, 1845
Hannah May	November 15, 1873
Michael Joseph	July 23, 1875
Alfred William	October 4, 1878
John Thomas	Mar 6, 1901
Richard Everly	September 12, 1921
Arthur Terence	December 25, 1923
Evelyn Grace	Aug 17, 1953
Elizabeth Erika	May 28, 1976
Anthony Paul	December 15, 1978

'We've had more births since my brother, Anthony, but they weren't recorded here.'

'It often happens. The old bibles get stored in attics or in boxes and people forget about them.' Jayne stared at the photocopy for a long time before continuing. 'Did you make a copy of the title page too?'

'What do you mean?'

'The page opposite this one, the front matter, giving the publisher and the publication date of this particular bible?'

'I didn't think to look. Do you need that information?'

Jayne ignored the implication that she was going to take up the case. 'It would be interesting to know when it was published. Was it before or after the letter was written?'

'I can check when I go home.'

Jayne stared at the photocopies, examining them closely. 'The front plate with Annie Kelly's name comes from the first page of the bible?'

Elizabeth nodded.

'And you believe this Annie Kelly is the same woman who founded Kelly's Emporium and is mentioned in the letter?'

'I do.'

'There are a couple of interesting things about this family record. Firstly, the handwriting itself. You notice the name and the note on the front plate and the first three births are all written in the same handwriting and in the same ink?'

'I had noticed that, yes. I presume Annie wrote those names.'

'But if you look at the letter, the writing is remarkably similar to that in the bible. See? The same curls and flourishes on the capital letters. And look at the ascender on the lower-case "h" with its inward hook. Quite distinctive in writing the name "Honorah".'

Elizabeth leant forward and compared the two. 'I hadn't noticed before, but you are right. They are very similar.'

'Now, it could be just a coincidence. If Annie did write these names, she may have been taught how to write by the same man who wrote the letter. Remember, everybody learnt to write by copying.'

'I don't know. There's nothing in the family history about another man.'

'There's a couple of other discrepancies I find interesting.'

'Really?'

'You said she arrived in Perth in 1861 with two young children.'

'That's what my father told me.'

'But there are three names here. John, Dominic and Honorah. And they are hardly young. John would have been twenty-one by the time he arrived. Plus, if Annie's birth date was in 1830, she would have only been ten years old when John was born. She can't have been the mother.'

'You're right, I've never thought about it. Perhaps the family history is wrong.'

'They often are. The timelines get mangled as they are handed down from generation to generation. Or perhaps there is another Annie we don't know about.' Jayne held up the photocopies. 'You asked me to come here this morning for a reason…'

Elizabeth took a deep breath. 'I want you to do two things. Firstly, I want you to find out who the man who wrote the letter was.'

'And the second?'

'I want to know everything about my three-times great-grandmother. If she was the Annie who received this letter, then how does it tally with the family history? Was this her husband? Did the man not die on the voyage?'

Jayne thought for a long time. Did she really want to get involved with this case?

She enjoyed her life lying beside the pool, not worrying about anything or anybody. But Robert was right, she couldn't do that for the rest of her life. She had to be busy, to discover new things, to constantly keep her brain working.

'If I take this case, and it's a big if, I must do it in my own way and at my own pace.'

'I'm in no rush. Annie Kelly arrived here over a hundred and fifty years ago, her secrets can wait a while longer.'

'And secondly, I may need help from other researchers in Australia or the UK. Unfortunately, these people have to be paid.'

'Money is not a concern.' Elizabeth reached into the backpack and brought out a cheque book. 'Shall we say five thousand dollars to get you started and ten thousand on completion of the case? If you need more, just let me know.' She handed a cheque over to Jayne.

'That's more than generous. I'll start right away. I should be able to give you my preliminary findings in a couple of days.'

'So quick?'

'It'll just be the first research and perhaps thoughts for further areas to explore.'

'Sounds great. Anything else you need from me?'

'A couple of things would help. If you could photocopy all the front matter of the bible and send it over to me. Plus if you could put together a rough family tree, it would help and save me time.'

'I'll do that as soon as I get home. I'm so excited. A mystery in my family and we're investigating it.'

Jayne stood up. 'Just to manage expectations, sometimes we genealogists hit road blocks where the documentation just isn't there to find out more.'

'I understand. Looking into the past can be difficult, but it is exciting, isn't it?'

'That's why I love it so much. I'll get back to you in a couple of days with my initial thoughts.'

Jayne turned and as she walked out of the café, she wondered whether she had made the right choice. Should she have taken on this new job or should she just enjoy the rest of her stay in Australia lying beside the pool, drinking pina coladas?

The next few days would tell her.

CHAPTER TEN

August to December, 1837
Aboard the *Sir Charles Forbes*

Annie was kept extremely busy throughout every one of the 136 days of the voyage to Australia.

Firstly, the ship itself, the *Sir Charles Forbes*, was overcrowded with convicts; 150 women from every corner of Ireland and every accent. Antrim, Cork, Clare, Carlow, Donegal, Dublin, County Down, Fermanagh, Galway, Kilkenny, King's County, Kildare, Kerry, Londonderry, Meath, Monaghan, Mayo, Roscommon, Tipperary, Armagh, Limerick, Louth, Leitrim, Waterford, and Wicklow – not forgetting her own Queen's County, of course – were all represented on board.

Most spoke a smattering of English but a few only conversed in Irish. With these women, she acted as a translator for the surgeon, describing their symptoms to Mr Clifford as best she could.

The women were not healthy, particularly those who had embarked at Cork when the ship had sailed round the island to pick up even more convicts, adding to the overcrowding.

The situation was not helped by the ship itself. As Mr Clifford described it to her one day, 'She's an ill-sailing lugger. See, she lies close to the water. No wonder the place is often wet and putrid.'

Every day at six bells, the women who thought themselves ill lined up in front of the small sick bay. Surgeon Clifford looked at them, quickly pronouncing both an illness and a cure.

'Croup. Use three drops of Dr Evans' mixture in water. Next.'

'Dropsy. Use the leeches to purge her blood. Next.'

'Fever. Warburg pills. Next.'

'Whooping cough. One hour in the fresh air above deck.'

'But it's raining, sir,' the woman protested loudly.

'Even better, the cold rain will purge your system. Next.'

Most times, though, the patient was sent off with the harsh words of the surgeon ringing in her ears. 'Don't waste my valuable time, woman. It's nothing but a small gash on your hand. Will do you good.'

Or 'I'm a surgeon, not a wet nurse. Your child has gripe, madam. Take him away and feed him properly.'

After they had been sailing for twenty days, Annie noticed that many of the women reported that they were feeling tired and their knees and elbows were painful. A few even said their gums were bleeding, with what teeth they still had loosening and falling out.

'Scurvy. Make up a mixture of six parts vinegar and one part sugar, to be drunk every morning.'

'Where do I get the vinegar and sugar, sir?'

'From the cook, tell him the surgeon sent you.'

Annie made up the liquid in an empty bucket, doling out a cupful to every woman on board each morning. Most complained of the taste, but few refused something that was free and ordered by the surgeon. Within a few days, the symptoms of scurvy became less and less visible, some of the women even demanding the drink when they weren't showing any effects of the disease at all.

The days passed quickly as the ship sailed further south, and life on board fell into a routine for Annie; the sick bay roll-call at six bells, followed by the surgeon going off for his breakfast and his morning constitutional around the deck while Annie administered the doses of medicines to the sick, or looked after them if they were confined to the sick bay.

She soon became used to the various pills, ointments, balms, and herbs the surgeon used in his treatments. The work was very similar to that which she had performed for her father. The only difference being he used fresh herbs and natural substances, while Surgeon Clifford had mysterious bottles and unguents secreted in his medicine chest as well as his natural cures.

She became adept at making diagnoses herself, sometimes adding pills without the surgeon's knowledge when she felt it would improve the condition of her fellow convicts.

Bridget was by her side on most days, protecting her from the demands of the more aggressive convicts.

'Hey you, Annie Kelly, give me another slug of that Chloro stuff. Better than a bottle of gin, it is.'

'Move along or get a fist in your face. The surgeon's assistant can only give out what the surgeon tells her, no more, no less.'

Now this wasn't strictly true, but the others weren't to know that.

All was going well and Annie was feeling confident in her new position, but after they rounded the Cape, the weather became progressively colder.

The harsh conditions ensured that more and more women were visiting the surgeon each morning. Catarrh, bronchitis and even pneumonia became prevalent the ship's population.

It was then that they lost their first patient, a young baby of seventeen months: George.

His mother had been sentenced to seven years' transportation for stealing, and rather than separate them, incurring all the costs of a wet nurse and childcare, the judge had decided the baby should accompany his mother to New South Wales.

One evening, the mother had rushed into the sick bay where Annie was nursing the patients with pneumonia.

'My baby, he's not well.'

In a dirty wet blanket, a young child lay still, a halo of sweat dampening his thin, ginger hair.

'He keeps bringing up his food and he's very weak.'

Annie bent over his thin body, holding a mirror to his mouth. It slowly fogged up.

'The breathing is there but it's shallow and fast.'

She stripped the baby of his damp soiled clothes and wrapped him in one of the army blankets, nestling him into the thin arms of his mother. She sent for Mr Clifford, who arrived in a temper.

'I'm at my dinner, woman, why have you disturbed me?'

'It's this woman's child, sir, I think he's ill. His breathing is shallow and he has a fever.'

The surgeon glanced at him quickly. 'Enteritis. Common in babies. Two drops of the Chlorodyne in water with a supplement of sugar water should solve the problem.'

The doctor left and Annie fed the baby the medicine and sugar water, giving the mother some oatmeal she had left over, which the woman devoured hungrily.

Despite her best efforts, the child died two days later, never waking from his fever. He was buried at sea hastily the following morning, the weighted body wrapped in one of the blankets, a few words said over the small shape, and then slid into the cold water.

Annie watched the blanket rest on the surface of the sea before slowly sinking beneath the white-capped waves. Another child who would not see another dawn.

She lost only two more passengers on the voyage: Mary Houlihan from Dublin, who died of pneumonia as they were crossing the Indian Ocean, and Peggy Fallon of Galway, an old and dissipated prostitute, sentenced to life for plying her trade and stealing from one of her clients, who passed away close to the shores of Australia on the second day of December.

Annie watched the surgeon write in his journal on that day.

One woman died today. I pray this voyage ends soon as, if it continues for much longer, or we become becalmed off the shores of New South Wales, I cannot answer to my maker for the lives of these wretched women. They are dirty, diseased and redolent of the morass from which they came; a country called Ireland, may I never see its shores or its people ever again.

Luckily for Annie, they were not becalmed but sailed briskly on, finally entering Port Jackson on Christmas Day, 1837.

On that day, she left the small sick bay and crept on deck, seeing the humble brick-and-wood houses of the port lined up behind the dock for the first time.

She crossed herself three times and said a Hail Mary to thank her for the safe deliverance to these far shores.

What would the future hold?

She did not know, but she did care.

How she cared.

CHAPTER ELEVEN

Tuesday, September 15, 2020
Perth, Australia

By the time Jayne returned to the house in Dalkeith, Elizabeth had already sent her the information she'd requested.

She made herself a pot of tea and sat down at her laptop, ready to begin. In the room next door, she could hear Vera moving around. Normally she and Robert would have gone out for their walk by now; it was strange they were still at home.

She opened Elizabeth's email. The covering letter was bright and bubbly, just like the woman herself.

Dear Jayne,

Great meeting you this morning. I'm so excited to be working with you to uncover my family tree and solve the mystery of the letter and its writer.

As you requested, I've copied the first page of the bible. It seems to have been printed in Dublin, which suggests an Irish connection, but I suppose they sent the bibles all over the world. I've also attached my handwritten family tree. Sorry, there are a few gaps but this is what I know. I'm sure you can help fill in the missing persons.

Hear from you soon,
Love
Liz

Jayne turned her attention to the attached files. The first was a copy of the front page of the bible. The paper had yellowed and foxed, but the type was still clear and distinct. The title page contained a lot of information in itself.

Title The / Holy Bible / Translated from / The Latin Vulgate, / Diligently Compared with the Hebrew, Greek, and / Other Editions, in Divers / Languages; / The / Old Testament, / First Published by / the English College, at Douay, A. D. 1609; / and the / New Testament, / First Published by / the English College, at Rhemes, A. D. 1582. / with Annotations, References, / and an Historical and Chronological Index. / The Whole Revised and Diligently Compared with / The Latin Vulgate. / The Stereotype Edition. / Dublin: / Printed by Richard Coyne, / Bookseller, Printer and Publisher to the Royal College of / St. Patrick, Maynooth. / MDCCCXXV.

Ronald would probably be able to give the complete history of this bible, but it was getting late in Manchester, so instead of calling him, Jayne sent an email along with the picture of the front page.

Hi Ronald,
Sorry to bother you, but can you tell me anything about this bible? A client just found it among her father's belongings.
Regards,
Jayne

Surprisingly, the answer came back within two minutes.

No bother, Jayne.
It's quite a well-known Catholic bible first printed in 1825. It's known as the 'Murray Bible' from Archbishop Daniel Murray, who approved this particular version. There was a lot of these bibles printed in the early years of the nineteenth century as the ability to read and write increased and the Catholic bishops wanted their flocks to read approved versions. They were printed in Dublin but distributed throughout the English-speaking world, particularly to America. They were often used as gifts from the devout to someone going abroad or emigrating. This

one followed the translations created by the Catholic seminaries in Douai and Rheims. I love the old-fashioned spelling of the names of the towns.

You can pick them up cheaply from bookshops, flea markets and house sales on the U.S. East Coast, particularly in Boston and Philadelphia. Not worth very much, I'm afraid, as lots were produced – unless, of course, somebody very famous owned it.

Best regards,
Your friend,
Ronald

PS. I never thought of Australia as a source for books, but there must have been a lot of first editions sent there. If you see anything interesting just zap a picture over to me.

She was quite touched on seeing Ronald's words at the end. Jayne realised she had crossed from being a business colleague to something far more personal for Ronald. 'Your friend' was not a term he used lightly. She sent a quick email back, thanking him for his response.

However, his note didn't add much to what she already knew.

Had Annie Kelly carried this bible with her when she sailed to Australia in 1861? The inscriptions regarding births suggested she had had it from at least 1840.

Jayne opened the next attachment. It was the handwritten family tree created by Liz.

Annie Kelly was at the top, with no indication of her parents' names or of the man who was her husband. There followed the three children's names that were noted first in the bible. It seemed that neither Honorah nor John Henry married, while Liz was a direct descendant of Dominic Kelly through his son, Michael Joseph Kelly, who was born in 1875. There were other sons and daughters of Dominic, all of whom had married and produced lines of their own.

Jayne decided to follow those families later. What was key at the moment was staying on track to answer the questions posed by Liz.

Who was the letter writer?

And where did Annie Kelly come from?

'Focus, Jayne, focus,' she said out loud to herself. Perhaps her six months off from genealogical research had affected her thinking. For once in her life, she wasn't sure how to proceed. Normally she could see instantly the issue at hand and how to cut to the chase.

She closed her eyes to think.

'Let's concentrate on Annie Kelly, she's the key to all this.'

She realised she was speaking out loud to the empty room, but she didn't care. She did miss Mr Smith, her cat, though. Normally he was her constant companion when she was deep in the bowels of a research project. But he was back in England, being looked after by one of her neighbours and ex-clients, Alice Taylor. She wondered if Mr Smith missed her as much as she missed him. She doubted it. Cats missed nobody… or at least they never showed it.

'Focus, Jayne, focus,' she scolded herself again.

What was it Liz had said? 'Annie Kelly died in 1904.' If she was such a well-known merchant in Perth, her death would have been noted in the local newspaper.

Jayne logged on to Trove. It was a free online resource to help explore amazing collections from Australian libraries, universities, museums, galleries and archives.

She typed 'Annie Kelly' followed by 'obituary, Perth' into the search box. Instantly a link came up, to the *West Australian* of September 27, 1904. She clicked on it and the old newspaper appeared on her screen.

The whole city of Perth regrets to hear of the passing yesterday evening of one of the rocks and matrons of our community.

Mrs Annie Kelly, founder of Kelly's Emporium on William Street, passed peacefully in her sleep, surrounded by her loving family.

Your communicant was privileged in recent weeks to interview Mrs Kelly directly and hear in her own words of her life in our fair city. Of course, before she

started our interview she offered me one of her famous apples, saying 'an apple a day, no doctor to pay'. An aphorism I will remember for the rest of my life.

'I was born the second daughter of the Kelly Family in 1830,' she told me. 'My father was a herbalist and I often acted as his assistant. My family all died when I was young and so, with nothing to keep me in the country of my birth, I came as a free migrant to Perth in 1854 aboard the *Amos Sadgrove*, when the city was but a small struggling community on the banks of the Swan River. My husband, Peter Brennan, had unfortunately died during the passage, leaving me with the task of bringing up a daughter and a son on my own. We struggled at the beginning, but through my own efforts and the assistance of the kind people of Perth, we gradually prospered, setting up our first Kelly's dispensing chemist in 1861, followed by the haberdashery three years later. Both stores expanded and flourished with the growth of the city. A few years later, I had the idea of combining the stores on one site and adding other ranges of merchandise. We must never rest on our laurels in business or in life. We must always renew and reinvent ourselves. The newly created Kelly's Emporium was an instant success. Recent years have seen this growth multiply ten-fold with the discovery of gold in Kalgoorlie. But in many ways, I miss the early days when Perth was a smaller, kinder place. However, you cannot hinder progress. The world, and life, always changes, as it will continue to do when I am gone and long forgotten.'

Perth, the city and its people, will never forget you, Annie Kelly, or your generosity, your kindness and the free apples you gave every child who visited your store. Here's Annie, telling the story of the famous Kelly's Emporium tradition of keeping a bowl of apples in the entrance which any child could eat.

'When I was young an old woman had a house nearby with an apple tree in her back garden. I used to look over the wall at the tree, watching as the apples became bigger, redder and juicier with each passing day of summer. One day, I remember being hungry and myself and my brothers couldn't stand it any longer. We decided to climb over the wall and take an apple each, just one, to taste how good they were. Well, of course, I had just taken my first bite of this wonderfully juicy apple when the old woman came rushing out of the house. My brothers were quick and managed to escape, but I was caught. I received such a beating that night from my mother, my legs were black and blue for weeks. From that day, I resolved to give away apples to any child who wanted one, a tradition we established in the very first Kelly's Emporium and which we have continued to this day.'

A wonderful story from a wonderful woman.

Your correspondent went to pay his respects to the family of this illustrious Perth family. While he was there, her grandson told me a wonderful story. On her deathbed, Annie asked him to go to the top drawer in her bureau. There he found an old English penny. As Annie held it tightly in her hand, she left this earth.

What was the story behind the penny? Nobody in her family would tell me. Was this the first penny she ever earned or was it something else? It is a secret Annie took with her to the heaven she has no doubt entered.

You will be missed, Annie Kelly. There are not many like you around any more, nor will there be many in the future.

Farewell, Annie Kelly.

Brilliant, thought Jayne. At last, here is the woman's life story, straight from the horse's mouth.

The first thing she noticed was the date anomaly. Annie didn't arrive in Australia in 1861, as told to her by Elizabeth, but earlier in 1854. Still before the date on the letter, but significantly closer. Perhaps the family oral history had confused the opening of the first store with the date of arrival. It happened often when the dates were handed down by word of mouth.

Secondly, the obituary confirmed the date of birth for

Annie: 1830. So she couldn't have been the mother of John and Honorah. Was there another Annie that nobody knew about? The obituary didn't give any clues. Strange. Two women with the same name and similar ages? Jayne wrote in her notebook:

Two Annies. Cousins?

Thirdly, there was a name for the husband, Peter Brennan, and the fact that he had died on the voyage. Jayne made a note to check the passenger lists for ships into Australia for the year 1854. The name of the ship on which she had sailed was the *Amos Sadgrove*.

Then Jayne noticed something strange. She thought for a moment, then added some more notes to her book.

Was 'Kelly' Annie's maiden name?
Why didn't they use Brennan?
Was Peter the author of the letter?
Did he also write in the bible?
Birth dates of children????

She sat back. None of it made sense, but at least she was beginning to work out the right questions to ask. In Jayne's experience, half the journey to solving a problem was asking the correct questions. And these certainly gave her plenty of new areas to explore.

She heard a noise at the door and saw Vera standing there.

'You didn't go for your walk this afternoon?'

She came into the kitchen. 'Not today, Jayne. Your dad's not feeling well so I thought we'd better stay inside. Of course, he wanted to go, stubborn old man that he is.'

'Is he okay?'

'I'm not sure at the moment. He's having problems with his breathing. It might be a return of the pneumonia he had a few Christmases ago in Manchester.'

'Can I go and see him?'

'I wouldn't at the moment. He's having a nap.'

'Not like him to sleep during the day.'

'I know, that's what's worrying me. He hasn't been eating for the last couple of days either, says he has no appetite.'

'Do you think we should call the doctor?'

'I'll check him when he wakes up and then we'll decide. Do you want another cup of tea?'

Jayne shook her head. 'I've drunk enough to float the *Titanic*.'

'How was the meeting? I can see you're sat at your computer, so you accepted the job?'

'You know me too well.'

'Your dad was worried. Thought you'd lost your drive and energy. Becoming lazy, he said.'

'Just like Robert. He can never understand people who

don't keep themselves busy.'

Vera laughed. 'That's him. He's always got to be doing something, even if it's just the *Guardian* crossword.'

As Vera made her tea, Jayne glanced back at the computer. Something was disturbing her about the obituary, but for the life of her, she couldn't work out what it was.

CHAPTER TWELVE

December 29, 1837
The Docks, Sydney

'Annie Kelly.'

She stepped forward as her name was called by the sergeant. To her unsteady legs, unused to walking on dry land after so long, the desk seemed a long way away at the end of the wharf. She wobbled as she walked on the cobblestones, her body still adjusting for the rocking of the boat that was no longer happening.

After what seemed like miles, but couldn't have been more than a few yards, she finally stopped before the desk. In front of her an officer was scribbling in a book.

That morning the convict women, all 150 of them, had been taken from the *Sir Charles Forbes* berthed in Neutral Bay and deposited unceremoniously at the docks. They had been kept on board the ship for four days after they arrived. Nobody knew why and even fewer people were going to tell the convicts.

A bishop, Polding by name, and an assortment of well-dressed women were there to greet them.

'Ladies, you have been brought to this new land because you have committed heinous crimes in your home country,' the bishop began. He took out a large white handkerchief and blew his nose loudly before continuing on.

'Do not look on this as a sentence for those crimes. Rather, regard it as an opportunity for redemption, just as Our Lord redeemed the sins of the heathens by his death on the cross.' He smiled as if remembering something amusing. 'Now I am not suggesting you nail your hands to a wooden cross and rest there for three days on Pitt Street, the area is no Golgotha, but through hard work, obedience to your masters and avoiding the temptations that have so far led you to this place, you may,' he raised his large index finger, 'find a semblance of hope and even happiness in your lot. Remember. Hard work will cleanse your soul and clean it of the impurities that have befallen you. Like the Garden of Eden, this benighted land has multiple temptations that will encourage you to leave the path of righteousness, and it is only through hard work and obedience that you will avoid the slough of their despond.'

As the bishop took a deep breath to continue his speech, Annie looked around her. A crowd had gathered to watch their arrival on one side, and a group of soldiers in their red coats stood on the other in case of trouble. All the women convicts were lined up along the quay, still dressed in the clothes that had been given to them in Ireland. Slightly worse for wear now, though, after the voyage.

She had said goodbye to Surgeon Clifford that morning. For the first time, his tone had been gentle towards her.

'I thank you for your assistance on this voyage, Annie. You have been a great help to me and to your fellow… passengers.'

'Thank you, Mr Clifford, I have learnt a lot from you. I am glad to have been of service.'

'I have sent word to an old friend, Captain Furlong, to see if you can be of service to him. But I have received no answer so I fear he may be away from the town at present. You may have to take whatever has been decided for you.'

'I don't understand, sir.'

'As the ship arrived in port, a notice was sent out that anybody who was in need of female servants was to apply using the established forms and pay the required fees. You will be assigned to those who have paid.'

Annie didn't understand. 'I am to have a job, sir, will I receive pay?'

'Of course, not,' he snapped, 'you are a convict. The assignees will pay the Crown for your services under a penalty of forty shillings if you abscond from your work. I advise you not to abscond.'

'Where would I run to, sir?'

'The bush. The city. There is a shortage of women in this hell hole. Many men would pay you to stay with them, but your honour would be ruined.'

'I am a convict, Mr Clifford, I have no honour.'

The surgeon sniffed loudly. 'That's as may be. I bid you good day and good luck, madam.'

With that, he turned on his heels and went below to his cabin. As Annie climbed into the boat that brought her to the docks, she hoped to see him waving her goodbye from the rail of the ship, but he never came.

'Work hard and work well for your masters!'

Bishop Polding's last words were shouted and they brought Annie out of her reverie.

'Those are my last comments on your welcome to Australia. You may proceed with the assignations, Lieutenant.'

The soldier sat down by his desk and opened a book. A sergeant beside him called out, 'Jane Meanagh.'

One of the oldest convicts stepped forward slowly, her grey hair wafting in the breeze.

'You are assigned to Matthew Oldfield of Darlinghurst.'

A dour-looking farmer stepped forward, accompanied by his mouse of a wife. 'Why have you given me an old one, Lieutenant? I specifically requested somebody young and strong who could help me around the farm.'

'The assignments have been made by the government,

Mr Oldfield, I suggest you take it up with them.'

The farmer snorted loudly, grabbed Jane Meanagh by the right arm and dragged her away with him, admonishing her to 'work hard and work long, I'll have no slackers on my farm'.

The same process continued on for each of the women convicts. Some of the applicants were happy with their assignees, others complained loudly and vociferously.

It was then that Annie heard her name.

She stepped forward nervously, wobbling as she approached the desk of the lieutenant.

'Wait there,' he ordered.

The sergeant then proceeded to read out other names, quickly and without stopping.

'Alicia Meally, Mary Connelly, Elizabeth McMullen, Ann Matthews, Sarah Gallagher, Catherine Cassidy, Jane Hanby, Catherine McCarthy, Catherine Dwyer, Matilda Finlay, Mary Kelly, Mary Keane, Mary Heffernan, Honorah Daly, Sarah McLoughlin.'

Slowly, the women whose names had been called out assembled in front of the lieutenant's desk.

'You ladies have been selected to go to Newcastle, where you will be assigned to families there and in Maitland and the Patrick Plains. Sergeant, take the convicts away. The steamer leaves in one hour.'

The sergeant saluted smartly. 'Yes, sir.'

'Just a minute, Lieutenant Joyce,' a well-dressed

woman said.

'Mrs Furlong. I didn't see you there.'

'I have only just arrived. I believe you have an Anne Kelly amongst your women.'

'I do, madam. She has just been assigned to Newcastle.'

Mrs Furlong turned to the line of convicts. 'Which one of you is Anne Kelly?'

Annie stepped forward, her head held high.

'You have been Mr Clifford's assistant on the voyage?'

'I was, ma'am.'

'And you learnt about poultices, medicines and caring for the sick from him?'

'I did, ma'am. Surgeon Clifford was generous with his knowledge.'

'But not so generous with his praise, I'll wager.'

'Not so much, no, ma'am.'

'You'll do.' She placed a sheet of paper down on the lieutenant's desk. 'This woman has been assigned to me. She will work in my household. The appointment has been approved by the Governor.'

'But... but... this is most irregular. She has already been assigned to Newcastle, and I thought you already had a convict working for you. Didn't I assign her myself just a month ago?'

'She ran off with some ruffian she met at the docks. Both have already been apprehended and are presently in gaol awaiting the pleasure of the magistrate. And so I have come here again.' Mrs Furlong tapped the paper in the lieutenant's hand. 'Can you not read the name on the warrant?'

His eyes dropped to the paper. 'Convict Anne Kelly assigned to the household of Captain and Mrs Furlong.'

'And the signature and seal?'

He answered slowly, knowing was beaten. 'The Governor's.'

'Come with me, Anne, you are to be in my household for the foreseeable future.'

'I'm usually called Annie, ma'am.'

'But this will mean I am one short for Newcastle,' the lieutenant spluttered.

'Take one of the others,' Mrs Furlong said over her shoulder as she led Annie away from the docks. 'There's plenty of convicts still there waiting.'

CHAPTER THIRTEEN

Tuesday, September 15, 2020
Perth, Australia

After Vera had returned to her bedroom to check on Robert, Jayne grabbed some chocolate from the fridge. Despite living in Australia for the last six months, her love of good chocolate had not lessened. Early on she had discovered the Margaret River Chocolate Company on Murray Street and became addicted to their Dark Chilli chocolate bar. It was a square of that which she placed in her mouth, allowing the chocolate to melt slowly, waiting for the little kick of chilli at the end.

Chocolate was a moment of indulgence she allowed herself during every research session. A moment to treat herself and give her energy to face the next task.

She decided to focus on Annie Kelly first rather than on the identity of the letter writer, reasoning that if she could work out her background then the letter writer's name would become apparent.

But where to start?

She wrote a few details from the obituary and some questions alongside those notes.

Born 1830. Where?

Family died. Any records of deaths? Church records? Any surviving relatives?

Arrived Perth 1854 aboard the *Amos Sadgrove*. Check records for ship's log and passenger lists. Where did it leave from? How long was the voyage?

Free migrant? Any list of passengers in the UK?

Husband Peter Brennan died on the voyage to Australia. Where and when were they married? Certificates? Church records? Banns? What religion? (Probably Catholic given the bible.)

Lived in Perth for the rest of her life? Censuses? Estate records? Wills?

Then she thought about the other source of her information: the bible. It gave her three of the family births linked to Annie and the dates:

John Henry   **Dec 8, 1840**
Dominic James   **Feb 27, 1842**
Honorah Bridget   **Mar 3, 1845**

She re-read the list. This was a good beginning; plenty of questions to answer to help her move forward. She wasn't an expert on Australian genealogical research, so she added two other areas she should look at:

Australian Censuses?
Australian passenger lists?
Talk to Duncan?

Duncan Morgan had helped her when she needed to find Harry in Australia. He would definitely know where to look and what to look for.

She sat back and treated herself to another square of chocolate. There was a lot of work to do. Perhaps she should have stayed on her lounger by the pool this morning?

And then a broad smile crossed her face. This was the moment she loved; when she was about to embark on a journey of discovery, not knowing what secrets she was going to find, what truths she would uncover, what the future – and the past – held.

Whoever said 'it's the journey, not the destination' knew how she felt right now.

CHAPTER FOURTEEN

January to June, 1838

Sydney, Australia

Annie's first month in the Furlong home passed in a blur; she was constantly kept busy attending to the needs of Mrs Furlong and her three children, one of whom had an affliction of the body that left her tired and bed-ridden.

The daily chores seemed never-ending; lighting the fires, emptying the chamber pots, cooking breakfast for the master, the children and then Mrs Furlong, who was a late riser. After breakfast the daily cleaning began; the parlour first, in case guests arrived, followed by the family room, the children's bedrooms and the Furlongs' room. Then it was time to cook lunch for the children and Mrs Furlong, followed by another round of cleaning and emptying. If Mrs Furlong's friends visited, it was afternoon teas and cakes from the bakery as the lady of the house held court.

The evening was more cooking, washing and cleaning (the dust got everywhere), the preparation of the children for bed, the dowsing of fires and the extinguishing of the numerous candles that lit the house after dark.

Finally, after ten o'clock, Annie dragged her weary bones back to the small, barely furnished room she slept in at the rear of the property. She threw herself down on her rickety bed and cried herself to sleep, remembering her parents and her life back in Ireland.

Would she ever see either of them again?

After the first month, Annie understood why the previous woman had run away with the first man she had met. In that short time Annie had never left the house, never had a day off, never had a minute to herself when she wasn't sleeping or working.

Mrs Furlong was not a bad woman, nor difficult to work for, but she was temperamental and prone to changing her mind.

After Annie had cooked dinner one evening for the children – a wholesome meal of potatoes, cabbage and pickled pig's ear – the woman became flustered.

'John is awfully fussy about his food. And today he has been dealing with the weekly punishment detail for his regiment. It always leaves him in such a bad mood. Let's kill one of the chickens and serve him that tonight. What do you think?'

'A whole chicken? For tonight?'

'Yes, it is an extravagance, but John will be so pleased.'

'If it is to be roasted, it will not be ready before he returns home.'

'What if you fricasseed it?'

'What, ma'am?'

'Fried it quickly, the French way.'

'Never heard of the "French way". I could joint it and soak the pieces in buttermilk like my mother does and then fry them. But we have no buttermilk and I don't believe there is any to be had in the city.'

'Roast it anyway, I will placate John until it is ready.'

Of course, Captain Furlong returned with a roaring hunger and wanted to eat immediately. He tucked into the pig's ear, pronouncing it the best he had ever eaten, and then spent the rest of the evening drinking port on the verandah with Lieutenant Higgins.

The chicken was not wasted, though. The children and Mrs Furlong had it for breakfast and Annie made a broth from the giblets and a few leftover vegetables, which she fed to Amy, the sickly child, who for the first time since the family's arrival in Australia, actually ate all of her food.

A result which Mrs Furlong pronounced in her best Essex accent as a 'passing success'.

That night, Annie overheard the Furlongs talking through the thin partition walls.

'You must make sure this one stays, Marjorie. We cannot afford the cost of another runaway. The two who have already gone since our arrival four months ago have had a dire effect on our finances and on my reputation.'

'I cannot help it if these women do not want to work. It is the reason why they are in this wretched country in the first place. They sought to steal their way out of their situation in life rather than earn their place in society through hard work and diligence.'

'I, of all people, know why they are here. I am just asking you to look after this one. We cannot afford to pay the fine if she breaks her contract.'

'I will attend to it, husband. It seems young Annie has taken an interest in Amy. And Surgeon Clifford gave her a strong recommendation for her skills with poultices, balms, the care of patients and her sewing.'

'Good. The child has been bed-ridden ever since the voyage.'

'The sea air was bad for her. She was raised in London where the smoke was much better for her lungs. Surgeon Clifford has prescribed a daily enema for Amy to rid her of the bad humours encouraged by the voyage.'

'Annie can begin the enemas tomorrow.'

'But I am not so sure that is the correct way to proceed.'

'You would go against the surgeon's advice in this matter?'

'I watched Amy eat a chicken broth that Annie had cooked. Afterwards she was the most animated I have seen her since we arrived in Australia.'

'Be careful, we cannot afford to lose another servant. Understand?'

A soft, emollient, coquettish voice. 'Of course, husband. I know exactly what to do.'

Annie stepped away from the thin wall that partitioned the hallway from the bedroom of the Furlongs. 'Knowledge is power,' she whispered.

It was a phrase used often by her father when he was trying to create a new balm or poultice for one of the myriad illnesses that afflicted the people of her home town.

She had not understood its meaning before.

She did now.

Her life, as it was, couldn't go on. She would have to do something about it, but what?

And then a thought occurred to her.

Perhaps that would work?

CHAPTER FIFTEEN

Tuesday, September 15, 2020

Perth, Australia

Jayne stared at all the questions she had asked herself and wondered where to begin. Normally she was always certain of how to proceed on a genealogical investigation; in some obscure way the ancestors just told her what to do. But this time she felt uncertain and unsure.

Why?

Was it because she was dealing with Australian migration, an area she'd only worked on a few times before? Or was it because she'd lost the knack of investigating after her six-month lay-off?

'Come on, Jayne, time to go back to basics. What do we know for certain?' she said out loud to herself.

She stared at the obituary.

Annie Kelly said she'd arrived in Australia as a free migrant in 1854. If Jayne could find Annie and her husband Peter on a passenger list, it would tell her where they'd embarked and even where they had lived.

Having used the Australian passenger lists when she was looking for Harry's departure from England, she was sure Findmypast had an extensive archive.

She logged on to the website and found a record called *Australia, Inward, Outward & Coastal Passenger Lists 1826–1972*.

She completed the information she had – name, surname, birth date, and date of arrival in Australia, 1854 – checked the 'name variants' tab in case Annie was down as Ann, Anne or Nan, and pressed send, crossing her fingers.

Four results, including variations on the Christian name. All Annes, but nobody using the name Annie.

First name	Last name	Departure Port	Arrival Port
Ann	Kelly	Launceston	Sydney
Ann R	Kelly	Colombo	Melbourne
Anne	Kelly	London	Sydney
Mary Ann	Kelly	Liverpool	Sydney

She clicked on each of the links. None of them matched what she knew of Annie Kelly.

The first was a 28-year-old single woman going from Tasmania to Sydney. The second was a woman travelling with just one child and her husband, John. Plus, Jayne was sure that if Annie Kelly had lived for a while in Sri Lanka then she would have mentioned it in the newspaper interview. The third entry was another single woman, this time aged 42, travelling from London. Finally, the last was a servant attached to a large English family with no other relations travelling.

Jayne scratched her head and then expanded the search to two years on either side of 1854, just in case Annie had the date of arrival or departure incorrect.

Thirty results.

Once again, Jayne went through them one by one. Most were single women or coastal passengers. None matched the family details given in the bible, and none had an arrival port as Perth or Fremantle.

Had Annie travelled with her husband, bringing the family over later?

Jayne went back to the obituary. It was very clear. *I came as a free migrant to Perth in 1854…* But it didn't say where she had departed from. Had she taken a coastal freighter from another port to Perth? But if she had, the record would have listed her and the family.

Jayne tried a different tack. Perhaps Annie had travelled under her married name, only reverting to her maiden name after the death of her husband.

She searched for Annie Brennan in 1854 using all the Christian and surname variations.

No results.

She expanded the search by two years once again, and this time received three hits. After checking them out, none matched as all were single women in their thirties.

Strange. No records at all.

Perhaps she was being too general in searching for arrivals to Australia. What if she narrowed it down to just arrivals into Western Australia?

She switched websites to Ancestry.com and searched in the *Western Australia, Australia, Crew and Passenger Lists, 1852–1930.*

Again Jayne put in Annie's maiden name and the married name of Brennan, restricting the search from 1852 to 1856.

No hits. Very strange.

Perhaps she was going about this the wrong way. Rather than search for the passengers, why didn't she search for the ship? At least then she would be able to narrow down the number of times, in 1854, that the *Amos Sadgrove* had visited Perth.

She put the ship's name in the search engine, leaving the passenger name blank.

Nothing. No hits.

Even stranger.

She then went to the Lloyd's Register of Shipping Heritage and Education site and typed in the name of the ship and the date, 1854. These books contained all the ships that had registered with and been insured by Lloyd's.

No results.

She broadened the search to include all years. Still no hits. It seemed the ship didn't exist on the Lloyd's site. Was it registered elsewhere?

Jayne got up, stretched and went to make herself a coffee. She selected the strongest espresso pod and put it in the machine, enjoying the delicious aroma as the hot water hit the coffee grounds.

She took the coffee back to her seat and sipped it slowly. What to do next?

She couldn't find Annie or her husband on any of the passenger lists from 1852 to 1856. She couldn't even find the ship they had supposedly sailed on. Had the ship's name been lost or misfiled? Should she expand her search to add more years at the beginning and the end?

She went back to the Western Australian records on Ancestry.com and removed the year tab completely. This time, she had over 1,250 hits for the full period to 1930, just for Annie Kelly. If she added another search for Annie Brennan, that number would probably double.

Searching that many records would take a long time. Too long.

There must be a smarter way of finding when Annie Kelly arrived in Western Australia. She had to find a parameter. A document that would state conclusively that Annie Kelly was in Perth on a particular date.

She knew exactly where to look.

By chance she had come across the fact that the first Census was taken in New South Wales in 1828, with other states performing their own Censuses until the first national one was taken in 1881.

Did Western Australia perform its own Census before 1881? Jayne checked online.

Familysearch had a Census for Western Australia in both 1829 and 1837. Too early for her needs. But there was a Census for 1859.

Perfect.

Jayne went online, only to find her hopes dashed within minutes. All the records for the 1859 Census had been destroyed except for those from a small town called York about 75 miles from Perth. She checked those records anyway.

No Annie Kelly.

She investigated further. The UK Census records were Jayne's first port of call in any search; as long as she had a name, a date of birth or even a place of residence, she could usually find someone. However, in Australia most of the physical Census records, the returns themselves, had been destroyed for privacy issues or in fires.

Blocked again.

She sipped her coffee. What would she do in similar circumstances in the UK?

She'd look for alternatives. Perhaps there were substitutes she could turn to.

She checked the possibilities for Western Australia. They seemed particularly sparse, only really starting after Annie's death in 1904. She eventually found a Perth post office directory published by Pierssene in 1893 that seemed as good a place as any to start.

There were three mentions for Kelly. The first was a rather plain alphabetical listing.

Kelly, Annie & family, merchants. Murray St. Tel. No. 23

The second was a listing for the street address that their business occupied.

Kelly, Annie & family, merchants. Station St (West Side).

Jayne presumed that the first was a home address. Interesting too that they had a telephone installed, number

23, even in 1893. It must of been one of the first phone lines.

The final listing was an advertisement for their shop.

Kelly's Emporium
Manufacturing and Dispensing
Homeopathic Chemists and Druggists
Haberdashery and Fabrics
All other merchandise available for the modern home
Station St

Prescriptions accurately dispensed with the purest drugs
The latest fashions from Europe
Catalogue available for immediate dispatch
Delivery to all parts of Western Australia

So, if Jayne were to understand these listings correctly, they confirmed that Annie Kelly was in Perth and an established shopkeeper by 1893. It matched both the obituary published in the newspaper and her client's description of her three-times great-grandmother's business.

But what had happened from her arrival in 1854 until 1893? Without specific documentation, Jayne could never find out where Annie had come from or who the mysterious 'D' was.

Jayne sipped her coffee and sighed. She hated to admit it but she needed help. She needed to talk to someone who really understood Australian records and how to overcome brick walls.

Luckily, she knew exactly who to call.

CHAPTER SIXTEEN

January to June, 1838

Sydney, Australia

The following morning, Mrs Furlong was more attentive than usual as Annie went about her duties: cleaning the parlour, setting the kitchen fire and preparing breakfast for the two elder girls.

'Is your room comfortable?' she asked.

'It is, ma'am,' answered Annie.

'Have you enough sheets?'

'Plenty, ma'am.'

'You can leave the sweeping of the verandah till after luncheon, if you prefer.'

'I cannot, ma'am, the master and his friend were smoking out there last night. There is ash everywhere.'

'I know, disgusting habit, but he does love it so.'

'I like the aroma of cigars too, ma'am. My father used to smoke them.'

'Did he? I'm surprised an Irish farmer could afford such luxuries.'

'He wasn't a farmer, ma'am.'

'What was he?'

Remembering her new-found dictum, Annie didn't answer the question but carried on sweeping.

'Annie?'

'Yes, ma'am.'

'I watched you with Amy yesterday. She enjoyed your broth.'

'It was easy to make, ma'am. My father often cooked it for sick people, to help build up their strength again.'

'Could you make it more often for Amy? She does need to recover her life after the voyage.'

'Of course, ma'am. But…'

'But what?'

'I thought Surgeon Clifford had prescribed enemas to cure Amy.'

Mrs Furlong's eyes narrowed suspiciously. 'How do you know that?

'When we were aboard ship, it was his usual cure for lassitude and torpor. That and being confined below decks to avoid the sea air.'

'But you don't agree?'

'It is not my place to agree or disagree with such an eminent person as the surgeon, however…'

'Out with it.'

'However, my father always said a body needed building up after it was ill, and nothing was better than bones.'

'Bones?'

'A broth of beef bones and herbs. The bones would be no problem, the abattoir has plenty. The herbs, however, only grow in Ireland. A shame one cannot get them here.'

'What do you need? I'm sure I can find them.'

'I doubt it, ma'am, but the dispensing chemist may have the dried versions available.'

'We will go this afternoon, you and I, to Mr Wiggs on the Quays. If he doesn't have them, nobody will.'

'There is a special ingredient, though…'

'What is that?'

Annie hesitated to tell the woman, but if she was to gain some sort of freedom from the drudgery of housework, she would have to prepare her father's broth correctly. 'It's poteen, a spirit distilled from potatoes. My father used to make his own till the revenue caught up with him.'

'Poteen? I don't know if there is any in Sydney, but John has a case of brandy. Wouldn't that work just as well?'

'I'm sure it would, ma'am.'

'Well, let us go now. Amy's health requires that we act quickly and I wouldn't mind trying a few glasses of your father's broth myself. Just to see its effects, mind.'

Annie smiled to herself.

After a month, she was finally to be allowed out of the house. Perhaps she could find a chance to escape from this hell hole, run away like all the others had done. She couldn't imagine spending seven years working like a slave for Mrs Furlong.

It would kill her.

CHAPTER SEVENTEEN

Tuesday, September 15, 2020
Perth, Australia

Jayne rang Duncan Morgan and he picked up immediately.

'Great to hear your voice again, how are you doing?'

They had met up a couple of times when she'd first arrived in Perth, for a coffee and a gossip about all things genealogical. But since Covid had reared its ugly head, they hadn't seen each other.

'Not bad, still hanging in there.'

'You didn't go back to Manchester then?'

Duncan had this peculiar Australian habit of ending his sentences on a high note. Jayne always found it amusing, it was like the question was a song.

'It seemed safer to stay here.'

'And a whole lot warmer, I bet.'

'You're not wrong.' Jayne thought it was time to cut to the chase. 'Listen, Duncan, I need to ask a favour.'

'Ask away, happy to help you in any way I can.'

Jayne always loved the openness of the Aussies. None of the stiff British pompousness she sometimes encountered.

'I need to pick your brains about Australian research. I'm working for a client and I think I've hit a brick wall.'

'Not uncommon here, there isn't the depth of government Censuses and church records that you can find in England.'

'That's exactly the problem.'

Duncan said he was free that evening and Jayne arranged to meet him at the unfortunately named Lucky Shag bar on the waterfront for an early glass of wine.

He was already there when Jayne arrived, a half-drunk schooner of Coopers draught in front of him.

He rose and kissed her on both cheeks. 'Sorry about this place. It's certainly not the swankiest restaurant in town but the view is to die for and it suits me to a tee.'

He was right, the view was amazing, overlooking the Swan River to the far side of the bay.

'It always tickles me that I'm drinking in the place where the first settlers under Captain Stirling probably landed nearly two hundred years ago. What're you having?'

'A glass of Chardonnay would be perfect.' Since coming to Perth, Jayne had given up her usual New Zealand Sauvignon Blancs for the richer butteriness of a Margaret

River Chardonnay. For some reason, it just worked so well with the cool breezes of Perth.

'Coming up.' Duncan made a few hand signals to a waitress. 'Now, let's get down to business, Jayne, you said you needed some help.'

Another trait Jayne loved. The straight-forward talking when doing business. It saved a lot of time, avoiding all the niceties of polite English conversation before getting down to the real point of the meeting.

She explained the problem and showed him a photocopy of Annie Kelly's obituary, and copies of the letter and the bible pages.

'This is all you have?'

'That's it, I'm afraid.'

'And your client wants to know where her three-times great-grandmother came from and who wrote the letter?'

'You got it in one.'

He picked up the obituary, read it through again and smiled. 'It's a bit gushing, isn't it? This reporter obviously knew on which side his bread was buttered.'

'I don't understand.'

'This old lady was the founder of Kelly's Emporium, wasn't she?'

Jayne nodded.

'In its day, Kelly's was the Sears, Roebuck of Western Australia. It had a large advertising budget and could allot it to whichever newspapers wrote the nicest articles praising its wares and its owners.'

Jayne understood. 'Nobody was going to write anything bad when it could cost them a lot of money in advertising revenue.'

'Now *you've* got it in one.' He took a deep breath and began to speak. 'There's something else you should understand about the Australia of the time, actually two things. We're not proud of it, but it happened and it can't be swept under the carpet.'

The waitress brought Jayne's glass of Chardonnay and Duncan paused before continuing his explanation.

'I notice there is no mention of a birthplace in Annie's obituary. It suggests a rural, or at least semi-rural, upbringing but doesn't name a place.'

'I thought that was a bit strange. Normally in such an effusive obituary, the full life story would be given. It's like she only came alive once she arrived in Australia.'

'It's not surprising, though, and the giveaway is her name.'

'I don't understand.'

'My bet is Annie Kelly was Irish.'

'Why was that a problem?'

'To be Irish at that time in Australia was to have come from the lowest of the low. To be in the class of labourers, the lowest rung in Australian society. If you wanted entry into polite Western Australian society of the time, it would be best not to shout from the rooftops where your antecedents were born.'

Jayne thought for a moment. 'It's like the England of the fifties. Landlords would put signs outside their lodging houses saying "No Irish need apply".'

'You have only to look at the *Punch* cartoons of the Victorian era to realise the Irish were seen as almost a sub-human species of people, with strange beliefs and practices, exacerbated by a devotion to what was pedantically known as the "Church of Rome" on official government documents.'

'Church of Rome? Catholics?'

'The Protestant ascendancy in Australia was always dubious of Catholicism and its Irish practitioners. Of course, it's all changed now, but back then they were seen as an existential threat to the true path of worshipping God.'

'So Annie could have been born in Ireland?'

'I'd say more than likely.'

Jayne nodded her head, trying to absorb this new information. 'You mentioned a second point to know.'

'This is similar but goes back to the founding of Australia itself. Your Annie claims to be a free migrant to Perth in 1854.'

'It's in the obituary.'

'What if she wasn't a free migrant?'

'What do you mean?'

'There weren't many free migrants to Perth in that period. But what is known is that in 1849 the colonial government needed a labour force to develop the port and its surrounding infrastructure. So they turned to one that was available and cheap.'

'I don't understand.'

'Convicts. They began to bring convicts from London with the first boat arriving in June 1850.'

'You think Annie could have been a convict?'

'I'm not certain, but it wouldn't surprise me if she was.'

'Why?'

'Again, it's that element of snobbishness that infected Australian society during the late Victorian period. Nowadays, people are proud if they have a convict as one of their ancestors. It's a talking point and a source of pride and toughness. But back then, it was a source of shame. To admit you had convict ancestors, or had been a convict yourself, was impossible if you wanted to enter high society.'

'Magwitch.'

'I'm sorry, Jayne, I don't understand you. Who's Magwitch?''

'From Charles Dickens' *Great Expectations*. A convict who made his fortune in Australia but who was shunned by polite society and lived his life through the main character, Pip.'

'I remember now. He died attempting to return to Australia.'

'So Annie would never have admitted she had a convict background?'

'Probably not.'

'But wouldn't people know, or at least be able to guess?'

'You mean like this reporter.' He jabbed the photocopy. 'Probably. But it was the Victorian era of "don't show, don't tell". Unspeakable things went on behind closed doors in Victorian homes, but the veneer of respectability and righteousness was always maintained. Didn't somebody once work out that, despite the Victorian facade of high morality, there were eighty thousand prostitutes working the streets of London in this period?'

'So the reporter knew but wouldn't write about it?'

'Polite society being very polite… If you had money and status, which this woman undoubtedly did.'

'So you're saying this obituary isn't true, it isn't her life story?'

'I'm sure parts of it are true. But doesn't she give it away herself when she says "we must always renew and reinvent ourselves"? Like many people, she created a story of her life that was acceptable to the mores of the day and to Western Australian society.'

Jayne was silent for a long time, before she finally said, 'But that means the story she told the reporter was false.' She picked up the photocopy of the obituary. 'All this could be lies. Where do I start if it's all lies?'

'You start at the beginning, not believing anything unless it is backed by documentary evidence.'

'Genealogy 101. Everything has to be supported by documentary proof. I can't find any proof of the assertions in the obituary, so I'll have to discard it...'

'Until you can find proof later.'

'But that means the only documentary evidence I have to work with is this.' She held up the photocopy of the family page in the bible.

'People don't lie in their bibles, do they?'

CHAPTER EIGHTEEN

April 13, 1839
Sydney, Australia

Annie Kelly walked with a spring in her step down George Street. She had just been to Paddy's Market and later would go to the wharves and see if any new fabrics had arrived on the latest ship from England.

The last year had seen a complete turnaround in her life. She could come and go as she pleased and worked just a few hours a day, creating poultices, herbal remedies and broths for Mrs Furlong and her growing list of friends.

Amy was now in rude health, gaily dancing and enjoying the many entertainments and balls that the social life of Sydney had to offer. Annie had been unable to find all the herbs she'd wanted to make that original restorative broth, but Mr Wiggs had enough for her to create a beef broth that would have brought back Brian Boru dancing from his grave.

The effect on Amy was almost immediate. She went from lying in bed all day long, to walking around the house, to striding along the dusty streets of Sydney, all in a couple of months.

Of course, the transformation didn't go unnoticed. Mrs Furlong was questioned by the women of the city on the miraculous recovery of her daughter. Soon, Annie was at work most days; roasting the bones, soaking the herbs, boiling the soup down until it became a thick broth, and finally straining it into small bottles.

At first, Mrs Furlong gave the broth away freely to her friends, but soon she realised that there was a commercial demand for what they now called 'The Elixir'. When her husband was posted to Newcastle for a long period, she encouraged Annie to make far more and began to charge for it.

Without the knowledge of her husband, Mrs Furlong even acquired two other convicts from the newest arrivals into the city, to cook, clean and maintain the house, leaving Annie with the sole duty of making her broth.

Mr Wiggs soon took an interest and each bottle was now being sold at his pharmacy for the princely sum of 2 shillings and sixpence. They flew off the shelves, requiring Annie to increase her production to two batches a day and buy new, much bigger roasting and boiling pots.

To her credit, Mrs Furlong shared her good fortune with her convict servant. For each bottle sold Annie receive threepence, and the money went into a box under her bed. Money that could be used to take her back to Ireland when her sentence was finished.

It was in this gay frame of mind that Annie strode down George Street, quietly adding up her profits from the sales in the last week, when a tall gentleman who was dressed rather shabbily accosted her in the street.

'Miss Kelly, is it?' he asked.

'Who wants to know?'

'I do.'

She attempted to walk around him but he stepped into her path. 'And who is "I"?'

'Daniel Sheehan at your service, ma'am.' He made a florid bow, stretching one leg in front of him.

A Dublin accent from the sound of him, she thought. 'Well, Mr Sheehan, I have my mistress's business to attend to, so if you would be so kind as to let me be on my way…' As she spoke she attempted to get past him, but each time he shifted position to block her.

'Mr Sheehan… please.' She raised her voice slightly.

'Your mistress is Mrs Furlong?'

Annie stopped. How did he know?

'I see from your reaction that I am correct.'

She reddened. 'It is none of your business who employs me, sir, so please let me be on my way.' She attempted to walk around him once again and this time she succeeded.

As she was walking away, he said, 'So you're the one who makes the broth?'

She stopped and turned back towards him angrily. 'It

is none of your business what I do or don't do, sir.'

'Oh, but it is. You see, I am a journalist for the *Sydney Gazette and New South Wales Advertiser*, and your new broth – your Elixir, as they have called it – is the talk of the town.'

She looked him up and down. 'You're not a journalist, you're nothing but a convict.'

'In Sydney, one can be both.' He bowed again. 'Daniel Sheehan, late of the *Morning Register* and the *Honest Dubliner*, now of the *Sydney Gazette and New South Wales Advertiser*, after a short interregnum as a guest of His Majesty in Kilmainham Gaol and on his good ship, the *Captain Cook*, stopping for a few months as a clerk at the Colonial Supply Office before being discovered by Mr Robert Howe, editor of the said newspaper.' He bowed once again.

'Pleased to meet you, Mr Sheehan,' she gave a polite curtsey, 'and I am even more pleased to wish you good day.'

With that, she turned on her heels and walked quickly down the street, swinging her bag in front of her, a broad smile on her lips.

She wasn't to know it yet, but in the following years, Daniel Sheehan was to make, and break, her heart many times.

CHAPTER NINETEEN

July 15, 1839

Sydney, Australia

She saw Daniel Sheehan many times over the next few months, bumping into him apparently by accident in the shops and on the street. At first she put it down to Sydney being a small town with only a few streets where people could shop or walk. But soon the sightings became so frequent, she knew that he was following her.

One day, she was delivering some bottles of broth to Mr Wiggs – they were now being labelled Wiggs' Energy Elixir – when Sheehan approached her again.

'It is good to see you, Miss Kelly.'

How did he know her name? Had he been checking on her? Did he even know where she lived?

The effrontery of the man, to accost her on the streets like a common trollop. She decided to go on the offence. 'Are you following me, Mr Sheehan?'

'Me?' he mouthed innocently. 'Of course I am.' He reached out and picked up one of the bottles she had in her basket. 'So this is where the famous Energy Elixir comes from; the kitchen of Mrs Furlong's home. What's inside? From your shopping habits, I would think roasted beef bones, assorted herbs, an onion or three, but I wonder what else? A dash of brandy, my tastebuds tell me. The stuff does have a kick to it.'

She took the bottle from him. 'As I have said before, that is none of your business. It is time for me to go.'

She turned to walk to the Furlong home.

'Haven't you forgotten to deliver your bottles to Mr Wiggs?'

She stopped. Damn the man for his impertinence. If her father were here, he'd beat him until he was black and blue.

She turned back and strode straight past him with her head held high, opening the door to the chemists, hearing the tinkle of the bell as she did.

Of course, he was waiting for her when she left.

'I am sorry if I have upset you, Miss Kelly.'

'How do you know my name?'

'It's a small place, easy to find anyone's name. Particularly a pretty girl who works for Captain and Mrs Furlong. You forget I am a journalist.'

She picked up her pace as she walked away from the shop, but he matched her stride for stride.

'Perhaps you could do your job and leave me alone.'

'But I am doing my job, Miss Kelly. Unfortunately that does include not leaving you alone. In fact, you will be the subject of my next article in the *Gazette*. The people of Sydney will be interested to discover who is the creator of the famous Elixir.'

She stopped once again. 'I do not want to appear between the sheets of your newspaper, Mr Sheehan.'

'I'm afraid the matter is of public interest, Miss Kelly, and my editor is an avowed supporter of your Elixir, so much so, he has asked me to purchase three bottles from you directly.'

'I am not a saleswoman, Mr Sheehan. The Elixir can only be purchased from Mrs Furlong or Mr Wiggs. I do not sell it, I merely make it.'

He smiled slowly. 'It is good to hear you confirm your role in its creation. Could I have a quote from you for the article?'

'Please do not approach me again. That is your quote, Mr Sheehan.' With that, she ran off down the road and didn't stop running until she reached the Furlongs' home.

That evening she told Mrs Furlong about her encounter with the journalist.

'Good, I have been pestering that editor, Howe, for the last month to write an article. He's had more than enough free bottles from me.'

'You don't mind?'

'Not at all. All publicity is good publicity. Between myself and Mr Wiggs, we will ensure the article is positive.'

'But Mr Sheehan says he will use my name.'

'I doubt it. But even if he does, it will be good publicity. People like to know where their medicines come from. It gives them an authenticity that is otherwise lacking.'

'I don't want to see my name in the paper.'

For the first time, Mrs Furlong softened her voice. 'Over the last year, I have come to enjoy your company and your work, Annie. You won't be a convict for ever. Your sentence was only seven years. With the money you are making and the reputation you are building, it will be easy to get your ticket-of-leave and the eventual commutation of your sentence. Listen to my advice. Build up your business and build a new life in this country. The old one holds nothing for you.'

'My family is still in Ireland.'

'Bring your family here. The colony is crying out for free migrants. The old days are nearly over. This country is going to be rich and prosperous. We are already sending wool back to England and the tonnage is increasing year on year. Captain Furlong and I have decided to make our home here when his army service comes to an end. You would be wise to do the same.' With those last words, she stood up. 'Now, don't you have some Elixir to make? It does not brew itself, you know.'

* * *

The next day, Mr Sheehan encountered her again as she was walking along George Street.

'Good morning, Miss Kelly. I have something for you.'

He produced a fresh newspaper from his bag, the ink barely dry.

'I hope you enjoy the article. I will not bother you again.'

He bowed once and then strode off down the street. She opened the newspaper and began reading the article under his byline.

Ireland's secret tonic is now available in Sydney
An Elixir so powerful, it was once drunk by the Kings of Ireland before battle

Readers of this column on life in our little community may have noticed a new preparation that has been available at the Pharmacy of Mr Wiggs and from the good offices of Mrs Furlong, wife of one of the leading soldiers of the 80th Regiment.

This preparation, called by its purveyors, The Elixir, has so far stunned the city with its efficacy particularly against the torrid effects of the Australian climate; torpidity, drowsiness, lassitude and as a balm during bouts of fever or restlessness.

Indeed, so effective is the Elixir that its potency has spread by word-of-mouth through the better class of citizen. Mrs Crawford, daughter of our head of the Commissary, has stated publicly, 'I have never felt better since drinking a bottle of the Elixir every morning. My health, appetite and constitution have all improved wondrously.'

This correspondent had the pleasure of meeting the creator of this fabulous tonic. She comes from the same poor country as the writer. A country rich in literature and history as well as the arcane knowledge of the herbal pharmacopeia. Her family has a long history of producing medicines, balms, tonics and elixirs for the ancient Kings of Ireland. Indeed, the famous Elixir was once drunk by King Brian Boru before the battle of Clontarf, to give him strength and energy for the day ahead.

When quizzed on the ingredients of the Elixir, its creator was circumspect. 'The ingredients are a secret handed down from generation to generation of herbalists in my family. I could not reveal them, sir, to anybody but on pain of death.'

Nobody could wish such a fate on the fair maker of the Elixir, so your correspondent did not press her further. But he has tried the Elixir himself and can vouch for its wondrous properties. Never has he felt so energetic or vitalised.

Indeed, he can add a new cure for one of the illnesses that plague the citizens of our little town. The Elixir is a marvellous tonic after a night out with friends at the various taverns and ale houses that lurk on the streets to tempt the innocent into a life of dissipation. The following morning, your correspondent drank one bottle and immediately felt as though he had spent the whole night sleeping soundly in his bed, his headache gone and his mind as fruitful and perspicacious as ever.

We thank the creator of this wonderful Elixir from the bottom of our hearts. It is rare that such a jewel of the ancient Irish medicinal arts is available in our town.

But we are lucky she has come here, bringing her Elixir with her.

THE ELIXIR IS AVAILABLE FROM MR WIGGS' CHEMIST AND MRS FURLONG AT THE EXTREMELY ATTRACTIVE PRICE OF 2 SHILLINGS AND SIXPENCE. TRY IT ONCE AND YOU WILL NEVER STOP,

She stopped reading. Of course, he had exaggerated the benefits of the Elixir and she never claimed it was drunk by the Kings of Ireland. Her father had merely created it for tiredness and anaemia. At least he had not mentioned her by name.

She glanced down the street. Mr Sheehan was nowhere in sight, vanished from view.

For a moment, she missed his attentions and his smile. Then she shook her head, told herself not to be a silly girl, and continued with her shopping.

But inside, she was secretly pleased with the write-up of her Elixir. At least she was keeping the memory of her father's work alive. And with a bit of luck, she would now be earning enough money to take a ship back to Ireland when her sentence was finished.

CHAPTER TWENTY

September 02, 1839
Sydney, Australia

Annie met him by chance six weeks later. At least, she thought it was by chance, as he appeared out of the blue in front of her.

'Good morning, Mr Sheehan. I haven't had the opportunity to thank you for the article you wrote in your newspaper.'

He attempted to edge past her. 'No need to thank me, ma'am, just doing my job.'

'There were, however, significant inaccuracies in the article. I never said my Elixir was given to the Kings of Ireland. In fact, I never told you anything about it.'

'Poetic licence, ma'am, newspapers are fond of it. Allows us to help the reader understand the qualities of your product. As for the personal details, they were supplied by your employers. I kept your name and any way of identifying you out of the article.'

He raised his hat. 'I bid you good day, ma'am.'

'Mr Sheehan, sales have almost trebled since your article. At least let me buy you some tea by way of recompense for your efforts on my behalf.'

'That is not necessary, ma'am.'

'I insist. Shall we go in here?' She pointed to the open door of a hotel. 'Unless you are too busy, of course.'

Daniel Sheehan smiled. 'Nobody could be too busy to refuse such an offer.'

They went inside and the proprietor approached them. 'Daniel, it's good to see you so early, what can I get you? The usual?'

'You seem to be well known here, Mr Sheehan. I presume you have written articles for them as well? What is your usual?'

'Even in Dublin, I was partial to a Lapsang Souchong from China. Will you join me?' He confirmed the order with the proprietor and added some petits fours.

A group of ladies at the next table waved at Daniel Sheehan, and he bowed in return.

'You *do* seem to be well known, Mr Sheehan.'

'The result of being a journalist, ma'am, one meets people from every walk of life.'

'Your acquaintances seem to be mostly women.'

'The *Gazette* has an avid readership amongst the fairer sex.'

The tea arrived in a large teapot. The proprietor arranged the china tea cups and silver spoons, placing a plate of petits fours on lace doilies in the middle of the table.

'Anything else, Daniel?'

'That looks grand, Mary, thank you.'

'Just call me if you need anything.'

With that, she walked away, her long black skirt trailing along the floor and her hips swaying from side to side.

There was silence at the table before Annie said, 'Shall I pour?'

'Please.'

She proceeded to pour the tea, and placed two petits fours on a plate for him using the silver tongs.

'For a country girl from Ireland, you do know the social niceties.'

'Firstly, Mr Sheehan, I am not a country girl from Ireland. As you already know, my father was a herbalist and we lived well.'

'And yet you are here?'

'And yet I am here,' she repeated, sipping a small mouthful of the Lapsang Souchong. The warm tea layered a scent of smoke and herbs on her tongue before softening to leave a wonderfully refreshing aftertaste.

'That is a very good choice, Mr Sheehan.'

'Thank you, I thought you would like it.'

Silence descended again.

'I wonder if—'

'I know nothing—'

They both spoke at the same time and then laughed.

'Ladies first,' said Daniel.

'I was going to say I know nothing about you, Mr Sheehan.'

'And yet here you are having tea with me. The gossiping women of Sydney town will be going wild with excitement.'

'Now you are teasing me.'

'Just a little. What would you like to know?'

'Whatever you would tell me.'

'I am here, that should tell you everything you want to know about me. A convict with a life sentence of transportation.'

'How did it happen? Did you commit murder?'

'Nothing so exciting. I was sentenced for a love of my country, Ireland, and a hatred of our coloniser, England.'

'I didn't know that was a defined as a criminal offence.'

'Ah, but it is. I was a journalist working for the *Honest Dubliner*. The authorities didn't like some of the more accurate articles I had written and I was charged with sedition.'

He reached into his jacket pocket, pulling out an old, leather wallet. From deep within, he selected a well-thumbed article clipped from a newspaper.

'You can read the story of my trial here, if you like. It was written by an Englishman for *The Times* but it is fair account of the proceedings, I think.'

She opened the folded and creased paper and began to read.

NEWSPAPER EDITOR IN COURT

CHARGED WITH SEDITION

Today Daniel Sheehan, the present editor of the *Honest Dubliner*, was arraigned at the Dublin Assizes charged with sedition and unlawful assembly…

'She stopped for a moment. 'It says you were the editor of the *Honest Dubliner*, not a journalist.'

'I did have that title. But what is an editor but a better-paid journalist with a green pencil?'

She continued to read.

The defendant was asked how he pled.

He raised himself up in the dock and answered, 'I plead not guilty and I do not recognise this court.'

Already a tall man, he now towered over his guards.

'What? What did the man say?' His Honour, Mr Justice Browne asked the question directly of the bailiff.

'He said he does not recognise the court, your honour.'

The judge's eyes flared red. 'Does not recognise this court? Well, sirrah, this court recognises you for the blackguard and disloyal miscreant that you are. Bring on the first witness.'

Mr Sheehan's answer seemed to have inflamed his lordship. It is this reporter's contention that it may have affected his sentence too.

In answer to the judge's call, a large, rotund man bustled his way through the crowd and bounded up to the witness box. The bailiff held a bible close to his right hand.

'Do you swear to tell the truth and nothing but the truth, so help you God?'

The witness replied that he did with a twinkle in his eye, which suggested to this correspondent that the truth was the last thing on his mind.

'Is your name Amos Sadgrove?' asked the prosecuting barrister.

He was an evil-looking soul called Hesaphiah Quigley with a scar across his right cheek. He looked more like a pugilist than a member of the bar. Indeed, it is whispered in the better drinking establishments in Dublin town that Mr Quigley obtained the scar whilst duelling when he was a Classics student at Trinity College.

It is interesting that so many proponents of the righteousness of the law have no problem breaking it in their own lives. However, that is an article for another day. Let us return to the trial of Mr Sheehan.

After agreeing that his name was Amos Sadgrove, the witness was asked about his profession by our duellist barrister.

'I am a publican, your honour, I have the rights to sell porter, ales and spirits at 7 Water Street in this city.'

'Do you know the man that stands before you in the witness stand?'

'I don't know him personally but I know of him.' The crowd in the courtroom laughed loudly at this response. The rotund man gained a little more confidence. 'Everybody knows of Daniel Sheehan, why, hasn't he been writing in the *Honest Dubliner* for the last year or so? Good articles too.'

'We will be the judge of Mr Sheehan's literary attributes, Mr Sadgrove, not you.' The prosecutor sniffed.

'Quite right, Mr Quigley, we will have no literary allusions in my court. This is a place of judgement, not a place of sentencing.'

The judge took another gulp of the claret, allowing the crowd to appreciate his *bon mot*, which they did with raucous laughter and a final round of applause.

His Lordship is famous in the legal profession for his aphorisms. Indeed, a book of his recent sayings, *Literary Judgements*, has been published and is available from Mr Harvie, bookseller of St Stephen's Green.

After this particular witticism, the prosecutor waited for the hubbub to die down before continuing.

'On January 14th in the fifth year of His Majesty's reign, did you see the man in the dock at your premises?'

'I did, your honour. The man and four others established themselves in a table at the corner and were whispering to each other.'

'Whispering? And what did they say?'

'Well, I couldn't hear everything but when I served them their port, I did hear him,' he pointed at Daniel Sheehan, 'say very clearly that it was time to attack Dublin Castle and overthrow all those damn'd English.'

A gasp of outrage flowed around the court.

The prosecutor allowed it to swell before shouting, 'Traitorous words, Mr Sadgrove.'

The man in the witness box touched his knuckle to his forehead. 'They were indeed, Mr Quigley, I was cut to the bone by them words.'

'So what did you do?'

'I sent a serving girl for the militia.'

'They came and arrested the men?'

'No, just Mr Sheehan. The rest had left before the militia arrived, but Mr Sheehan was still drinking his port.'

'Thank you, Sadgrove, for your honesty in coming here today.'

The bailiff asked, 'Who is acting for the defendant today?'

A clerk turned and whispered loudly, 'The defendant is acting for himself.'

'Proceed, Mr Sheehan.'

It was now the turn of the defendant to attempt to refute these heinous allegations by cross-examining the witness.

The defendant, a tolerably handsome man with an attractive ginger mane of hair, grasped his lapel with his right hand and threw out his left hand.

'I am standing here today, but I have done nothing wrong and am innocent of all the charges laid before me by the agents of the Crown. A Crown, I might say, that occupies my land illegally…'

At these words, the judge's gavel banged loudly on his desk three times. 'Mr Sheehan, the only person who makes speeches in my court is me. If you continue with your attempts at oratory, I will simply continue the trial without you.'

'Am I not allowed to argue the case for my defence?'

'Not in my court, no. You may question the witness but I will not stand for none of your Irish speechifying.'

Daniel Sheehan stood there for a few moments before turning to the witness. 'Have you seen me before at your establishment, Mr Sadgrove?'

'You have often frequented it with your friends, sir.'

'What language do we speak when we are sitting together?'

'What?' asked the judge. 'What language? The only language you should be speaking is the King's English.'

This produced many a 'here, here' and 'well said, sir' from the crowd.

'What language do we speak?' persisted Daniel Sheehan.

'I am not so sure, Mr Sheehan, but it could have been the Irish. I do not have the ear for the language myself.'

'And yet you said you understood what I was saying. How could that be if I was speaking Irish?'

The witness's mouth flapped open and shut twice and he glanced at the prosecutor for help.

'That is quite easy to answer, isn't it, Mr Sadgrove?' interrupted the judge. 'When you were serving these miscreants their port, they were speaking the King's English, just as Mr Sheehan is speaking it now. Isn't that correct, Mr Sadgrove?'

'It is correct, it is that, your honour. He was speaking the King's English as plain as the nose on your face.'

Annie Kelly stopped her reading and looked at Daniel. 'Did you know this man, this Sadgrove?'

'I used to drink at his ale house regularly with friends. He was forced to give evidence against me on pain of losing his licence. People often choose themselves or their families over Ireland. It is only to be expected.'

Annie didn't answer but continued reading.

The nails in Mr Sheehan's coffin were sealed by the next three witnesses.

Major Howard, who arrested Sheehan, swore that the defendant shouted 'Down with the King' as he was being arrested.

As an officer of the law, it was apparent that this testimony had a profound effect on the jury.

The next person called, a serving girl of just seventeen years named Molly McGinn, stated that she saw Daniel Sheehan writing treasonous words on a piece of paper.

'Can you read, Molly?' asked the defendant.

'A little, sir. I can read my name.'

'Can you write?'

'No, sir, I do not have the writing nor the grip for a pen.'

'So how do you know what I wrote on this mythical piece of paper?'

'It wasn't mystical, it was white with grey lines on it.'

The final witness was a Martin Duffy.

'Mr Duffy. You were one of the people in Mr Sheehan's party that night, were you not?'

'I was, your honour.'

'And you have come here to testify against Mr Sheehan at no little threat to yourself, your property, and the welfare of your family?'

'I have, your honour.'

'And did you hear Daniel Sheehan say the words heard by the innkeeper, Mr Sadgrove?'

'I did, my lord. As soon as I heard them, I decided that to stay in Mr Sheehan's company was treasonous and treacherous…'

'Treasonous and treacherous, you say?' interrupted the judge.

'Yes, m'lud, that is why I left as soon as the words were spoken and reported them to the militia.'

'Well done, exactly the correct behaviour of any responsible citizen.'

Daniel Sheehan questioned the man next. 'How long have I been acquainted with you, Mr Duffy?'

'I would think about a year, Mr Sheehan, off and on.'

'And had you ever heard me utter treasonous words before?'

'Not as such, and not with such venom against our sovereign lord, the King.'

'But you never reported me to the authorities before now?'

The man smiled, looking to the judge. 'The words were never so bad or so vehement as they were on that night.'

'Is it a coincidence, Mr Duffy, that my arrest by the police happened just after an article calling for the disestablishment of the Crown was published in the *Honest Dubliner*?'

'I wouldn't know anything about that.'

'And is it not true, Mr Duffy, that you are an agent of the Crown, planted amongst my friends to report back to Dublin Castle on our every action, word and deed?'

The judge banged heavily on his gavel. 'Mr Sheehan, you are not to impugn the character of this witness. He is simply an honest Irishman doing his utmost to show his loyalty to the Crown and the country.'

'The man Duffy was an informer?' Annie asked.

'It has always been the problem with Ireland. Too many people are willing to sell their souls for English gold. This man was just the latest in a long line…'

Annie looked down at the article again.

The prosecutor stood up. 'I will be brief, m'lud. You have heard the witnesses who said Mr Sheehan spoke words that were treasonous to the Crown. He is guilty.'

The man bowed once towards the judge and sat down, indicating his case was finished.

'I do like a brief summary, Mr Quigley. This time you have surpassed yourself with your brevity and your precision. I congratulate you.'

Mr Quigley bowed again.

'It is now your turn, Mr Sheehan, but if I were you, I would learn a lesson from the prosecuting barrister. Be brief.'

Daniel Sheehan stood up, grabbing his lapel in his right hand and began.

'It is my intention to say a few words only. I desire that the last act of a proceeding which has occupied so much of the public time should be of short duration. Nor have I the indelicate wish to close the dreary ceremony of a state prosecution with a vain display of

words. Had I a fear that hereafter, when I shall be no more, the country I tried to serve would speak ill of me, I might indeed avail myself of this solemn moment to vindicate my sentiments and my conduct. '

He paused dramatically for a second like an actor on a stage, letting the crowd understand and appreciate the sentiment behind his words before continuing.

'But I have no such fear. The country will judge of those sentiments and that conduct in a light far different from that in which the man sitting behind his high bench has viewed them, and by the country the sentence which you, my friends in the jury, are about to pronounce, will be remembered only as the severe and solemn attestation of my rectitude and truth…'

The judge's gavel banged loudly. 'Enough, enough, Mr Sheehan, you have gone on too long. Anyway, I am ready to give my judgement.'

'But I have not finished speaking in my defence.'

'But I have finished listening to you, Mr Sheehan. Gentlemen of the jury, have you reached your verdict?'

The foreman glanced towards his fellow jurors who all nodded. 'We have, your honour.'

'And what is that verdict?'

'Guilty as charged, your honour.'

'Daniel Sheehan, you have been found guilty of the charge. Normally, with such a heinous contravention of the King's Law, I would now be donning my black cap and sentencing you to be taken from the place and hanged.'

A few shouts of 'make it happen' and 'get on with it' came from the crowd.

The judge stared at the offenders and they immediately shut up.

'But in this case, thanks to the swift action of the authorities, no actual offence was committed, merely the intention to commit the offence. In addition, even though five people were present, there seems to be no conspiracy to commit sedition. Indeed, we heard from Mr Duffy that upon hearing your words, the others promptly left the inn.'

'They left because they were agents of the Crown.'

The judge ignored him, carrying on. 'The sentence is transportation for life to the colony of Australia.'

'But that means I will never able to see Ireland again.'

'Ireland will no doubt prosper in your absence,' the judge said, then squeezed himself out of his chair and walked back to his chambers with wig in hand.

The court was in uproar.

The reporters were shouting. The crowd was baying. A young woman was screaming but nobody could hear what she was saying.

In the middle of the maelstrom, Daniel Sheehan was standing tall and quiet, the calm at the eye of the storm. A prisoner of Ireland to the last.

Annie stopped, she had read enough. 'So on this evidence you were sentenced to life here in this colony?'

'I shipped out on the *Captain Cook* on July fifth from Cork, three months after my trial, and I have been here ever since.' A long pause as he looked away from Annie, staring out through the open window, before whispering, 'I miss the green of Ireland so…'

She reached over and touched the back of his hand, quickly pulling back her arm when she realised what she had done.

'It is time for me to leave, Mr Sheehan.' She brought out her purse and signalled to the waitress to bring her the bill.

The woman sidled over. 'Daniel does not pay for tea here. It's always on the house.'

'But he didn't buy it, I did.'

The woman shook her head. 'Sorry, we owe Daniel for the articles he wrote on our behalf. He does not pay and neither do his guests.'

'I insist on paying.'

'And I insist you don't.'

'Ladies, ladies, fighting over a bill? Will wonders never cease.'

Annie glared at him. 'I insist on paying.'

The woman folded her arms across her chest. 'I won't accept your money.'

Daniel put his hand up. 'Perhaps I can suggest a compromise.' He reached over to Annie's purse and took one penny from it, William IV's broad forehead and curly locks proudly stamped on one side.

'You can pay me, Miss Kelly, for the article.'

'But the tea costs far more than one penny.'

'Nonetheless, that is what I am charging. Do you accept my bill?'

Annie nodded quickly.

'Good, we are finished here. Let me escort you to the street, Miss Kelly.'

They stood up and he took her arm.

At that moment, she didn't know how or why, but she knew she loved him.

CHAPTER TWENTY-ONE

Tuesday, September 15, 2020

Perth, Australia

Jayne Sinclair had just stepped through the doorway of the house in Dalkeith when Vera came rushing out to meet her.

'Thank goodness you're back. Your dad…'

Vera hadn't finished the sentence before Jayne ran past her into their bedroom. Robert was lying in bed, his face white and his breathing laboured.

'He was okay until five minutes ago, when he woke and was struggling to breathe and complaining of a pain in his chest and tingles down his left arm. I've raised him up in the bed and checked his air passages. He's a bit better than he was but I've already called an ambulance, they should be here any second. I think he may have had a heart attack.'

Jayne stared at her stepfather. Sweat dampened his forehead and his grey hair was already soaking.

'Are you okay, Dad?'

Robert attempted a weak smile and nodded a 'yes', but Jayne could see he was in difficulty.

'I've given him some aspirin but we need to check the oxygen levels in his blood. The medics will do that when they arrive.'

Vera was rearranging the pillows around Robert's back to give him more support.

'I'm alright, love,' he whispered.

'No, you are not, Robert Cartwright. You are going to the hospital for a proper check-up and that's the last I will hear of the discussion.'

Robert started to argue and then realised he didn't have the strength.

The door-bell rang and Vera ran down to open the door. In seconds, two medics – one male and one female, both heavily masked – walked in, checking the doors and corridors. They were soon quickly examining Robert.

'Are you having difficulty breathing, mate?' asked one, while the other attached a pulse oximeter to his index finger.

Robert nodded.

'Any pain?'

Robert pointed to his chest and to his arm.

'Feels like an elephant sitting on your chest, mate?'

'He's also been reporting a tingling sensation down his left arm. I gave him an aspirin five minutes ago.'

'Has he been unwell recently?'

Vera answered, 'He has been complaining of tiredness and shortness of breath. He's spent most of the day sleeping but woke up a short while ago with difficulty breathing and chest pains.'

As Vera spoke, the male medic examined Robert's chest and eyes while the female medic attached electrodes from an electro-cardiograph to his chest.

'Any history of asthma or breathing problems?'

'A bout of pneumonia two years ago.'

'Right.'

'Eighty-nine per cent oxygen,' said the female medic.

'We need to get you to hospital immediately, mate, but before we move you I'm going to give you some oxygen to help you breathe easier.'

He reached into the bag and pulled out an oxygen bottle and mask, which he attached over Robert's head, checking the oxygen was flowing freely.

'STEMI is elevated,' said the female medic.

Robert took three deep breaths and immediately his face seemed less pale.

'I'll just go and get the gurney,' said the female medic.

'Is that better, mate?'

Robert nodded and gave a thumbs-up.

'Still pain?'

Robert pointed to his chest.

'On a scale of one to ten, with ten being the worst, how bad is it?'

Robert put five fingers up, then increased the number to seven.

'That's not too bad, is it? Right, we're going to take you to the hospital as you may be having a heart attack. But the ECG can only tell us so much. The way to be sure is to check the levels of troponin in your blood. I've sent your results to a cardiologist, he'll let us know if we should go to the emergency department or direct to a catheter lab. I'll give you something for the pain.'

He turned to Vera. 'Is he allergic to any medicines?'

'No, not at all.'

The medic pulled back the mask and popped a small tablet into Robert's mouth. 'Do you need any water, mate?'

Robert shook his head.

He placed the mask carefully over Robert's mouth, checking the straps were firmly attached. Then he stood up and spoke to Vera and Jayne.

'His oxygen levels are too low, so he definitely needs to be checked out. He could have Covid but he's not showing any symptoms. The doctors will only know for sure when they test.'

'I used to be a nurse, I don't think it's Covid,' Vera said.

'He could be asymptomatic, one can never be sure. Or it could be his heart. Any history of heart problems?'

'None that we know of. We had a medical before we came to Australia and he was okay. Just the usual signs of old age. He was diagnosed with early-onset Alzheimer's seven years ago, but he hasn't declined greatly in that time.'

As Vera spoke, the medic was writing all this down on his tablet.

The female medic returned with the gurney.

'Let's get you on here, mate, and we'll put you in the ambulance.'

'Where are you taking him?' asked Jayne.

'The Royal. Who is coming with us? Because of Covid, you'll have to mask up.'

'I think you should, Vera, I'll follow in an Uber. Do you want me to bring anything?'

The female medic was already wheeling Robert out of the bedroom. Vera followed her closely. 'My knitting and a book. I'll message you where I am.'

Jayne followed the medics as they carefully placed Robert in the back of the ambulance. One climbed in the back to stay with Robert and Vera, the other sat in the driver's seat.

As they drove away, Jayne swallowed and held back the tears.

Would she see her stepdad again?

CHAPTER TWENTY-TWO

Tuesday, September 15, 2020

Perth, Australia

'He'll be okay, don't worry, Jayne.'

Vera took her daughter-in-law's hand in hers, holding it tightly.

They were sitting in the emergency department of the Royal Perth Hospital. Jayne had arrived thirty minutes ago after packing a spare change of clothes and some things for Vera in a bag.

She had been through this before with Robert and knew exactly what to do.

'How was he when he went in?'

Vera stared into mid-air. 'Not good,' she said slowly. 'He had a greyness to his face which I've never seen before. His cheeks are normally so rosy and his eyes so vibrant. They're what drew me to him in the first place. That and his kindness.' Vera swallowed and her voice broke. 'I don't know what I'll do if anything happens to him, Jayne.'

This was the first time Jayne had ever seen Vera upset. Normally, she was always so down-to-earth and in control.

It was Jayne's turn to squeeze her hand. 'I don't know either, Vera. He's our rock.'

At that moment, a doctor appeared in front of them. 'Mrs Cartwright?'

'That's me,' said Vera.

'I'm afraid your husband is not at all well. The good news is he doesn't have Covid. We've tested him and he's negative.'

'That's a relief, at his age…' Vera didn't finish her sentence.

'Does he have any history of heart problems?'

They both shook their heads.

'As I told the medics,' Vera said, 'we had medicals before we travelled and we were both okay. He has had pneumonia before and was diagnosed with early-onset Alzheimer's seven years ago.'

'Right.' The doctor looked down at his pad.

'Please tell us what's going on.'

The doctor took a deep breath. 'We think he may have had a heart attack. We're still waiting for the results of the tests, but we've decided to admit him for observation.'

'Heart attack?' said Jayne.

'It's a distinct possibility, but we'll know more later. We're going to move him up to a room shortly. A nurse will be along to take all his details. I presume he was being treated by the NHS?'

'For the pneumonia and the Alzheimer's, but nothing else. He doesn't like hospitals much.'

'Nobody does, not even those of us who work in them.'

'How is he really, Doctor?' asked Vera.

'He's very ill, Mrs Cartwright, but luckily you spotted the symptoms early and called for an ambulance. Now he's here, we'll give him the best treatment we can.' He patted her on the shoulder. 'I need to arrange his ward now. The nurse will take the details and you can go up and see him once we have settled him in.'

'Thank you, Doctor.'

The man strode back to his department, walking with an effortless speed that all emergency doctors seemed innately to possess.

Jayne and Vera were left standing there, watching him vanish from view, unable to say anything to each other and understanding that, at times like these, words were never necessary.

CHAPTER TWENTY-THREE

February 14, 1840
Sydney, Australia

They were married on a warm February day by Father John Therry in St Mary's Chapel.

'I, Annie Kelly, take you, Daniel Sheehan, for my lawful husband. To have and to hold from this day forward; for better, for worse; for richer, for poorer; in sickness and in health; until death do us part. I will love and honour you all the days of my life.'

They had both obtained permission from the colonial authorities before posting their banns in the church. At first, they had been refused permission to marry but, after the intercession of Captain Furlong and his wife, it was finally granted.

Annie had spent the intervening time sewing the dress herself from a long piece of white brocade she had bought in Simpson's Haberdasher's, enjoying the whole process of dress-making once more.

Daniel was in a new three-quarter-length frock coat and waistcoat, a present from Mr Howe, the editor of the *Sydney Gazette and New South Wales Advertiser*. 'No employee of mine is going to get married in the same clothes he interviews his clients.'

Daniel looked more like one of the newly rich landowners of New South Wales than the convict he was. He looked at himself in the mirror and thought that, for the first time since his trial, he looked vaguely human, not a criminal. He placed the penny he had taken from Annie's purse when they first had tea together in his fob pocket and patted it for good luck.

A penny and a wife, he thought. Not a bad bargain.

After they had exchanged vows, the priest blessed both of them with the words, 'You have declared your consent before the Church. May the Lord in his goodness strengthen your consent and fill you both with his blessings. What God has joined, men must not divide. Amen.'

With that, they repaired to Mrs Furlong's house where cakes, wine, ale and music were provided long into the night.

Their first child, John, arrived nine months later, on a beautiful December day. Annie had been drinking her own Elixir in the last months of her pregnancy, as well as applying poultices across her stomach created from recipes her father had sent her from Ireland. He had long specialised in the correct herbs and tonic for pregnant women. Annie recreated these now for herself, in the process making a new line to be sold by Mr Wiggs and Mrs Furlong.

During her pregnancy, two more female convicts from Ireland were hired to help do the more physical work, with Annie elevated to the post of supervisor. From a chair in the outhouse, she now watched over as the four women made each new batch of the Elixir and created the new tonics for pregnant women, which she first tried on herself.

The results were plain to see. A big, bright, bonny baby boy weighing just under eight pounds and in possession of the thickest mop of ginger hair they had ever seen.

'They are all saying how much he looks like you, Daniel.'

'It's the hair, the ginger runs in our family.'

'It can't be from my side.'

The baby was in her arms sleeping peacefully, his pert nose like a little button on his face.

'We must take care of him properly. I have instructed the girls to make a tonic to ensure my milk is rich and strong. Afterwards, when he starts to take solids, we must ensure he has the right food. Too many babies die young in Sydney before the end of their first year. That will not be the fate of my firstborn.'

From behind his back, Daniel produced a book.

'This is a bible given to me by my parents before I left Ireland. It is the only thing I still have of them. Inside I have inscribed his name and date of birth.'

He opened the bible to show the initial pages. Annie saw the name of her son, John Henry, written at the top in Daniel's wonderfully ornate hand.

'It is yours now, for ever.'

He placed it on the coverlet next to the baby.

'It is ours,' Annie emphasised, 'and I see there is plenty of room for you to write more names. We will have many more children in Australia, you and I, many more children.'

For a moment, Annie remembered her father and mother back in Ireland. She would write to them today to give them the good news of the birth.

Would they ever see their first grandchild?

CHAPTER TWENTY-FOUR

Wednesday, September 16, 2020
Perth, Australia

After two hours at the hospital, Jayne had returned to the house in Dalkeith at 12.30. They decided to split the time spent with Robert so that somebody was always there with him. Vera would spend the first night and Jayne would go the next day at noon.

They had talked with Harry over the phone, who offered to come in from the farm to be with them both, but decided it wasn't necessary until they knew the full extent of Robert's illness.

The last memory Jayne had was seeing him asleep with an oxygen mask over his face and the heart monitor beeping beside the bed. At least he was asleep, the sedatives having finally kicked in.

Now she stood in the open-plan kitchen, not knowing what to do. She should try to get some sleep but her mind was racing.

What if Robert had another heart attack?

What if he died?

How would they get back to England?

What would she do without him?

She looked down at her hands and found they were shaking. The last time she had been like this was when she was in the police.

Her partner had been shot in Moss Side right in front of her. She had watched him die in her arms before the medics had arrived. She had been uninjured, but afterwards, the lasting trauma had meant she could no longer function as a police officer. In the end she had left the force, taking early retirement when it was offered.

For a long time she had been at a loose end, not knowing what to do and not committing to anything.

It was Robert who had saved her. He had involved her in the research of his own family tree, and she found she enjoyed it more than anything else she had done for a long time.

It was also Robert who had encouraged her to take professional courses in genealogy and set up a company specialising in investigating genealogical cases, her skills as a detective and a researcher finally reaching their full potential.

That had been six years ago now, and she thanked him every day for pushing her and encouraging her. In her new career.

He was her rock and she didn't know what she would do without him.

She stood there, wondering if she should make herself a coffee, pour a glass of wine, watch television or just go to bed.

Then she heard his voice just as clearly as if he were standing next to her.

Don't mope around, lass. Nowt will come from worrying about me all night long. You've got a client who's expecting work from you. Get on with it.

She stared at her laptop. Should she get on with investigating Liz's family? At least it would keep her mind from worrying about Robert.

She opened the laptop and keyed in her password. Where to start?

Duncan had made it clear that he thought most of Annie's obituary was made up; an attempt to comply with the social mores of the day. Was her birth date or any of the information correct?

Jayne thought even that date might be suspect. After all, if you were going to invent a history for yourself then why not start with something as simple as a birth date?

She got up and made herself a coffee. If she was going to work tonight, she should at least try to give her brain a kickstart.

She brought the coffee back to the table and inhaled the aroma. She could feel the scent of the beans drift up to her brain and infuse it with energy. A quick sip and she felt the jolt of the caffeine.

Duncan had also said two other things. He thought Annie was Irish because of her surname, and that she had been a convict at one time.

Luckily, there were extensive records for the convicts that arrived in Australia.

Jayne logged on to the Convict Records website and typed in the name 'Annie Kelly'.

A lot of records, but unfortunately they weren't filtered. The site gave her everybody surnamed 'Kelly' and everyone with the Christian name 'Annie'.

Scanning them, she could see they contained a few people with just the name 'Anne Kelly' but they didn't really help her identify the person she was looking for. Even worse, these records were mainly from England, Wales and Scotland, with only a few Irish records included. If Annie Kelly was Irish, as Duncan thought, her record might not even be on the list.

She would have to narrow down the list of alternatives before using this site. She took another sip of coffee and logged on to Findmypast. At least here she could use filters to narrow her search.

The first record she checked was the one entitled *Australian Convict Ships 1786–1849*.

The records weren't complete in this archive, but at least it would give her a start. They included indents and muster records for the convicts in Australia, but some years and some records were missing.

She reasoned Annie wouldn't have been transported before 1820, so she entered this as a filter. With name variants ticked, this gave her 45 possibilities. She checked a few of them, seeing the records of convict women transported so long ago for such trivial offences as burglary, stealing spoons, and even vagrancy.

The level of detail included in the record was astonishing. Name, religion, marital status, birthplace, profession, crime, place and date of trial, sentence, height, complexion, hair and eye colour. The physical descriptions were the best she had ever read. One Anne Kelly was described as having:

A scar on the right eyebrow, mole on the right side of neck. Tattoo of the letters M A L M A H J. BH. S, Tattoo of a woman and glass on the upper right arm. Ring on the middle finger of the right hand. JF heart surrounded by ten dots. Flag, woman, and anchor on the upper left arm. Anchor in lower part of same. Ring on forefinger of left hand.

Added to the height description of 4 feet 10 inches and 'a fair, ruddy, pock-pitted complexion with sandy hair', Jayne could imagine an exact picture of the woman.

'It's almost as good as a modern photofit,' she said to herself. 'Not a woman I'd like to meet on a dark night in an even darker alley somewhere in the back streets of Dublin.'

She went through ten of the Anne Kellys listed before realising that none of this was helping her isolate the one woman she needed. The problem was, she had no physical description of Annie and wasn't even sure she was a convict.

She quickly checked another record which was held on Findmypast: The convict transportation records for 1787–1870. These were the original hand-written records for the convicts and their ships.

She filtered the record to 1820 and received 16 hits. Checking these results, she could see where the convicts were tried and sentenced, what their crime was, the ships they sailed on, and their date of arrival in Australia.

But once again, she couldn't isolate the Anne Kelly she wanted.

Jayne checked the clock. It was now 2.30 a.m. and she hadn't really made any progress. She wondered how Robert was doing and sent a text.

How is he?

She received a reply almost immediately.

He's fine, sleeping soundly. You need to get some sleep too.

Vera was right. If she was going to be at the hospital by noon, she would have to get at least a few hours' sleep otherwise she would be a basket case tomorrow. And anyway, she wasn't making much progress at the moment. Perhaps tomorrow would bring her better luck.

She shut her laptop and texted Vera.

Off to bed now. Call me if anything happens.
Will do. Now SLEEEEEEP!!!

Jayne smiled at Vera's reply, so typical of her stepmother. She stood up and walked wearily to her bedroom.

Was Robert going to be alright?

CHAPTER TWENTY-FIVE

February 1840 to December 1845
Sydney, Australia

Annie spent the next few years in married bliss. Two other children followed in quick succession to John: Dominic born in 1842, and Honorah in 1845.

Of course, there were many changes during this time. Sydney was a city that was expanding and growing at an incredible pace.

In 1841, Captain Furlong was appointed the police magistrate in Mudgee and the family moved with him. Annie obtained permission from the colonial authorities to remain in Sydney, still under the nominal employ of Mrs Furlong, producing the Elixir and expanding the range of her wares into tinctures and tonics for infirmity, old age, growing children, and pregnant and postpartum mothers. All these new medicines were created from the recipes her father had sent her in his letters, with adaptations to the ingredients available in Sydney.

Both Mr Wiggs and Mrs Furlong increased the amount of money she received for each product to sixpence. Now she was producing and selling over two hundred items a month, the money was adding up considerably. Despite Daniel's misgivings, it all still went into a box under her bed.

The only time it was opened was when she took money out to send to her parents in Ireland. As a convict she couldn't open a bank account, but Mrs Furlong agreed to send the money using her resources. After being forced to move from Durrow to Kilkenny, her father had never been able to re-establish his clientele. Her brother and sister were forced to work to support their aging parents. Annie sent what she could, but she knew it was never enough.

In 1843, after Annie was introduced to an Aboriginal woman called Frances living in Woolloomooloo, she began to use indigenous plants in her formulations. She went out on foraging expeditions along the shoreline and in the bush with the Aboriginal woman, learning the medicinal properties of these strange plants not found in her native Ireland.

She soon began experimenting with the leaves of the eucalyptus tree to treat coughs and colds, with the bark being used against scabies. The yellow vine was added to her balms to treat sores and rashes. She used the leaves of the corkwood tree as an antiseptic to help clean wounds, while the dried and ground-up fruit of the snakeberry were added to her creams against ringworm and skin infections in children.

At first she proudly explained to her customers and to Mr Wiggs how she was incorporating these native herbs in her traditional medicines, but she found they wouldn't use them.

As Mr Wiggs patiently explained one day, 'My customers are looking for the tinctures and lotions they are used to from Europe, not some useless medicine from the natives. You only have to look at how ill and ill-kept these people are to realise their medicines have no efficacy.'

'But I assure you, Mr Wiggs, they work. I have tried them myself.'

'You may think they work, Mrs Sheehan, but your customers do not. We will not be taking any more orders of your medicines if they contain those native materials. Stick to the Elixir and your father's recipes, Annie, we know they work and your customers love them.'

So Annie decided to continue to use the native materials, but simply not tell her customers. She kept the recipes of her various balms, tinctures, lotions and creams a closely guarded secret. Even the four convict girls Mrs Furlong employed to make the medicines did not know the recipe or the ingredients. They were simply employed in physically boiling the mixtures or parcelling them out into the various bottles and jars.

Annie's business continued to grow, but Daniel had

more ups and downs. One day in 1842, he returned home to reveal the *Sydney Gazette and New South Wales Advertiser* was going to close.

'They've been losing money for a long time, and I am not surprised. The new paper, the *Morning Herald* founded by Mr Fairfax, has taken most of the advertising money from the *Gazette*.'

'What are you going to do?'

'I don't know. A convict is not allowed to do nothing in this place. I suppose I will go back to being a clerk.'

'Couldn't you ask Mr Fairfax for a position?'

'I have tried already. All his journalists are "currently well employed and he has no need of any further assistance".'

Annie thought for a while. 'Why don't you open your own newspaper? Be the editor as you were in Dublin, be your own boss.'

'Newspapers cost money, Annie. There's printing, paper and distribution costs, not to mention an office where people can work and salaries to pay.'

'I have some money saved up.'

'But your sentence will end next year, you could apply for your Certificate of Freedom and return to Ireland.'

'And leave you and the children here? I can't do that.' She placed her hand on his arm. 'I have written to my family telling them my life is here in Australia with you now. My father understands, it is too late to go back.'

'Don't say that. It is never too late to go back to Ireland. One day we will all return, leaving this country and its wildness behind.'

'Think about opening the paper, it would be the right thing to do.'

'Free publicity for your wares?'

She laughed. 'Another article from Daniel Sheehan would work wonders.'

Daniel did think about this new project even as he toiled away each day at the supply department, writing inventories of blankets, picks, shovels and other building sundries in his neat hand.

'We should call it the *Sydney Irishman*. It should talk to all the Irish settlers, both freemen and convicts, giving them news of home as well as from Sydney and the other regions. We could use the newspapers from Ireland that come with the ships, but I have had a new idea…' Daniel said.

'And what is that?'

'We'll ask people to show us the letters they receive from home and we'll print those. It will be like having reporters in every county of Ireland.'

'Are there that many letters?'

'Those who can't read or write use professional letter writers to communicate with their loved ones. I used to write letters for people if they were illiterate. I'd add a few details about Dublin and how the city was doing, but mostly people told me what they wanted to say and I put it into good English or Irish for them. It's those sorts of letters we should print. They give a true flavour of home.'

Annie noticed that Daniel still referred to Ireland as home despite having lived in Australia for nearly eight years.

The more she thought about her husband's idea, the more attractive it seemed. If they could persuade people to print their letters, it would be direct personal experience of home. A point of difference from the *Herald* and all the other papers.

'We'll need advertisers to support us, and what better than the church and its congregations? People want to read about home and the *Herald* concentrates on news from England. We will keep the love for Ireland alive here.'

The following day they went to see Archbishop Polding at St Mary's after an introduction from Father Therry.

The archbishop was a sharp, austere man. He met them in his rooms sat behind a high desk and wearing the robes of his office.

After Daniel explained his idea for the newspaper and asked for his support, the archbishop paused and brought his fingers together as if in prayer, gold rings glinting in the late afternoon light.

'Why should I support another paper? We already have the *Australasian Chronicle* to spread the Church's views to its flock.'

'Begging your Grace's pardon,' began Daniel, 'but the *Sydney Irishman* would have a much wider remit than simply spreading the views of the Church. It would give the Irish population of Australia – currently numbering twenty-two thousand men and women – news from home, the prices of woollen products and manufactures, as well as championing the rights of the smallholders, farmers and workers in Australia. We would even have articles helping to educate these workers in their rights, duties and obligations. In fact, we will devote two pages to education in every issue, teaching people how to read and write and about the issues of the day, particularly as they relate to Ireland.'

The archbishop smiled. 'You have done your homework, Mr Sheehan. You know well that I have a particular interest and desire to see the Catholic flock educated in this society. Without education we cannot advance.'

'You have created eleven Catholic schools in the area and brought in the Sisters of Charity to help educate your flock. Your commitment to their education is well known, your Grace. I too agree that the Irish will only advance by being as educated, or better educated, than the English.'

'Will the newspaper support the Church in all its activities in this country? We are expanding rapidly as the population grows. I will be appointing bishops for Adelaide, Perth and Melbourne as soon as I find suitable candidates.'

'Of course, your Grace, we will always support the Church.'

He made the sign of the cross over both of them. 'Then you have my blessing. Now before you go, Annie, do you have anything for the arthritis? The pain in my wrist and fingers is excruciating.'

The rest of Sydney society was more difficult to win over, but with Annie's connections and the support of the Furlongs, the *Sydney Irishman* launched its first edition in February 1844.

Daniel ran home with the first printed paper tucked under his arm. He strode into the house and presented it to Annie as she was feeding a young Dominic.

'We've sold out the first edition, Annie. Next week, we will print one hundred extra copies.'

Annie looked at the paper. The front page was full of adverts, including a large one from Mr Wiggs, as well as the comings and goings of the various ships entering the docks and the cargoes they carried.

But it was the inside pages of the newspaper of which Daniel was most proud.

'See, my father sent me the latest news from Dublin with the arrival of the *Maitland* as well as copies of the *Freeman's Journal*, the *Nation* and the *Dublin Evening Mail*. The *Morning Register* has closed, though. A shame. I started my career working there in 1827: a lovely man, the editor. The news is fascinating. O'Connell has been charged with conspiracy and the Devon Commission appointed to look into the land leases. O'Connell will survive, though, the man's a true Irish leader.'

She had never seen him so excited or happy and it filled her heart with joy.

'You can read my leader, if you want. I want to give the paper a meaning for the Irish in Australia.'

She read it out loud.

'"The *Sydney Irishman* will provide the Irish of Australia with a weekly newspaper which will tell all the news of their home and their new world, relying on the principles of candour, honesty and honour, reporting the news without fear or favour. In Ireland, it will support the right of the country to rule itself without the interference of foreign powers. In Australia, it will provide readers with a champion of their rights as workers and landholders in their new country. We will be a voice for the poor and down-trodden everywhere."'

She stopped reading and looked over at her husband, standing proudly beside the hearth. 'It's a big promise, Daniel.'

'But it's one we will deliver, Annie.'

'What if the authorities object?'

'We will continue to fight, as we have always fought, here and in Ireland.'

Annie folded the paper neatly and placed it next to the

baby in his crib.

She loved her husband but hoped his love of Ireland didn't put them all into danger.

CHAPTER TWENTY-SIX

January 13, 1845
Sydney, Australia

Annie had prepared herself for this moment for seven years. On a bright, sunny Monday morning, the former Captain Furlong – now Major after his promotion – called her into his office at Hyde Park Barracks.

'I think you know what's coming, Mrs Sheehan. The Governor is pleased to present you with this.'

He handed over a fairly heavy weight of paper. Annie unrolled it and immediately tears began to well in the corners of her eyes.

She read the contents.

Certificate of Freedom.

By Order of His Excellency, the Right Honourable George Gipps, Kt, a member of Her Majesty's Privy Council in Ireland, Governor and Commander-in-Chief of the Colony of New South Wales and its dependencies.

This is to certify that SEVEN years having elapsed since the Sentence of Penal Servitude for that Term was passed on ANNE

SHEEHAN NEE KELLY, No: 47261, was tried at KILKENNY ASSIZES on the 7TH day of OCTOBER, 1836 and who arrived in this colony by the Ship SIR CHARLES FORBES, JAMES LESLIE, Master, in the year 1837, the said ANNE SHEEHAN, who is described on the other side, is restored to all the rights of Free Subject under such circumstances.

Given at the office of the Convict Department, Sydney, this 13TH day of JANUARY in the year of one thousand eighteen hundred and FORTY-FIVE.

**Signed: Chief Clerk
Signed: Inspector General of Police**

'Mrs Sheehan, you must keep this certificate safely about your person at all times and you are required to produce it when asked to do so by a lawfully constituted member of the police or officer of the colonial government.'

Annie just nodded without saying a word, still staring at the words on the piece of paper.

'Can I also add my personal note of congratulations to you,' Major Furlong said. 'You have become an upstanding member of our community in the colony and the Governor wanted me to pass on his personal thanks to you. He has found your Elixir particularly stimulating in these troubled times, the squatters and their wealthy friends giving him no end of trouble.'

Annie barely mumbled 'thank you' before carefully folding the paper into four and placing it into a wallet for safekeeping.

'There is, however, a condition attached to the Certificate of Freedom. It is only valid in Australia and the colonies.'

'What does that mean?' she asked suspiciously.

'The certificate is not valid in Ireland or the rest of the United Kingdom.'

These last words stunned Annie. She couldn't return home? She couldn't go back to Ireland? Never see her parents, brother and sister again?

'But I have served my sentence, why are there conditions attached to my freedom?'

Major Furlong shrugged his newly epauletted shoulders. 'The order of the resident magistrate, I'm afraid. Anyway, you have a husband and children in Sydney. Your husband has been transported for life, how could you leave him?'

He was right, she could never leave Daniel. Not now, not ever.

'My wife and Mr Wiggs have asked that you think about remaining in Sydney. In consideration of the time and effort you have put into the development of your medicines in the last few years, they would like to make you a junior partner in the company formed to make and distribute your products. It would mean that you would receive a director's salary of one pound a year plus a share of the profits of the enterprise. What do you say to that, Mrs Sheehan?'

Annie smiled to herself. She had expected this to happen ever since she knew her Certificate of Freedom would be granted at the end of her sentence. She had thought about going out on her own, making and selling the products herself. But she realised very quickly that the whole process would be expensive and costly, particularly as Mr Wiggs was the only retailer of pharmaceutical products in Sydney, and Mrs Furlong had the only distribution channels into the interior.

In the future, she could consider going out on her own, but not yet.

'A partnership, you say, Major Furlong? And what percentage of the company would I own?'

'A significant percentage. Mrs Furlong and Mr Wiggs are prepared to offer you a ten per cent partnership.'

It was better than she thought. She had expected only five per cent from them. Even that would have been generous for an ex-convict.

'I'm afraid I couldn't accept an offer less than fifteen per cent,' she finally said.

Major Furlong looked surprised. 'I can go no higher than twelve per cent, and that is final.'

His words were interesting, betraying who really made the decisions in the company. The offer came from Major Furlong without recourse to anybody else.

'I accept,' she said. 'I also have some new products I

am working on. A new balm for the rheumatism and an inhalant for children with asthma.'

'That is good news, Mrs Sheehan. My wife will be pleased.'

And then it hit Annie.

She had committed to staying in Australia. She would never see her family or Ireland again.

'As a free citizen, you could even invite your family to join you here in Sydney. We are looking for many new immigrants now that the convict transportation has ceased.'

It was as if he had been reading her thoughts. She would write to her father and mother that evening and invite them to come to Australia. Would they ever leave Ireland?

While she had Major Furlong's attention, she decided to ask him something that had been troubling her since her marriage.

'My husband, will he ever get his freedom?'

Major Furlong looked down for a moment and then said, 'It is possible, but he was sentenced to transportation for life and the crime was sedition, a most serious offence. However, it is in the Governor's power to grant him a pardon if he sees fit. For such a serious offence, Mr Sheehan would have to show his contrition and be supportive of the government in everything it does. Do you understand me?'

Annie understood.

Daniel would have to give up everything he held dear to obtain his freedom.

Would he do it?

CHAPTER TWENTY-SEVEN

Wednesday, September 16, 2020

Perth, Australia

The next morning Jayne woke up with a start and sat up in bed.

Something had been nagging her all night, a voice whispering in her dreams. She realised that she had started in the wrong place with her investigation into Annie Kelly. The only information she could really trust was the family bible, with its names of the children and their birth dates.

She jumped out of bed, ready to rush to her laptop, but then she remembered Robert. How was he?

She quickly messaged Vera.

How is he? Sleeping well?

A good night, he slept well. The doctor checked on him and we'll know more later. I'll ask them to tell us what is happening at noon when you arrive.

I'll be there before then. You must be tired…

I'm okay, just spent the night worrying.

Jayne felt immediately guilty. While she had been sleeping, Vera had been up all night at Robert's bedside. She would go well before noon and then at least Vera could take a break.

She went into the kitchen and fixed herself a coffee. Her laptop was lying closed on the countertop. Did she have time to check out her idea before leaving for the hospital?

Jayne recognised this obsessive streak in herself. Once she was on the trail of an investigation she focused solely on it, often to the exclusion of everything else, even forgetting to eat sometimes. It had been the same when she was in the police and was one of the reasons she was promoted so rapidly.

It was a part of her personality that Robert recognised.

'It's the only way to work, lass, you give it everything or you don't do it. It's all or nothing.'

But now he was lying in hospital, gravely ill, and all she had thought about was work and finding out the truth about Annie Kelly.

She ignored her laptop and sipped her coffee. She checked the time on the large clock on the wall: 7.30 a.m.

She would leave at eleven o'clock for the hospital, perhaps stopping off somewhere en route to get Vera a good latte and a muffin.

What was she going to do until eleven?

She stared at the laptop and it stared back at her.

She finally reached out to open it up, inputting her password. Robert would understand, he knew how important work was.

She stopped for a moment, her fingers hovering over the keyboard. What was the thought she'd had last night?

She focused on remembering until it finally came to her. She had dreamt of a large hand coming in to sweep away the obituary, knocking it on to the floor, bringing the bible in and jabbing its finger against the names listed at the top.

John Henry   Dec 8, 1840
Dominic James   Feb 27, 1842
Honorah Bridget Mar 3, 1845

What if the family tree was correct and these were Annie's children? What if they weren't born in England or Ireland? What if the records of the family actually started in Australia, not in any of the home countries?

As these questions swirled around her brain, Jayne knew exactly where to look to find out if her hypothesis was correct. The Australian Census records may be missing, but the registers for births, marriages and deaths were still available.

Records were divided by state in Australia, so she decided to search in Western Australia first. She logged on to the index search tool on the WA.gov website for births, marriages and deaths.

Then she realised her first problem. She had no idea of the surname of Annie's husband. In the obituary it was stated as Peter Brennan, but was this true?

She decided to leave the field blank for now, simply entering the years 1841 to 1851 and the name of the mother as Annie Kelly with the box for all name versions checked.

She pressed enter and crossed her fingers.

No hits.

She tried entering the surname Brennan, leaving everything else as it was.

No hits.

Maybe the family had always used Kelly as a surname, not Brennan nor even any other name. She tried entering 'Kelly' into the surname field on the form.

Still no hits.

Were the entries in the family bible another tissue of lies? She checked the one fact she did know for certain – Annie's date of death.

She opened the death registry and entered the correct information, changing the year to 1904.

Immediately, she had a result. There was one Annie on her own at the top.

All the information was correct, except in the section where parents' names were supposed to be entered, the registrar at the time had written 'UNKNOWN'.

Jayne rolled her eyes and said, 'Annie, you are not making this easy.'

But then she noticed the age. This Annie had been 84 years old.

After a quick calculation, Jayne worked out that this would give her a birth date of 1820, not 1830 as the obituary stated. Had Annie taken some years off her age? She wouldn't be the first woman to do it and she wouldn't be the last.

But this also meant that Jayne would have to use a much wider range of birth dates in any subsequent searches.

For a moment, she sat back in her chair and sipped her now cold coffee. There were no birth records for the children, but the death record was exactly right. Had Annie simply not registered her children? John Henry was born just before registration began, but the others were born after it had been introduced.

From what she knew of Annie's character, Jayne couldn't imagine she would not register the children. That left only one possibility. Annie didn't have her children in Western Australia but somewhere else.

The UK?

Ireland?

Or in another Australian state?

She glanced at the clock: 10.17 a.m. Once again, time had flown by while she was researching.

She tried one last search before she would have to start showering and then head for the hospital.

She looked at the marriage records. The available information stretched from 1841 to 1946. She typed in Annie's name and entered a wide date range of 1841 to 1881.

She realised this was a long shot, as Annie would probably have married before 1840 if her first child was born in that year. Again, she couldn't imagine Annie having children out of wedlock.

No hits.

'Right, that means I have to come up with a whole new strategy. You are not making this easy, Ms Annie Kelly.'

She closed the laptop and put it in her bag. She would do more research at the hospital while watching over Robert.

She glanced again at the clock. It was now 10.32 a.m.

Time to hurry, she really didn't want to be late. Not for Robert or Vera.

CHAPTER TWENTY-EIGHT

January 1845 to December 1848

Sydney, Australia

For the first year after she received her Certificate of Freedom, all went well for Annie Kelly.

Their family was increased by the birth of a girl in 1845. Honorah Bridget arrived on the scene and immediately lit up their lives with her good humour and amiability. It was almost as if all the happiness of her mother and the innocence of her father had merged into this one child, and it all sparkled with the verve of the woman she had been named after: Honorah Duffy.

Annie often wondered what had happened to her friend from Grangegorman. Was she still tweaking the noses of those in authority?

Baby Honorah never seemed to cry, was always happy and cheerful, and loved being around people.

For Annie, Honorah was the joy and centre of her life in Sydney.

Each morning she spent time feeding her with a mixture of oatmeal and buttermilk sprinkled with a few herbs and berries she had foraged. The child seemed to thrive on this diet, avoiding most of the illnesses that beset the young of Sydney.

Daniel's newspaper prospered, gaining a wide readership amongst the Irish population of New South Wales and the rest of the country, particularly as news began to arrive in 1845 of the failure of the potato crop in many parts of Ireland.

'People are dying of starvation in a country that is one of the most fertile on earth, the Emerald Isle. How can this be happening?' he asked Annie one day.

She had no answer.

That morning she had received a letter from her father in Kilkenny. He described the suffering of the population.

Dearest Annie,

My news is not so good.

The potato crop has failed again and the peasantry who rely on it for sustenance have nothing to eat. The people have nothing. Their homes are hovels containing the bare rudiments of life; a stool or two, a box serving as a table, straw strewn on the ground serving as a bed, kept in by a few stones or a stick, and with half a blanket or a rough sheet. The children and adults both wear clothes that are nothing more than rags. All has been sold to buy what little food there is.

The city has created work schemes for the poor, build-

ing roads and the like, but these do not last long and the expenditure of energy required is often more than the food given.

The workhouse is a shambles; overcrowded, desperate and disease-ridden. It is so bad that people often take their chances on the street rather than risk entering through the steel-bound doors.

Your mother and I barely survive. There is no money for people to pay for our medicine and I would not take it even if there was. Your mother scolds me, but what should I do? Take money from a family whose children are just bones and skin?

I cannot do it.

Your brother and sister have taken advantage of the emigration schemes to leave our blighted country. They have decided to go to Canada, there is nothing left for them here in Ireland. There is nothing here for anybody any more.

I believe the situation can only get worse in the following years. It is best they leave now, before they too suffer the horrors of starvation.

I am glad you decided to stay in Australia when you finished your sentence.

Your loving father,
Liam

Of course, Daniel printed the letter on a prominent

page in the *Sydney Irishman*, ensuring the recipient remained anonymous as he always did.

The authorities became more suspicious of Daniel's activities after 1846. The newspaper had taken a strident line against the government when news of another failure of the potato crop reached Sydney. It particularly angered Daniel that even as people were dying of starvation, beef, wheat, oats and barley were still being exported from the ports of the country to feed the workers of England.

As the years wore on, the editorials of the paper became more aggressive, supporting the Young Ireland movement when Daniel O'Connell allied himself with the Whigs.

'Annie, the man has betrayed us. How can he be in cahoots with the very people who have starved our people to death?'

By 1848, Daniel was calling for revolution in Ireland and the establishment of a Republican government as espoused by William O'Brien, Thomas Meagher and Richard O'Gorman. The last straw for the authorities was when he placed the new flag of the Irish Republic – the orange, green and white tricolour – on the masthead of the *Sydney Irishman*.

They acted swiftly, closing down the newspaper overnight and destroying all copies of the latest issue. It was only through the intercession of Annie's friends and Archbishop Polding that the paper was allowed to be circulated again, with the tricolour removed and after a promise from Daniel that he would be more temperate in his language and reporting.

It was at this time that the first major tragedy befell the family.

In late 1848, John Henry fell ill with scarlatina. Daniel had been writing about the disease since the previous year, after six out of thirty free migrants staying at a flop house in Clarence Street had died of it.

He campaigned for the authorities to better people's living conditions so that the young victims could withstand the coughs, sore throats and the red itchy rash that covered their bodies. It was not the first time the disease had devastated Sydney. In 1841, many young people had died when the working-class areas had been badly affected. Now it was back again, and Daniel was determined that the authorities should act to stop it from spreading.

But the more he pushed, the harder the authorities worked to convince themselves that no such epidemic existed, even employing the *Sydney Morning Herald* to criticise Daniel indirectly:

The disease, such as it is, still exists among us in a small way, though not to such an alarming extent as some who write in our newspapers are wont to impress on the public mind. Indeed, only a few cases

have occurred recently, none of which have terminated fatally.

So far, the disease had been found in the north-west corner of the town in the working-class area of The Rocks, with Moore's Wharf at Millers Point pinpointed as the epicentre.

But in late 1848, it spread to other parts of the city. John Henry was one of the first to succumb to its effects, showing the classic symptoms; sore throat, fever and the red rash. Annie tried her best to save him using her balms and poultices, feeding him chicken soup laced with herbs even though it was painful for him to swallow. She even sought help from Mr Wiggs and Dr Ellison, the assistant surgeon of the 80th Regiment.

But nothing worked.

After four days of terrible pain, John Henry passed away on the morning of December 18, 1848. Daniel and Annie were bereft, their home a house of desolation.

Annie felt the guilt most. After all, hadn't she spent most of her time with their youngest, neglecting John Henry? And wasn't she the great herbalist whose cures could prevent disease, save the sick, and strengthen the living? Yet she had been unable to save her own son.

It was Daniel who dragged her back from her slough of despond. After they had buried John Henry in the Devonshire Street cemetery in a service presided over by

Father Therry, he sat her down in her favourite chair in the house.

'You must take the children away.'

'What?'

'The authorities have played down the seriousness of the disease for too long and John Henry has died as a result. Scarlatina will take more children before it is finished. They must not be our children.'

Annie glanced across at Dominic and Honorah playing together on the floor, and realised that Daniel was right.

'But where shall I take them?'

'We have friends in Morpeth, the Nainbys. I have asked if they can accommodate yourself and the children and they have agreed.'

'But what about you?'

'I cannot leave now, the news from Ireland is not good. The famine is worsening. Shocking reports have come in from Schull and Skibbereen and the whole of Connacht is suffering. I will be safe here, the disease mainly affects young children.'

Annie looked across at their children once more. Nothing mattered more than their health and wellbeing. But she didn't want to leave Daniel alone in Sydney.

'I don't want to go.'

'I think you should. I can book a steamer to take you tomorrow morning.' He looked down at this wife in her black dress, her hair coiled tightly around her head. 'It is for the best, Annie.'

'I do not want to leave you. How will you look after yourself? And the authorities, you know they disapprove of your editorials on Ireland and their governance of this scarlatina outbreak…'

'I will not adjust my beliefs to suit the ideas of a group of jackasses in Government House.'

'You don't have to. Just be a little bit more circumspect is all I am asking. You owe it to the children and the memory of John.'

He stared into mid-air, nodded once and walked out. Annie was left sitting on her own, her hands clenched together tightly in her lap.

The following morning, Annie remained with the children in the house. She spent the day brewing balms to be rubbed on chests, a draught made from lamb bones to build the children's strength, and a steam inhaler using dried eucalyptus leaves and a tincture of tea tree oil to clear the lungs and the nasal passages.

Each morning the children and Daniel were forced by Annie to drink the draught, rub the balm on their chests and spend fifteen minutes inhaling the purifying steam.

Despite other families falling sick around them, the Sheehans remained strong and unaffected. Annie was beginning to think they had weathered the storm when, on Christmas Day in 1847, exactly ten years to the day since she had arrived on the *Sir Charles Forbes*, an age and half a lifetime ago, a letter was delivered. It had just come in with the arrival of the *Tippoo Sultan*, a merchant vessel from England.

Annie didn't recognise the handwriting on the front, but opened it anyway, expecting news from Ireland.

Dear Mrs Sheehan,

I regret to inform you of the demise of both your parents, Liam and Margaret Kelly, at the Kilkenny Workhouse on September 12, 1848.

They had both been ill and weak for a long time before being admitted to the workhouse on the evening of September 11.

As the priest assigned to the said place, I performed the last rites for them and they died within hours of each other. They remained together in death as they had been in life.

As there are no living relatives in Kilkenny, the parish arranged a pauper's burial on consecrated ground.

I found letters from you in Australia and another brother and sister in Canada. I have written to all of you, recounting the details of their death.

May God have mercy on their souls.

Yours in God,
Fr Brendan Walsh pp

Annie stared at the letter for five minutes and then read it again and again.

She knew now what she had to do.

CHAPTER TWENTY-NINE

Wednesday, September 16, 2020

Perth, Australia

Jayne entered Robert's room to one side of Ward 4F in the Royal Perth. She quickly gave Vera a hug without saying a word.

Robert was lying in his bed, unmoving. An oxygen mask covered his face and his body was wired up to a series of machines next to the bed. His face had a grey paleness she had never seen before and there was a thinness, almost a translucency, to his skin. A thin plastic tube led from his arm to a saline drip attached to a stand.

'How is he?' Jayne whispered.

It was strange, Robert had no chance of being woken by their voices but Jayne and Vera still whispered.

'Same as last night. He hasn't moved at all. The doctor has been round twice and said he would have a chat with us when you arrived.'

Just as she spoke, there was a knock on the door and the doctor popped his head round, accompanied by a nurse.

After he had finished examining Robert, he pulled Vera and Jayne to one side.

'We have now confirmed that Mr Cartwright suffered a myocardial infarction yesterday evening. Luckily, you called the ambulance quickly and we were able to stabilise his condition. But I'm afraid he isn't out of danger yet. His heart rhythms are irregular. After he becomes more stable, we may have to perform surgery on him to insert a stent in one of his cardiac arteries. Are you sure there has been no history of heart problems?'

'None that I know of, Doctor,' answered Vera. 'His heart has always been the strongest part of him.'

'We'll keep monitoring the situation and perform further tests. You are his carer, Mrs Cartwright?'

'I am. Since his diagnosis of early-onset Alzheimer's and our marriage, I was appointed his official carer.'

'Good, then you will be allowed to stay with him. Unfortunately, hospital rules mean you will have to leave at eight p.m., Mrs…'

'It's Ms Sinclair, Jayne Sinclair. I understand.'

'I'm afraid there is some bureaucracy involved in his care as Robert isn't an Australian citizen, but we have a reciprocal agreement with the NHS. If you could come with me, Mrs Cartwright, we can sort that out now.'

'You go, Vera, I'll stay here. You should go home and take a shower afterwards. I can remain with Robert this afternoon.'

'Are you sure, Jayne?'

She stared at her stepfather lying inert on the bed. 'It's the least I can do.'

Vera and the doctor left, leaving Jayne alone in the room with Robert. The only sound was the constant electronic buzz of the machines keeping him alive and the soft beep of the heart monitor.

Her stepfather had been a fighter all his life. He wasn't going to give up now, no matter how weak his heart was.

She settled herself in the armchair, pulling out her laptop. She took one long look at Robert before opening it and logging on.

At least work would keep her mind from worrying.

CHAPTER THIRTY

December 29, 1848

Morpeth, New South Wales

Their friend, Frederick Nainby, was waiting for them at the wharf of the Hunter River Steam Navigation Company when they arrived in Morpeth.

Annie had travelled by the steamer, *Clonmel*, from Sydney, stopping for a brief period at the rather desolate town of Newcastle. She had said goodbye to Daniel, giving him a quick hug and warning him to be careful, before hustling the children on board the steamer and down into the cabin she had booked.

The news of the death of her parents, following so soon after the death of her young son, had shocked her to the marrow. She had spent a long time thinking about them and her life since she had arrived in Australia.

Should she have gone back in 1844 rather than stay here? Should she have insisted that her parents join her in Sydney? She had offered to pay for their passage but her father had said no. He was too old and frail to leave Ireland and start a new life halfway around the world.

Should she at least have brought her brother and sister here? But they had preferred to go to Canada, rather than to a penal colony.

After a long night's soul searching, she realised that she could spend her life having regrets and wondering what could have been, but she couldn't change anything that had happened.

She couldn't change stealing the apples.

She couldn't change the judge's verdict.

She couldn't change her voyage to Australia.

She couldn't change anything.

What she could do was keep her children, Dominic and Honorah, safe from the disease that was rife in Sydney right now.

On Christmas evening, she told Daniel of her decision to leave.

'I'm so glad you have finally come round to my way of thinking, Annie. But what about your business making the medicines?'

'The children are more important. Rosie has been making the balms and the Elixir for seven years now, she can manage. I will leave her the recipe and I will reduce the number of products we make.'

'Is that wise?'

'There is nothing else to be done. I must take the children from here before the scarlatina claims them too.'

'I agree, it is the best for their future.'

She didn't want to tell Daniel she had been up all night worrying about the past, the present and the future.

'I will book passage for you to Morpeth as soon as possible.'

They had embarked on the regular, daily steamer and now here they were, a day later, standing on the wharf of the town, deep in the Hunter Valley.

'It is good to see you again, Mrs Sheehan.'

Frederick Nainby's wife, Lydia, stepped forward to kiss her on both cheeks. 'Are these the children we have heard so much about?'

Dominic and Honorah stood together, holding hands on the wharf, obviously overawed by their new surroundings. Dominic nodded shyly.

'You will enjoy playing on our land. We have horses, sheep, and even Frederick's pride and joy, our pigs.'

'You have horses?' asked Dominic. 'Can I ride one?'

'If your mother agrees, of course you can.'

Frederick picked up their bags.

'You must be exhausted after your journey, let us take you back to Richmond Vale and settle you in. The horse and trap is over there.'

Frederick loaded the bags and the people on to the small trap and clicked his tongue to encourage the tiny horse to walk on.

Annie checked out the town as they drove through it on the way to the Nainbys' cottage.

Morpeth was busy, with a long wharf next to the Hunter River. It was the major loading place for goods from the interior farms and settlements that went on the daily steamers down to Newcastle and on around the coast to Sydney. The trip was then repeated in reverse for manufactured goods made in the town or imported from England.

One long street stretched away from the wharf, lined on either side with brick and wooden houses. To Annie's eyes, there seemed to be a lot of hotels, inns, and wine and spirit merchants for such a small town. But she also spotted a variety of general stores, corn merchants, churches, and even schools.

Annie breathed deeply. 'The air is clean and fresh here compared with Sydney.'

'The breezes from the river keep the town cool even on the hottest days of summer.'

'Where is the soap factory?'

'About ten miles from here, on the farm in Richmond Vale.'

They had all met in 1843. Frederick had been a pharmacist in England and, on arrival from Melbourne, had discovered Annie's wares on sale at Mr Wiggs'. He soon sounded her out about their provenance and manufacture. Of course, she didn't reveal her trade secrets but they had talked for a long time about the efficacy of certain herbs and tinctures.

He then explained that he had obtained the lease for some Crown land in the Hunter Valley, at a place called Richmond Vale, and had the idea of producing soap in a factory there.

'There is an abundant supply of raw materials; the carcasses of sheep and cattle from the nearby farms. Out in the country, the smell of boiling the animals down will not be noticeable, better than placing it in the middle of the city. On my walks through Sydney, I have noticed the residents have a desperate want of soap.'

'It has to be imported from England so it is very expensive.'

Frederick Nainby soon agreed with Mr Wiggs to sell his new soaps in his shop, and opened the factory in 1844.

He and Daniel became firm friends, even more so when Frederick joined the committee to provide relief for the victims of the Irish Famine, a cause dear to Daniel's heart. He often stayed at their home during his visits to Sydney and, when he married Lydia in 1847, Daniel had been his best man.

'Mr Close has opened a new coal mine on the other side of the river. According to the engineers, there is a good coalfield underneath the land in these parts. There may even be gold, too.'

'You haven't got gold fever as well?'

Gold had recently been found near Bathurst and reports had come of discoveries in Victoria and Western Australia.

'The land is rich, Mrs Sheehan, but what is beneath the land is even richer.'

Annie glanced towards Lydia's stomach. 'That is indeed true, Mr Nainby, but it seems your wife's body is the richest of all. When are you due?'

'In June, God willing. But how do you know? I though I wasn't showing yet.'

'What is due, Mother?' asked Dominic.

'Mrs Nainby is going to have a baby, that's what is due. It is a gift from God.'

'I'd like some gifts from Him too.'

She ruffled his hair. 'You have many gifts, but let's hope a baby is not one of them.'

'Here is our home.' Frederick Nainby turned the horse and trap into a short drive leading to a wooden cottage surrounded by a verandah in the Indian style.

'It looks beautiful, Mrs Nainby.'

'I hope you will be comfortable during your stay with us.'

Annie stared at the cottage, thinking of their small house in the crowded streets of Sydney. 'I'm sure I will.'

CHAPTER THIRTY-ONE

Wednesday, September 16, 2020

Perth, Australia

Jayne took a deep breath. The only sound in the hospital room was the noise of the machines keeping her stepfather alive.

'Focus,' she admonished herself. 'What do you really know?'

She thought hard. She could find no documentary evidence to support Annie Kelly's story of her arrival in Perth. Indeed, the one fact she had discovered was a discrepancy in the reports of her birth date. The obituary said 1830, while the death registration gave a date of 1820.

Jayne was inclined to believe the latter year but, in truth, it could have been anywhere in between.

The only accurate dates seemed to be those of the children's births named in the family bible. But where were they born? She had already eliminated Western Australia, as birth registration started in 1841 and there were no records of any of the children there.

That left a couple of options; either they were born in Great Britain, including Ireland, or they were born in another part of Australia.

Which to go with first? She could ask Ronald to go through the English records, but as she was in Australia it seemed better for her to concentrate on this country.

The three children's dates of birth were given as 1840, 1842 and 1845. At this time in Australia's history there were only two major ports of entry into the country; Sydney and Van Diemen's Land, now known as Tasmania.

She decided to concentrate on Sydney. A quick search told her that civil birth registration didn't start there until 1856.

'Damn,' she said out loud, 'why is this so difficult?'

She breathed deeply again. She should be used to brick walls by now. Wasn't that why clients appointed her rather than doing it themselves? She always had a few techniques to get around obstacles.

She logged on to Findmypast, discovering that many of the early parish records for Sydney had been transcribed. She decided to search in the New South Wales births section, which included those records as well as the civil registration.

She typed 'John Henry' into the 'Who' box, leaving the surname blank. Then she added a registration year of 1840, plus or minus one year, reasoning that if he was born in December, Annie Kelly may not have got round to registering his birth with a church until January of the next year.

In the 'Denomination' box she typed 'Roman Catholic'. She could have put Peter for the father's first name, but decided to leave it blank. In the last box of 'Mother's Name' she entered 'Anne'. There was no place for a surname, so perhaps these records didn't collect the mother's surnames.

Then she pressed search and crossed her fingers.

She saw nine hits.

'Right, we are finally getting somewhere.'

She scanned the lines, noting there was a Kelly in the second entry, and that four of the births happened in 1840 but weren't registered until 1841.

She knew exactly what to do next. She went back to the search details for the New South Wales births, this time entering Dominic's name instead of John's, and changing the birth date.

Once again, she pressed search and crossed her fingers.

One hit.

A child born to Daniel Sheehan and an Anne without a surname in 1842.

'Get in,' she shouted, punching the air and then suddenly remembering where she was.

She looked across at her stepfather. He was still lying motionless, the machines beeping close to his head.

There was a knock on the door and a nurse entered. 'I thought I heard a shout from this room. Is everything okay?'

Jayne felt even more guilty. She mumbled something about stubbing her toe and the nurse left, reminding her before she went that the call button was by the side of the bed in case of an emergency.

Red-faced, Jayne returned to her screen.

It looked like Daniel Sheehan was possibly the father of Annie's second son, Dominic as well as John. But it wasn't definitive. Perhaps Annie had not registered the births or it was simply a coincidence.

She decided to do one last check. She changed the date to 1845 and the name to Honorah Bridget, pressing search one more time.

Just one hit again.

Honorah Sheehan fathered by Daniel and Anne.

This time she punched the air silently. She was sure she now had the correct family. After all, what were the chances of the three children's names and dates of birth matching exactly? Dominic and Honorah Bridget were hardly common names even then.

Then it hit her.

She had made one big assumption. She had assumed the Annie named in the family bible was the same Annie she was searching for.

But what if they weren't the same person?

What if they were cousins with the same Christian name? It was quite common in Irish naming practices for the same forenames to be used again and again in families.

Then an even worse thought hit her. What if this family bible had nothing to do with the Kellys at all, and one of Liz's relatives had simply bought it at the Australian equivalent of a car boot sale? Ronald had told her that these Irish Catholic bibles were fairly common.

She put her head in her hands and whispered, 'You are not making this easy, Annie Kelly.'

CHAPTER THIRTY-TWO

January to June 1849

Morpeth, New South Wales

Annie and the children very quickly settled into life with the Nainbys in Morpeth. Honorah loved the fresh air and playing in the garden. Dominic started to go to the small town's school, discovering new friends amongst the children of the area.

With her children settled and happy, Annie spent most mornings working on new recipes for medicines or developing her father's recipes using ingredients that she found growing on the banks of the Hunter River and in the fields surrounding it. Frances had told her that hop bush could be used for toothache and cuts, so she added it to a calendula balm and thought it might aid in the recovery from burns, while she ground up the bark of the wattle tree and created an infusion with it that acted as a mild sedative to aid sleep.

One day, almost four months after their arrival, Frederick and Lydia took her for a walk into the centre of town while the children were being looked after by a neighbour. Opposite the Wheat Sheaf Inn, Frederick pointed to a small stone building.

'What do you think of that?'

'Are you planning to move here from the cottage?' she asked.

He laughed. 'Not at all, it's going to be my new pharmacy.'

'What? You're opening a pharmacy? What about the soap factory?'

'I've put it up for sale. You look shocked.'

'You only opened it less than four years ago.'

'It is too far to travel and to manage.' He smiled at his wife. 'We have decided that now we have a baby on the way, we should live in Morpeth and earn a living here. What better way than by opening a pharmacy? I have already talked with Mr Wiggs and he has agreed to supply me with the latest drugs and pharmacopeia on consignment. If you would be so kind as to supply us with your medicines too, we should be set from beginning.'

'Of course, I will send you anything you want. Have you thought of developing your own?'

'If I am honest, that is the plan. I had some experience in mixing medicines when I was apprentice to Mr Hoggett in York.'

'Congratulations, to the both of you. The beginning of a new family and of a new business, all in the same year.'

'Shall we go and celebrate?'

They repaired to the Wheat Sheaf Inn, where tea and scones were served.

'Have you heard from Daniel?'

'Not for two weeks. In his last letter, he said that all was well in Sydney. The onset of the winter season has seen the decline of scarlatina in the city. I think we will return home soon.'

'But not before I have my child?' said Lydia.

'I want to be here for when your firstborn opens their eyes and screams at the top of their lungs as they discover the world.' She thought of her own children. 'There are no words to describe the feeling of utter joy.'

'I am so happy that you will be there. But I will be sorry to see you go. We love Dominic and Honorah,' said Lydia.

'They will both be sorry to leave. But you will have a family of your own soon to look after.'

They both stopped talking, comfortable in their friendship. It was Frederick who broke the silence. 'Did Daniel tell you anything about the latest moves regarding transportation?'

'He said there are moves by some to re-introduce it to New South Wales after the suspension by Governor Bourke in 1840. The landowners particularly are saying there is a shortage of labour.'

'They simple don't want to pay people properly. I have organised meetings in this area to support the suspension and even to abolish transportation altogether, but there is a strong lobby wanting it to return. In my view, Australia can only prosper based on the free movement of people, not on the transportation of convicts.'

'I have heard the orphans have already started to arrive under Earl Grey's scheme,' said Lydia.

Frederick laughed. 'They have, but there are complaints already about the quality of the girls brought from Ireland. The only people who seem to be happy at their arrival are the sailors and men of ill repute in the city.'

They talked for the next hour over the topics facing the settlers in Australia. Morpeth was the centre of trade in the Hunter Valley and Frederick, through his many contacts, was well aware of the problems facing the country.

After finishing their afternoon tea they walked slowly home, enjoying the cool of the season. As they approached the cottage, the children didn't run out to greet them.

'Is something wrong?' asked Annie.

'They mustn't have heard us coming up the drive.'

They walked into the sitting room to find a young man sat on the armchair, his hat in his hands, being watched over by the children and the neighbour, Mrs Harris.

He stood up and bowed. 'I am so sorry to have bothered you at this time of the day. Anthony Ridding at your convenience, sir.'

'Welcome to our house, Mr Ridding. What can I do for you?'

'I have a letter for Mrs Sheehan, sir. If I could give it to her?'

He pulled out a sealed letter and passed it over to Annie.

'What is this, sir?'

'A letter from your husband, Daniel Sheehan.'

'Daniel? What has happened to Daniel?'

'I implore you to read the letter, ma'am.'

Annie ripped it open and began to read.

Dear Annie,

I am writing this to you from Darlinghurst Gaol. The colonial government has seen fit to place me here as I am apparently 'a danger to the wellbeing and security of the colony'.

I haven't eaten for three days and my guts are strangled.

Could you come back to Sydney and help free me? The outbreak of scarlatina has ended now, though no doubt it will return due to the incompetence of those in charge.

I miss you terribly and do not want to spend another day in this hell hole. Perhaps I have become soft since my arrival in Australia, but I cannot bear the smell, noise and company of the other prisoners any longer.

I implore you, please come to rescue me.
Your husband,
D

Annie turned to Frederick. 'Could you book passage for myself and the children back to Sydney? It seems we must return.'

CHAPTER THIRTY-THREE

Wednesday, September 16, 2020
Perth, Australia

Jayne took three deep breaths, glancing across at her stepfather, still motionless in the bed. She watched as his chest rose slightly with each inhalation and fell again.

How funny it is, she thought, that we rely on these functions; a heart beating, lungs inflating and deflating, blood being purified through the kidneys and liver, and yet we are never really aware they are happening until they go wrong.

She'd always thought that Robert's problems with Alzheimer's would one day become so bad he could no longer remember who she was or her relationship to him. But instead, it was his heart that had given out. A heart she had always presumed would go on beating till the end of time. We never contemplate our parents' deaths; we assume they will always be there for us, as they were there when we were growing up.

To kiss a grazed knee better.

To hold hands as you crossed a busy road.

To welcome us home with a hot drink after our first extremely wet camping trip.

To console us when that first love turns into first hate.

We think they will always be there, but they won't. If genealogy had taught Jayne one thing, it was that we all die in the end, we just don't know exactly when it will happen.

Jayne shook her head. She must stop thinking these morbid thoughts. Robert was strong, he would pull through. Meanwhile, she had to solve the problem of Annie Kelly.

How could she do that?

She focused her mind on her work. How could she prove that the Annie Kelly she had found was the correct ancestor of her client?

She was pretty certain she had the correct people. But being 'pretty certain' wasn't good enough, she had to know definitively.

Also, simply telling Liz that her three-times great-grandmother had invented her life, telling a story to a reporter which he repeated as the truth, wasn't good enough. As shows like *Who Do You Think You Are?* had shown, family history was all about stories.

What was the real story of Annie Kelly?

And then it occurred to her. Was the 'D' who had signed the letter Daniel Sheehan? If it was, it would explain everything.

'Hold on, Jayne, don't jump ahead of yourself. Take it step by step. Prove you have the right Annie Kelly first.'

She glanced once more at Robert, checking if her words had woken him, but he lay quietly in his bed, sleeping, the drip and electrodes still attached to his body and the machines quietly beeping.

She went back on to Findmypast and found the *New South Wales Marriages 1788–1945* listing, typing in the groom's details.

It immediately gave her a transcript of Annie and Daniel's wedding, giving their names and registration years, but little else she didn't already know.

Now she had these details, she could order a marriage certificate from the NSW Registry of Births, Deaths & Marriages. She searched again on the site, finding their marriage was listed even though official registration didn't begin until 1856. While she was there, she also ordered birth certificates for all the children. Each one cost 35 Australian dollars, but it was worth it if she needed to build a family tree.

But none of these certificates would prove she had the correct Annie Kelly. She checked the list of resources available on Findmypast and noticed one record entitled *New South Wales Registers of Convicts' Applications to Marry 1825–1851*.

Duncan had said he thought Annie was possibly a convict. Apparently, convicts were encouraged to marry as it promoted the morality and stability of the colony, but they had to apply for permission to the Governor first.

If Annie was a convict, she would have needed such a permission. Jayne entered Annie's name and the year of marriage into the search field.

Two records came up.

The first was beautifully written in a rich copperplate script.

Name	Age	Ship	Date of Refusal	Clergyman
Daniel Sheehan	26	Captain Cook	December 16, 1839	Rev Therry, Sydney
Annie Kelly	19	Sir Charles Forbes	Ditto	Ditto

Beneath the record, the clerk had written:

The consent of the visiting magistrate is required before this application from Daniel Sheehan can be submitted for the approval of H. E. The Governor.

It seemed the marriage had originally been refused by some minor clerk in the government. Why did Daniel Sheehan have to gain the consent of a visiting magistrate? She checked the other records on the same page – a record of refusals. Most involved underage women needing the approval of their parents, whilst others were denied because one of the parties had stated they were already married when they entered the colony. One even stated baldly:

Disallowed. The female having being sentenced to the factory since the date of the application.

Jayne knew the factory was intended to be a place where unassigned female convicts would be gainfully employed in tasks that were beneficial to the colony; where their basic need for shelter was provided and where 'corrupting influences' could be kept at bay.

But nobody else listed had required the consent of a visiting magistrate. Strange. What had he done?

She clicked the other record for Annie Kelly and Daniel Sheehan. It was an entry in a ledger recording approval of the marriage.

Jayne scanned the record. If this was the correct Annie Kelly – and it was still a big IF in Jayne's mind – this document showed that Duncan had been correct in his belief.

Annie Kelly was a convict who had been sentenced to seven years' transportation and had arrived on the ship, *Sir Charles Forbes*. If she was still in bond, it meant that she hadn't finished serving her sentence or obtained her ticket-of-leave or her Certificate of Freedom.

She must have arrived in Australia seven years before her marriage at most.

Her husband's crime must have been far more serious; he had been sentenced to transportation for life and had arrived on a different ship.

Jayne knew exactly what to do now. She checked the records for *Australian Convict Ships 1788–1849* and typed in the name of the ship, along with Annie's name. These records weren't just a list of who was transported, they were also a copy of the indents of the convicts transported on a particular ship. These records allowed the colonial authorities to check and track each convict in Australia.

She pressed send and, as she always did, crossed her fingers, praying to the gods of genealogy for a successful result.

The record came up immediately. It had been typed and gave immense detail of each and every convict.

LIST of 150 FEMALE CONVICTS, by the Ship, SIR CHARLES FORBES, JAMES LESLIE, Master, WILLIAM CLIFFORD, Surgeon Superintendent, arrived from IRELAND 25th December 1837.

There in the middle was the record for Annie Kelly.

Kelly, Annie, 17, Read and Write, Rom. Cath., Single, Queen's County, Herbalist's Assistant, Stealing 3 baskets of apples, Kilkenny, 20 February 1837, Sir Charles Forbes, 7 years, none, 5ft 1in, dark, ruddy and a little freckled, brown, hazel. Nose a little cocked, small mole on left side of neck, small scar on top of right index finger.

Jayne could immediately imagine Annie standing in front of her. A small woman but with strength in her eyes and body. A woman who could make a life for herself in the rough and tough world of the Australia of the time. Actually, more than that, a woman who could rise to the top and run her own business, setting up a commercial dynasty that lasted for more than eighty years.

Then one detail in the description suddenly shouted at her. *Herbalist's assistant?* Where had she seen that before?

She dug into her bag, pulling out a copy of the obituary. There it was in black and white:

My father was a herbalist and I often acted as his assistant.

Jayne punched the air. That was it, she had the correct Annie Kelly. She quickly checked if there were any other Annie Kellys on the same ship.

Luckily, there weren't.

She went through every convicts' occupation for that ship and three others that arrived in Sydney after the *Sir Charles Forbes*. None of them had another herbalist's assistant. In fact, most of the poor wretches who were sentenced to transportation had been labourers, maids or servants.

She was sure she had the right Annie Kelly.

At last, Jayne felt she was making progress. Now it was time to check out Annie's husband, Daniel. Why had he been sentenced to life?

And who was Peter Brennan, the man who, according to Annie's obituary, had died on the voyage?

CHAPTER THIRTY-FOUR

June 10, 1849

On board the vessel *Gambit*, en route to Sydney

While the children played on the deck of the steamer, Annie was lost in her thoughts.

What had Daniel done to be imprisoned?

Was it something he had written?

Or was it worse?

She strode across the narrow deck from one side to the other, the aroma of burning coal assaulting her nostrils. She couldn't be in her cabin at the moment. She had to be somewhere in the open air where she could move and think.

As soon as they arrived in Sydney, she would take the children home where they could be looked after by one of the indentured servants.

Then she would immediately go to Mr Brown, their solicitor, to arrange for Daniel to be released.

She would probably have to put up a surety for his good behaviour, but that should be no problem. It would have been better to have stayed behind to help Lydia with the birth of her first child, but it wasn't possible. Daniel needed her and she had to return to his side.

She read his letter again. What had he been charged with?

There was no information other than that he had somehow offended the colonial authorities. Hadn't she advised him to be careful? The *Sydney Irishman* had been closed once already, hadn't he learnt his lesson from that?

She moved up to the bow of the ship. The wind was stronger on her face now they had left Newcastle and headed out to the open sea, always keeping the coast on their starboard bow.

The engines fought to keep the ship moving forward against the prevailing currents and a long stream of wine-dark smoke trailed being them, a dark smudge against the eggshell blue sky. The boat rocked from one side to the other, throwing spray up against the side of the bow, but still it moved forward through the tide and the waves.

She stepped back and walked towards the children, the sun peeping through the rigging, playing with the light across her face.

She always noticed the light had a different tone in Australia compared to Ireland. It was clearer, drier, more translucent. Objects seemed starker and sharper. She could even see each individual tree picked out against the coast on their right. In Ireland, everything was suffused with a soft, hazy light, as if the damp of the country had insinuated itself into the particles of light themselves.

She stared at the children playing together on the deck of the ship, her daughter watching with awe and love as her elder brother produced a drawing of a seagull in flight.

'Oh, Daniel, what have you done?' Annie said out loud.

Both children turned towards her.

'Mother, what is wrong, why are you crying?'

She wiped her eyes. 'It is nothing, Dominic, the sea air stings.'

'You should go down to our cabin then.'

He carried on with his drawing. How grown-up he sounded. He even looked like his father, with that little quiff of ginger hair that drooped over one eye, giving him an almost piratical air.

'Make sure you pull your coat around your throat, and you too, Honorah. The sea air at this time of year can be cold and piercing.'

'I'm not worried, Mother, I like the sea.'

John, her son who had died, had looked more like her. She missed him every day; his kindness and love of books, the way he held his head when he looked at people. But most of all she missed his voice, calling to her in the morning as he woke from his sleep.

How she missed him.

CHAPTER THIRTY-FIVE

June 11, 1849
Sydney, Australia

Annie was surprised to see Major Furlong waiting for her when she returned home with the children.

'I need to talk to you.'

She bustled about, ensuring that they knew exactly what to feed Dominic and Honorah.

'Can we talk later? I need to go to see Daniel. He has been imprisoned in Darlinghurst Gaol.'

'It is about Mr Sheehan that we have to speak. Please sit down.'

Annie adjusted her headscarf and headed towards the door.

'Annie, I need to speak to you.'

In all the years they had known each other, Annie could never remember Major Furlong using her first name. His wife often did, when they were alone together in private, but the Major had always been courteously formal.

To him, she had always been Miss Kelly, or Mrs Sheehan after she had married.

She stopped in her tracks, turned and walked back to where he was standing beside the fire.

'Please sit yourself down. Please…' His tone was no longer sharp and commanding, but soft and almost regretful.

'You want to speak to me about Daniel and his incarceration?'

'I do.' He paused for a moment, brushing a strand of hair from his forehead. 'As you are aware, your husband was sentenced to life transportation. He has not received a pardon nor a ticket-of-leave in his time in the colony. As such, he remains on the convict register. It was with great regret that I heard, in your absence, his articles had become far more strident in their criticism of the colonial governments both here and in Ireland.'

'There is much to criticise about the behaviour of both governments.'

He held his hands up.

'I will not argue with you. But in recent months, his writing has crossed the border of fair criticism and entered the realm of incitement to rebellion both here and in Ireland.'

'I don't understand.'

He passed across a folded copy of the *Sydney Irishman*. 'Read his latest editorial.'

She opened the paper. In stark black type a headline

cried:

CITIZENS OF AUSTRALIA AND IRELAND
THROW OFF YOUR SHACKLES
YOU HAVE NOTHING TO LOSE BUT YOUR CHAINS

The time has come. We can resist it no longer. Famine has decimated the population of Ireland, forcing thousands to flee from their emerald homeland.

In our own fair city, disease and corruption has killed thousands, forcing many others to escape into the hinterland, far away from the ravages of pestilence and plague.

Did not my own dear son, John, suffer the ultimate penalty in his battle against pestilence? A life taken away by a colonial government more interested in the profits of its supporters and the advancement of its own wealth rather than the wellbeing and health of its citizens.

I say to you once and I will say it again:
NO MORE!
The revolutions in Europe and the actions of those brave young Irishmen, William Smith O'Brien and Thomas Meagher, have shown the way forward for our compatriots here in Sydney.

We must rise up against our colonial masters,

throw them and their fellow lickspittle conspirators into the depths of Sydney Harbour.

They are but the few and we are the many.

Rise up, I say, rise up today and free yourselves from the yoke of servitude.

Either we are free or we are dead. We cannot be both.

RISE UP, RISE UP TODAY.
THROW OFF YOUR SHACKLES!

Annie placed her hand across her mouth when she had finished reading. What had happened to Daniel?

Major Furlong coughed and she turned her attention back to him.

'Luckily, we were informed by the printer of the contents of this rag and we were able to stop its distribution. In recent months, as your husband's editorials have become increasingly vituperative and strident, we have been monitoring his work and his attitudes. He has been meeting secretly with a gang of ruffians who call themselves Irish Nationalists, in an inn near the docks. After this editorial was delivered to the printer, he and his gang of ne'er-do-wells were arrested by order of a magistrate.'

'How can I get him out?'

'I am afraid that is not possible. The Governor has decided that they will not be tried. Such a trial would only make certain their views were to be known more widely.

Instead, he has decided that through an order in council, all the offenders are to be transported to Norfolk Island at Her Majesty's pleasure.'

Annie's hand flew to her mouth once more. 'That cannot be. You would not deprive the children of their father…'

He held up his hand to stop her speaking. 'Because of our long relationship and the particular friendship you have with my wife, and you being a partner in the company she founded, I interceded with His Excellency on your husband's behalf. We have agreed a compromise. He will not accompany the others to Norfolk Island. Instead he will pay a fine and be sent to Perth in Western Australia. The government, or should I say the Commissary, is still his Master as a sentenced convict. It can decide when and where it sends him and Perth will be his new destination along with a few other recalcitrants. They will help with the construction of new government buildings, roads and dock facilities in the town. It will remove the human flotsam and jetsam of Darlinghurst and Parramatta Gaols, allowing the government of New South Wales to transfer the cost of their upkeep to the Western Australian authorities. Of course, the Governor is pleased with the solution as it allows us to rid ourselves of a problem and save money at the same time.'

'But… but that would mean he would leave Sydney. Leaving everything he has built here over the last twelve years. He has a family and a wife…'

Major Furlong steepled his fingers in front of his sharp face. 'He should have thought of that before he called for insurrection against Her Majesty's colonial government. You will have the choice of going with your husband or remaining here in Sydney. Obviously, because of your mutual business relationship, my wife would prefer you to remain here. However, the choice is yours. Move to Perth with your husband, or remain here while he is sent to the town alone.'

Annie closed her eyes. 'When would we have to leave?'

'If you decide to go, a ship is departing for Perth in two weeks. If you decide to stay, my wife has decided to make over this house and all its contents to you as a gift. The gift would be contingent, of course, on the continuance of your business relationship.'

Annie nodded. She understood. As ever, the carrot and the stick were being applied to equal effect.

His voice softened once more. 'Annie, my wife would dearly love you to stay in Sydney. She feels it would be better for your future and the future of your children. To be frank, Perth is no place for the young, not at the moment.'

'It is certainly better than Norfolk Island.'

'I thought I made it clear that Daniel was not going to be sent there. His fellow…' Major Furlong struggled to find the word, '…conspirators have already departed for the island. They will remain there for at least seven years.'

'So I have just two weeks to make a decision?'

Major Furlong smiled and licked his thin lips. 'Can I be blunt, madam? Your husband is a rebel, a dreamer and a wastrel. The Governor has tolerated his editorials, his rudeness and his sarcasm for one reason and one reason only. You have friends in this town, Annie. Your medicines have saved many and enriched the lives of others. Frankly, without you, he would have been sent to Norfolk Island long ago.'

'Is that supposed to please me?'

'No, but it is supposed to indicate to you the perilousness of your husband's position and the strength of your own. You have a strong future in Sydney, madam, even if your husband doesn't.'

'So you present me with an impossible decision.'

'No, your husband has presented you with a simple choice through his madness; you can accompany him to Perth to the detriment of your own life and that of your children. Or you can stay here, build your business and ensure you live a life of respect and repose. Stay in Sydney, in this house where your life is comfortable, or go to a new place where you will be dependent on the kindness of strangers. For me, it is a simple choice, one that does not require much thought at all.'

'And if the boot were on the other foot? If your wife had committed an act that meant you had to choose between her and your career, what would you do, Major?'

'My wife would never put me in that position, madam. Before performing any action, she would consider the effect it would produce on the life of myself and our children. Something your husband has singularly failed to do.'

'But he is still my husband.'

'And your children are still your children. You have already lost one child to disease, are you to lose others to poverty and misery? The lives of a convict's children in Perth would not be ones of ease or comfort, not to mention the lack of educational facilities in the town. Would you subject your children to such misery?' Major Furlong raised his eyebrow sardonically. 'So which choice are you going to make? Your children or your husband?'

Annie stared at him, her eyes ablaze. 'Major Furlong, I choose both,' she snapped.

He smiled again and stood up. 'I have tried my best to convince you of the hopelessness of your husband's position. If you decide to leave, my wife will, of course, continue to make your Elixir and your various tinctures, balms and syrups.'

'What?'

'You look surprised. Did you think you could receive letters from home without us reading them? We have known about your recipes for years.'

'But you don't know the changes I have made to them.'

'But we do. Why do you think we put one of our own to be your assistant? She knows the recipes off by heart. But all this will not be necessary if you stay here with us. My wife would prefer that outcome, naturally. I will bid you good day, madam.'

'And what about my share of the company?'

'What share? What company? That will all be forfeited if you leave Sydney.'

He walked towards the exit, then stopped and turned back. 'We do hope you make the right choice.'

'You forget, sir, what I have created since I arrived in this town. I have a will to succeed.'

'You can't eat a will to succeed, madam. Your children can't eat it either.'

His words crushed Annie. She had no answer.

He bowed once and left.

She was left on her own in the living room. A place she had once enjoyed but now seemed alien to her, a cell, not a place of refuge.

Should she stay or should she go?

CHAPTER THIRTY-SIX

Wednesday, September 16, 2020

Perth, Australia

Jayne knew she was finally making progress. From Annie's ship record, she now knew her birthplace in Ireland – Queen's County, now known as Laois. Civil records didn't begin until 1864 in Ireland, so she would have to rely on parish records if she was to find out who Annie's parents were. She could ask Ronald to go through them to see if her birth had been written down.

She hated going through those records herself, finding the handwriting of the parish priests extremely difficult to decipher. Of course, the records might not even exist. If that was the case, she could check the Tithe Applotments for the county, taken from 1818 to 1834. They only listed heads of families, but at least she would know the location of those with the surname Kelly and that could help Ronald later.

But that was for another time. Now she had to focus on Annie's husband, Daniel Sheehan. Where had he come from and why was he sentenced to life?

She went back to the Australian convict ships records and typed in the name 'Captain Cook', plus Daniel's surname.

It was apparent this ship had made three voyages with convicts to Australia. Daniel was on the last voyage in 1836.

LIST of MALE CONVICTS, by the SHIP, CAPTAIN COOK, GEORGE BROWN, Master, ARTHUR SAVAGE, Surgeon Superintendent, arrived from IRELAND on November 13th, 1836.

Daniel Sheehan's indent was as well described as his wife's.

Sheehan, Daniel, 26, Read and Write, Rom. Cath., Single, Dublin, Publisher, Sedition. Dublin, 14 January 1836, Captain Cook, Life, none, 5ft 9in, fair, ginger, green. Long visage, nose crooked to the right, scar above right eyebrow, fingers long and stained.

Again, Jayne could imagine him standing in front of her right here in the hospital room, his ginger hair slightly long and tousled, and green eyes that pierced her soul. But why was he imprisoned for life? Sedition was a serious charge at any time. Had he been part of the movement for Irish independence? Had he somehow offended the authorities?

She read through it again. A publisher. Was he the writer of the letter to Annie? The copperplate writing made him the prime suspect.

Just then there was a light tap on the door and it opened. Vera walked in looking much better, having had a shower and a little nap.

Was it 8 p.m. already? Jayne checked the time – 7.45. She had been lost in the world of research for hours.

'How is he?' Vera asked.

Jayne instantly felt guilty; she hadn't checked Robert for two hours. She looked across at him and he hadn't moved. His chest still rose with each breath and the machines continued to beep.

'He's fine, Vera, still no change.'

'I suppose that's for the best, sleep will give him a chance to recover. I just had a chat with the nurse and she says the doctor will come round at ten thirty. She also wanted me to remind you that no visitors are allowed after eight p.m.'

Jayne understood. She began to pack up her computer and the various notes on Annie Kelly and Daniel Sheehan.

'Have you been working?'

Jayne looked sheepish and nodded.

'Any luck?'

'I think so. I've finally tracked the three-times great-grandmother of my client.'

'That's great news, Jayne. See, you haven't lost your touch despite having taken six months off.'

Jayne smiled. Vera always made her feel better about herself.

She bent forward and gave Robert a peck on the forehead to say goodbye. For a second, she thought she saw his eyes blink in reaction. But then he remained still again, his face half-hidden behind the oxygen mask.

'I'll come back at eight o' clock in the morning. to relieve you, Vera.'

'No need to rush. Shouldn't you be informing your client if you've made progress?'

Vera was right. In her happiness at discovering the records for Annie Kelly, Jayne had forgotten she had a client who needed updating. 'You're right, I'll do it tomorrow morning at nine thirty. I know where she'll be. Is it okay if I come in after that?'

'As I said, it's not a problem. I love sitting here with Robert. If anything happens, I'll let you know.'

'Great, I'll see you around eleven-ish tomorrow.'

As she was going out, Vera shouted, 'Don't work too late tonight, get some sleep.'

Jayne smiled again. Vera knew her so well. 'I promise I won't work *too* late.'

As Vera settled herself in the armchair, Jayne took one glance at Robert before closing the door. He would be better tomorrow, wouldn't he?

CHAPTER THIRTY-SEVEN

July 15, 1849
On board the ship, *Racine*

Annie stood on the deck of the ship, her hair whipping around her face. The sails flapped above her head, the canvas and ropes snapping against each other in the breeze.

She had come on deck thirty minutes ago, leaving the children to sleep in the tiny cabin, Dominic's arms wrapped protectively around the shoulders of his little sister.

The voyage so far had been hard.

The first two weeks they had encountered winter storms, the ship lurching and rolling like a bucking mare. The children had spent most of the time being sick, while her condition was no better.

Gradually, the conditions improved and the captain had estimated that they should arrive at their destination in ten days with a fair wind.

She had purchased passage for herself and the children on the same ship that had been charted for the ten convicts going to Perth, one of whom was her own husband, Daniel.

Paying Daniel's extortionate fine had taken most of her savings. They would arrive in Perth with very little money.

There were only two other passengers, a merchant called Lilley and his wife. At first the couple had been friendly, but when they realised that Annie was the wife of one of the convicts, their demeanour turned hard and cold. These days, they didn't even say good morning when she met them on deck. And while they dined with the captain in his cabin, she was left on her own to eat with the children.

The highlight of their day happened at eight bells, when the convicts were brought up from their quarters in the depths of the ship for one hour, to exercise and move around the deck. The children waited for their father as he shuffled out on deck, blinking as the half-light of the bowels of the ship was replaced by the bright light of day.

They hugged, watched by the other convicts, all of whom were men of the worst type; murderers, thieves, rapists and arsonists. All sentenced to life transportation and, like Daniel, unable to obtain a pardon.

Daniel had changed during his incarceration. Annie had gone to see him in Darlinghurst and had been shocked by his deterioration. Gone was the extravagant quiff of a ginger mane that hung across the right side of his forehead, replaced by a few straggly hairs flecked with grey. His face had become more gaunt; the cheeks pinched with a row of pink gums on the right side of his mouth where teeth had once been.

What she noticed above all were his eyes. She had always loved their brightness, their sparkle, their wit as his voice played with words and his eyes played with her image. Now they were dead, lifeless, the spark vanished as if a dirty film had been placed across them.

In that first meeting in Darlinghurst Gaol, she'd felt his body through his rough shirt as they hugged. It was sharp, bony and angular, not the man she remembered.

'Oh, Daniel, what have they done to you?'

'They have done nothing, Annie, I have done it to myself.'

She heard the words, heard his breathing as he said them; shallow and hoarse.

'I am undone yet again. I would have thought I had learnt my lesson the first time.'

'What do you mean? I don't understand.'

'We were betrayed by infiltrators, but at least we managed to print the paper before we were arrested. Its words will be read by the Irishmen living in Australia.'

'Daniel, the paper was never distributed, the printer called the authorities before it was sent out.'

Daniel's face fell. 'He called the authorities?'

'They had been watching you for a long time. Oh, Daniel, how could you do this to us?'

'I do not know, Annie. I didn't do it for you, I did it for Ireland and for freedom.'

'Does Ireland care?' She waved her hands around the cell. 'And everybody has freedom except you.'

'What is going to happen, Annie?'

'According to Major Furlong, you will be sent to Perth while the others will go to Norfolk Island.'

Daniel buried his head deep in his hands. 'What have I done? What have I done?'

Annie knew what she had to do.

The answer was simple.

She had to follow her husband to Perth, leave everything she had created in Sydney.

Now, four weeks later, here she was, halfway to Perth with her children asleep in their small cabin, her husband chained to the deck below her feet, and herself, standing at the bow of the ship, worrying about the future and their new life in a place she had never seen before.

'You've done it once, Annie Kelly, you can do it again.'

But this time she wasn't so sure she would succeed.

CHAPTER THIRTY-EIGHT

Wednesday, September 16, 2020
Perth, Australia

Jayne returned to an empty house in Dalkeith. As she closed the front door, the sound echoed through the hallway. Normally Vera and Robert filled the house with their presence, but both were missing now and Jayne felt their absence keenly.

She put her keys down on the counter in the kitchen and went to make a cup of tea for herself. For a second she stopped as she reached for the PG Tips. These had been a special purchase for Robert because he loved a cup of tea in the morning and couldn't drink anything else.

'I was brought up on PG Tips and I can't change now. I've been drinking it since I was fourteen.'

They even had to make special trips to the Best of British store in Joondalup just to make sure he had his daily fix. As the teabags were used up, he began to panic.

'I think we need to get another box. Perhaps we should buy two this time.'

She put two bags in the heated teapot just as he did, filled it with water just as he did, even though there was only her to drink it and she only wanted one cup. She poured some milk into a mug and waited.

'You can't hurry tea, lass, you've got to give it time to brew, but not too long, otherwise you'll end up drinking a thick soup.'

According to Robert, exactly five minutes was the best time to wait, but Jayne rarely had the patience. After a couple of minutes, she filled up her mug and drank the first mouthful. There was something wonderfully warming and comforting about that first sip; the heat flowing through her body followed by the taste of the tannins in her mouth.

'Too milky,' Robert would have probably said, but she preferred it like this.

Her phone buzzed with a message.

Driving in from the farm early tomorrow morning, will go straight to the hospital. How is Rob?

Jayne smiled. Harry always called her stepfather Rob, even though Robert hated it when his name was shortened.

No change. Doctors talking about an operation.

Vera will look forward to you being there.

Harry's answer came almost immediately.

Will get there about 8.30. When will you arrive?

Around 11. Only two people allowed at any one time to visit a patient. I have a client meeting at 9.30.

Sounds good. We can stay and give Vera a break. I want to have a chat with you anyway.

Jayne was intrigued. What did Harry want to chat about?

See you tomorrow at 11.

Ok.

Jayne realised she hadn't yet booked Liz for their meeting. She immediately sent a text.

I have some updates on Annie Kelly and her husband for you. Can we meet at 9.30 in the Botanical again?

The reply was even swifter than Harry's.

Sounds wonderful. See you at 9 30 am. I can't wait!!!

So everything was set up. Jayne took another sip of her tea and switched on her computer. She had to get her notes in order for Liz tomorrow and, if she had time, find out more about Daniel Sheehan.

She immediately got to work, planning a true narrative of Annie Kelly's life and contrasting it with the story remembered by the family and recounted in her obituary in 1904. As Jayne worked, she realised the obvious starting point in the story was the obituary, as it reinforced what Liz had told her even though it was completely invented. Then it would be a simple task to show how no documentary evidence supported this family history and how Jayne had discovered the true story through the convict documents.

As she finished writing, she realised that the details on Daniel Sheehan were quite weak; all she had was his convict description, the ship he arrived on, and his marriage to Annie in 1840.

She glanced at the clock. It was 10.30 p.m.

Perhaps she could put in a few more hours before bed, just to flesh out more details. As he was described as a 'publisher' in the ship's manifest, she decided to see if he had appeared in any newspapers in Australia.

She logged on to Trove and entered his name followed by the years 1836 to 1850.

Immediately, 263 articles appeared.

'You were a prolific writer, Mr Sheehan,' she said out loud, sipping her tea and topping up the cup from the pot.

Most of his articles in the early years were written for the *Sydney Gazette and New South Wales Advertiser* and covered a gamut of topics, ranging from the price of wheat and how to raise a prize ewe, to the correct way to fold clothes and the news of Lord Melbourne's resignation as prime minister in 1841.

He was obviously a jack-of-all-trades journalist, one who could write about anything and everything.

Then in 1842 the articles stopped, with nothing appearing from him again until 1844. Had he been ill or had he lost his job? A quick Wikipedia search showed that the newspaper he worked for had closed in 1842. Despite being a convict, he could still suffer the problem of being made redundant.

In 1844, the articles continued under his byline for a newspaper called the *Sydney Irishman*. His writing increased during this period and Jayne noticed he sometimes had three or more articles in each bi-weekly issue of the paper. It wasn't until 1846, as she was reading the first reports of the famine in Ireland under his byline but with information supplied by a 'special correspondent', that she realised he was the publisher.

'To go from convict to publisher of a newspaper in eight years. Hats off to you, Mr Sheehan.'

She carried on reading the articles written by him. They spent a lot of time criticising the attitudes and actions of the British government regarding the famine. The descriptions she read of the actual conditions of the time were harrowing. Despite being on the opposite side of the world, Daniel Sheehan still had his finger on the pulse of the problems of Ireland.

As she read more and more through the years 1847, 1848 and 1849, the articles became even more strident, criticising the colonial authorities in Sydney for their handling of the health of the city, rejecting the appeals to re-introduce the transportation of convicts into New South Wales, and calling for the independence of Ireland and the sending of material relief to the country to assuage the problems of the famine.

Then, in 1849, the articles stopped.

She checked her search parameters, changing the years and looking for new work from Daniel Sheehan.

Nothing.

For some reason, he stopped writing in 1849. Had he died?

She went back to the birth, marriages and death records.

There were three records for Daniel Sheehan, but none of the details matched her man.

What had happened to him?

She glanced up at the clock. Somehow it was now 3.30 a.m.

She really needed to get some sleep. Should she send a message to Vera to check on Robert?

She decided against it. No point in waking her up too.

She got up, stretched and yawned. Perhaps in the morning she would get up early and see if she could discover what had happened to Daniel Sheehan.

Then she thought about the letter signed with the enigmatic initial, 'D'. Didn't it mention Fremantle?

She scrabbled amongst her notes, looking for the photocopy.

There it was. The letter was headed 'Fremantle, 1852'. That's where she would look next. Had he been sent to Fremantle and then decided to take a ship from there to leave Australia?

But how could he do that if he was sentenced to be transported for life?

Had he obtained his ticket-of-leave or a pardon? Or did he just escape?

She yawned loudly.

That would have to wait for morning. With luck, she would find the answer before she met Liz. If not, she would continue her research as she sat beside Robert's bedside.

At last, Jayne felt she was making real progress in the

case. Daniel Sheehan was beginning to come to life in her mind. All she had to do now was find out what had happened to him and how he had travelled from Sydney to Perth.

Shouldn't be too difficult, should it?

'Famous last words, Jayne,' she said out loud as she closed her laptop.

Her bed was calling her name, loudly.

CHAPTER THIRTY-NINE

August 19, 1849

Perth, Australia

Their ship finally docked and unloaded its human cargo in the city of Perth on a bright, cool winter's day on August 19, 1849.

Annie and the children were allowed by a friendly guard to say goodbye to their father before he was clapped in irons and shuffled off the ship. The guard informed them that he was to be taken to Fremantle where he would be housed and assigned work.

The children didn't cry as they watched their father being led away. Dominic was the only one who asked a question.

'When will we see Father again?'

Annie couldn't answer, as she didn't know.

Instead, she bustled around collecting their various cases, the only possessions they could bring with them from Sydney, placing them under her arms and marching off the ship into the Freemason's Hotel on the corner of William Street and St George's Terrace.

That night, after she had put the children to bed, she sat alone in the room listening to their gentle snores. They could afford to stay in the hotel for just two weeks. The move and the cost of coming to Perth had made a serious impact on her savings. She had to find work, a place to stay, and a school for the children in that short time. Otherwise, the money would run out and they would be left destitute and hopeless.

She thought of Daniel chained up in some awful cell in Fremantle and her heart reached out to him.

They would survive this struggle.

She would survive this struggle.

* * *

The next morning she was up bright and early, eating breakfast with the children in the dining room of the hotel. She spotted a copy of the *Inquirer*, dated 15 August. In amongst the notices for the sale of horses, ewes and rams, the arrival and departure of ships, the requests for tender and the sales of sundries, two small items caught her attention. The first was an advertisement for a general store that sold 'a variety of household goods, medicines, wines and spirits, and leather goods'. She decided to talk to the proprietor, Mr Davis, to see if she could sell him some samples of her wares she had brought from Sydney.

The second advertisement was from the Sisters of Mercy.

The Sisters of Mercy, possessing every facility, have arranged to open, on the 3rd September, a distinct Day School for a limited number of young ladies. Besides a solid English education, comprising Grammar, Geography, History, Arithmetic, Writing, Etc. Etc., the French language will be taught; also Music, Drawing and Plain and Ornamental Works.

Parents wishing to avail themselves of this opportunity, and be informed of the terms and conditions, will have the goodness to call at the Convent of the Sisters of Mercy, Perth on any day from the 16th August, Sundays excepted.

She didn't particularly like the part about 'terms and conditions'. It suggested that she would have to pay for Honorah's education, but at least the opportunity was available, and at a school run by the Sisters. She decided to visit there after seeing Mr Davis.

At precisely 10 a.m., she dressed herself and the children in their finest Sunday best and they all marched to the corner of Goderich Street and Pier Street, dodging the overladen wagons taking sandalwood down to the docks.

She opened the front door of the general merchandise store and a bell rang above her head. Instantly, a large florid man appeared by her side, wringing his hands and enquiring, 'What can I do for you, madam? Isaac Davis is yours to command. We have the latest fine fustians and linens, just arrived on the *Merope* last week. I always pride myself on being able to purchase the best of Captain Robert's stock.'

Annie ushered the children in and they stood to one side.

'My, my, these are two fine children. I haven't seen them in my store recently. My wife makes the most delicious fudge, even if I do say so myself, only tuppence per piece but worth four times the price. Isn't that true, m'dear?'

Annie hadn't noticed the small, slim woman behind the girth of Mr Davis.

She stepped out into full view and seemed even thinner. She obviously did not partake of her own fudge when she was making it.

'Actually, Mr Davis, I have something you might be able to sell in your shop.'

Instantly the man's face fell as flat as the Swan River. 'Tradespeople, madam, enter around the back, they don't come in through the front door. That is reserved for paying customers.'

Annie made to leave.

'But now you are here, you should at least show us what you have.'

It was the wife who spoke. Annie expected her voice to be as thin and reedy as the woman herself, but instead it was deep and booming. Despite his bulk, Mr Davis shrank into the background as his wife took over. She was obviously the power behind the throne.

Annie brought out her case of samples; the Elixir which had sold so well in Sydney, plus a selection of the balms, poultices, tinctures and rubs she had created.

The woman peered, sniffed and poked at them all without saying a word.

Then Annie produced the articles created by Daniel and others about her products, with two letters of recommendation written in their florid handwriting by Mr Wiggs and Mrs Furlong.

The woman read them slowly, her lips moving as her eyes scanned the pages. She put them down carelessly on the counter.

'If, as you say, your products were so successful in Sydney, why have you come all the way to Perth? The town is small and the facilities limited. Surely it would have been much better to stay in Sydney with its larger population?'

'I'm afraid I had to accompany my husband, as he was sent here.'

The woman's face brightened. 'Your husband is a member of the colonial administration.'

'No, my husband is a convict. He was sent here from New South Wales.'

The woman began immediately to put all the samples and the articles back in the case.

'I think you have mistaken our establishment, Mrs…'

'Sheehan, Annie Sheehan.'

'This establishment only deals with the very best people in Western Australia. We could not possibly sell the wares of a convict's wife, we would die of shame. We are free migrants,' she said proudly, 'and I will thank you to take yourself and your children elsewhere.'

Annie's ears flamed bright red. She pulled the children to her and picked up the case. She turned to go and then stopped.

'Before I leave your shop, Mrs Davis, I would like to purchase six pieces of your fudge. My children love it so.'

Mrs Davis glanced at her husband before greed finally overcame any scruples she may have possessed about selling her wares to a convict's wife.

She hurriedly placed six pieces of the best fudge into a paper bag. Annie gave her the money and passed the bag to Dominic.

'Don't eat it all at once, children, you know such sweetness could upset your stomach. And it appears this store has nothing to cure such an illness.'

Outside, Annie instantly regretted the pride that had let her waste one shilling of her vastly depleted resources on fudge.

The children, though, were extremely happy. As Mr Davis had promised, the fudge was very good.

CHAPTER FORTY

August 20, 1849
Perth, Australia

That afternoon, Annie decided to visit her second port of call; the convent of the Sisters of Mercy. It was situated next to the newly built St John's Church at the other end of Hay Street.

The hustle and bustle of the morning had given way to a quieter, more serene atmosphere. There were very few townspeople walking the streets, and even Honorah remarked on it.

'Where is everybody?' she asked, her bonnet moving from left to right as she searched for people on the streets of the city.

'I expect they are having something to eat,' answered Annie.

'When are we going to eat?'

Annie had forgotten how large children's appetites could be. Ever since they had arrived in Perth, they had been for ever hungry. Perhaps it was the air, or perhaps simply a result of leaving the constant rocking of the boat. Whatever it was, they were making up for lost time on their food consumption.

'After we have had a chat with the nuns, then we can go to find something for you.'

'I don't know if I can wait that long,' said Dominic with a long sigh. 'Is Father eating?'

'I hope so,' Annie said quickly before adding, 'I'm sure he is.'

'Father is so thin these days, he used to be much fatter.'

Dominic was correct, their father had lost a lot of weight on the boat. Annie would try to take him some food; a bowl of stirabout, perhaps, or some broth. If she could find somewhere to make it, she would create a pot of Elixir for him. Even without the herbs, it was better than anything a convict would eat.

They saw the small squat shape of the church on their left, with the buildings of the convent behind it. Annie had never been to a convent before.

There was one next to the church in Durrow, but it wasn't a place where one normally went and the nuns were from a silent order, keeping themselves to themselves and not participating in the life of the town. Her father had gone there when a nun had fallen ill once, but he wasn't allowed inside. Instead the nun had described her symptoms from a high window and he had created a balm for her skin rash, leaving it at the front door where it promptly vanished, being replaced by tuppence as payment.

She stood in front of the large old door, grasped the iron knocker and rapped it twice on the wood. The sound seemed enormous to her ears, echoing around the entry hall.

Her knock was answered ten seconds later by a young nun who spoke English with a heavy accent. She was dressed in the normal black and white habit of the Sisters of Mercy.

'How can I help you?'

'I am wanting to bring my daughter to the school.'

'Ah, please come in.'

She stepped aside to let Annie enter the hallway. A strange scent permeated the place; a mixture of incense, furniture wax and piety. On their way through, an image of Christ on the cross stared down at them, his face lifted up to the heavens in suffering.

'This is the child you want to be educated?'

'Yes, this is Honorah.'

'A good name.' The nun knelt down in front of Annie's daughter. 'And do you want to go to school?'

Honorah nodded without saying anything.

'She's a little young, but we have three other children of her age starting with us in September so she will fit in. The cost is three shillings a week and the children will attend mass every day at eight a.m.'

Annie closed her eyes. 'Three shillings?'

'Is that a problem?'

'I don't think so. I will find the money.' Annie pulled Dominic to her. 'I also have a son.'

'Are you looking to educate him too?'

Annie nodded while Dominic squirmed away.

'I could talk to the Brothers and see if they have a place. The cost is five shillings a week for the boys.'

Annie blanched. Eight shillings a week just for education. How would she find the money? Nevertheless, the words 'that will be fine' tumbled from her mouth.

'Good, the starting date will be September third. Your child's name is Honorah and the surname is…?'

The nun paused her pen over a large ledger.

'She…' Annie stopped herself from saying the name. After her experience that morning with the shopkeeper, she couldn't risk the same reaction from the nun too. 'Kelly,' she finally blurted.

'Honorah Kelly,' the nun mouthed as she wrote the name down. 'And the father is here too?'

'He's in Fremantle,' answered Dominic before Annie could react.

'He's working there at the docks,' added Annie, saying a silent Hail Mary as penance for not telling the truth to a nun.

'So the family is separated? It's all too common in this area. At least he is not in Bunbury or Albany. Fremantle is just a short boat ride away. You have just arrived in Perth?'

'Is it so obvious?'

'It is, but we are all new arrivals in one shape or form. I have just been here for two years. I hear from your speech that you are Irish. Most of our pupils are Irish too. I am French, as you may have gathered. It is Sister Magdalena.'

'I am pleased to meet you, Sister.'

'One last thing. What is your address?'

'At the moment we are living at the Freemason's Hotel, but we are looking for somewhere permanent to live.'

'The search is never easy. Freemason's Hotel is not really a suitable place for young children.'

'I hope it will be just temporary.'

'It would be best. One final question, what is your husband's profession?'

Annie didn't know whether to tell the truth or to lie. She finally said simply, 'He was a journalist.'

'An educated profession. You said "was". What does he do now?'

The young nun looked up at her with such an open, innocent expression, Annie could lie no more.

'He is a convict. The government of New South Wales sent him here.'

The nun seemed undisturbed by the information. 'And were you a convict too?'

'I was, but I received my Certificate of Freedom in 1844. I was transported from Ireland for seven years.'

'And what did you do in Ireland?'

'I was my father's assistant. He was a herbalist.'

The young nun smiled. 'It is similar to me. My father has a pharmacy in Dijon, you know, the place of the mustard? I used to help him too.' The nun looked at her for a long time before asking, 'Did you cook and clean for your family?'

'I did. All the girls in Ireland are taught to look after the family while the boys can go out to play.'

'It is the same in France. If you would wait a few minutes, Mrs Kelly, I will return.'

Annie stood in the small white-washed room. Next to her, Dominic and Honorah were playing together on the floor, moving an imaginary horse and cart along a village street.

Annie expected the Sister to return at any minute with the news that the school wouldn't accept the daughters and sons of convicts, particularly not ones who couldn't possibly pay the school fees.

Instead, the nun returned with an older woman.

'This is Mother Superior.'

Annie curtseyed in front of the older woman.

'You say you are Irish?'

'I am, Mother Superior, from Durrow in Queens County.'

'I know it well, I was born in Abbeyleix. Your surname is Kelly?'

Annie reddened. 'My maiden name is Kelly, my married name is Sheehan.'

'So you must be Liam Kelly's daughter, the herbalist. I often used to buy his balm for the rheumatism when he came to the fair. He was a good man.'

Annie thought of her father and a tear appeared in the corner of her eye.

'You can cook and clean?' asked the older nun.

'I can.'

'And you are a Catholic?'

'I am.'

'Good. We are in need of a housekeeper. Your duties are to cook for the six nuns and myself, twice a day, while on Sunday we fast. You will also be responsible for the cleanliness of the schoolrooms at the end of day. There will be a small salary of five shillings a week, but you will live in a small cottage in the grounds, with all food and board. Obviously, your children will be educated for free. Do you accept the position, Mrs Kelly?'

'I do. When do you want me to start?'

'Immediately. Our present cook has run off with some soldier and Sister Magdalena's cooking leaves much to be desired.' She glanced at the younger nun. 'It is far too… French.'

'Good, I will move from the hotel tomorrow and start the day after. I must ask for Sunday off once every month, though. The children must go to see their father in Fremantle.'

'Agreed. Start the day after tomorrow. Welcome to our small convent, Mrs Kelly. Or should I call you Mrs Sheehan?'

Annie thought for a moment before answering, 'Either will do.'

'One last thing, Sister Magdalena tells me you used to be your father's assistant. Would you know how to make his balm against the rheumatism? The pain in my wrists is more than I can bear at the moment.'

CHAPTER FORTY-ONE

Thursday, September 17, 2020

Perth, Australia

Jayne woke up bright and early the following morning. After texting Vera to check on Robert and receiving a 'no change' answer, she sat in front of her laptop, coffee in hand, at 6.30 a.m.

'Time to get to work, Ms Sinclair.'

She checked the 'all record sets' button on Findmypast first. Western Australian births, marriages, deaths and directories, but nothing on convicts to the area.

She switched to Ancestry.com and searched the card collection. Immediately a record named *Western Australia, Convict Records, 1846–1930* leapt out at her.

She entered 'Daniel Sheehan' and pressed send.

No records.

Weird. Had she missed something? From the letter signed 'D', he was in Fremantle in 1852 and there was no record of him receiving a pardon.

She checked the source and noticed it was from the States Record Office of Western Australia. Logging on to their website, she found a whole host of convict records and documents.

Apparently, the Swan River Settlement, as Western Australia was known until 1832, had elected to become a British penal settlement in 1849. From then until 1868, a total of 9,925 convicts were transported and spread throughout the state to work on public works buildings. Generally, though, the convict system in Western Australia was more relaxed and less formal than that employed in New South Wales, with the prisoners enjoying a greater sense of freedom and less restrictions.

Jayne scanned the list of available resources: transportation records for the ships, convict registers, correspondence from the Comptroller General to the Colonial Secretary, medical registers and journals, occurrence books, staff registers, ticket-of-leave records and re-convictions.

The first two looked like what she needed but, unfortunately, they weren't online. She checked the clock. It was now 7.30 a.m. The records office opened at 9.30. Could she pay a quick visit to find the documentary proof that Daniel Sheehan was a convict in the area in 1852?

She'd have to put her meeting with Liz back for an hour or so. Plus, she would be late getting to the hospital to see Robert, but at least Harry would be able to relieve Vera – and all three of them couldn't be with him at the same time anyway.

She sent a text to Liz.

Will be an hour late, sorry. Just discovered an exciting new lead and need to go to the States Record Office. See you at 10.30 instead?

No problem. If you are on Francis Street, I can meet you in a coffee shop, *Ground and Co*, inside the library building at 10.30. Saves you coming to the Botanical.

Perfect. See you at 10.30.

This was followed by another text to Vera.

Won't be at the hospital until 11am. Is that ok?

Of course, Harry will be here anyway. See you at 11.

Everything sorted, it was time to get down to work.

CHAPTER FORTY-TWO

September 18, 1849
Perth, Australia

It was a month before Annie could take a boat with the children to see their father in Fremantle.

After early mass at St John's, they all dressed in their Sunday best and walked down to the pier.

'Will Father be pleased to see us?' asked Dominic.

'I'm sure he will. He hasn't seen you for a month.'

'I'll tell him all about the Brothers teaching me how to write. I'll show him how I write my name.'

'Your father has beautiful handwriting, you should get him to show you how he makes his letters.'

'I hope he can.'

Throughout all this, Honorah was silent, her small face screwed up tightly as if she were concentrating on some object far away to make sure it didn't move.

'Are you looking forward to meeting your father, Honorah?'

'I suppose so,' she said thoughtfully, 'but I'm trying to remember his face and I can't.'

Annie didn't answer. She grabbed both children's hands and rushed to board the ferry, making sure they bagged a seat at the bow, away from the smoke of the funnel.

It was funny that, for a woman born many miles away from the sea, in a county that had no large bodies of water, her life now revolved around it. Luckily the Swan River Bay was as flat as a millpond today; their crossing to Fremantle should finish almost before it had started.

As the ferry blasted two toots from its horn, the sailors threw off the ropes and the boat began to pull away from the shore.

Although she wasn't going to let the children know, she too was nervous about today's meeting. Of course, she had written to Daniel to tell him of her good fortune but had received nothing in reply.

The post of housekeeper to the Sisters of Mercy was relatively easy to manage. When the nuns weren't teaching, they kept mostly to their rooms, praying or reading. The only time she saw all of them together was in the morning after early prayers, and before mass. They assembled in the dining room and she served them breakfast prepared by a cook she had hired. Her own efforts in the kitchen had not been as successful as she'd wished, and the nuns had quickly decided that a proper cook was worth the negligible cost.

She got on well with all the nuns; they had a singular focus to their life which she admired. It was to devote themselves to God through the teaching of children. None of them had any desire for material gains or wealth, in fact, austerity seemed to give them more satisfaction than anything else. Annie realised very quickly that her job was to ensure they could spend their time with God and educating the children to the exclusion of all else.

With both the children at school all day, it was a job she enjoyed and relished. Within the first month, she had everything running smoothly, particularly the accounts. She found quite a few discrepancies from the last holder of the post, discovering that a lot of the money given to run the household had vanished or been frittered away.

She had presented a whole new set of accounts to the Mother Superior in her first week.

'Buying wholesale in the market rather than retail at Mr Davis's store will save the Sisters at least eight pounds a month, if not more.'

'A saving we can use to buy equipment and resources for the new school for girls. Thank you, Mrs Kelly, for your work.'

The new purchase system was set up the following week, much to Mr Davis's annoyance, but within the first couple of weeks it had drastically reduced the running costs for the nuns.

That morning at breakfast, she had told the Mother Superior of her intention to visit her husband.

'Do be careful, Mrs Kelly, on your journey. Perth is not as safe as it once was.'

'I'll be back by six o'clock to check that Cook has prepared the evening meal correctly and see if you need anything before you retire.'

'All is good, Mrs Kelly. Truthfully, it seems you have been here for years rather than just one short month. I don't know what we would do without you. I really don't know how we managed before.'

The words pleased Annie. It seemed that, after the upheaval of the last six months, her life, and that of her children, was back on an even keel.

There she was again, using the imagery of the sea. How her life had been taken over by it!

As if in answer to her thoughts, the ferry gave two long blasts on its horn.

The docks and town of Fremantle were rapidly approaching. She had already seen them once when she had arrived a month ago, and now she was about to set foot in the area for the first time. A little shiver of excitement ran down her spine. She tightened her grip on the children's hands so much that Dominic squeaked in pain.

'You're holding my hand too tightly, Mother, I'm not a child any more.'

The sailors assembled along the port side, ropes in hand, ready to toss them to the stevedores waiting on the dock.

Another long blast from the horn and the gangway was run out. The passengers gathered in a tight scrum around the entrance.

Annie waited, holding back until the crowd had disembarked.

When there were only a few people left, she walked down the gangway, her eyes gazing along the wharf, looking for Daniel.

It was Dominic who spotted him first, shouting 'Father!' and running down the gangway towards a man standing away from the crowds next to a half-constructed wall.

Was that her Daniel?

His clothes were dirty and grey, hanging off thin drooping shoulders like rags on a scarecrow.

She walked slowly towards him. As she approached, the stench of stale beer and whisky became stronger. His face was creased and sallow, the hair thin and grey.

But it was his eyes she noticed most.

Dull, lifeless, as if every little bit of joy had been dashed from them, leaving nothing but a trace of the life of the man she had once loved.

She hugged him, feeling his bones through his rough jacket.

'Hello, Annie,' he mumbled, before bending down to try to hug Honorah. The child turned away and buried herself deep in her mother's skirts.

Despite herself, Annie said, 'You've been drinking.'

He smiled briefly. 'Just a little, it helps brighten the day.'

Dominic was standing to one side, uncertain if he should speak to his father. Finally he said, 'I've started to learn to write, I can write my name now.'

'Be careful, Dominic, writing can lead to no good. No good at all.'

They spent the rest of the day together until Annie and the children had to catch the five o'clock ferry and return to the convent.

She told him of her life and her good luck at finding a position with the nuns. How it would give her a few years to build up her contacts and resources in Perth while the children were educated, and then she could restart her medical business, this time working for herself.

All the time she was speaking with such passion for the future, he seemed lost in his own private world.

'I'm sorry, Daniel, I have spoken so much of my life that I haven't asked you about yours.'

'I'm a convict, there is little to discuss.'

She bit her tongue. Where was the joy and life that Daniel used to possess in overflowing abundance?

'What do you do?' she asked.

'I am in the clerk's department at the dockyard. We write tallies of the ships that arrive, the stores unshipped, the goods stored in the godowns. I write long lists in my copperplate handwriting, which the supervisor enjoys because he has no fist himself. His writing looks like a goose has stepped in ink.'

'Couldn't you get a job with a newspaper? There seem to be many in Perth and Fremantle.'

'I tried, but my reputation precedes me. Nobody will use me as a journalist.' He took a deep breath. 'Annie, I wish I had never written the articles. If I had just held my tongue, and my pen, we would all still be in Sydney, not in this Godforsaken place.'

She wanted to agree with him, but what she actually said was, 'You could no more hold your tongue than an apple would remain on its tree in autumn.'

They carried on speaking for another hour. But try as she might, she couldn't raise him from his profound depression and unhappiness.

As five o'clock approached, she called the children to her. 'Say goodbye to your father.'

Dominic, like the growing man he was at the tender age of eight, shook his father's hand. Honorah, however, refused to leave her mother's side, not even looking at her father.

Two toots from the ferry announced it was about to depart.

They both hugged, Annie feeling once again the sharp bones beneath his shirt. 'Look after yourself, Daniel. Eat more and drink less.'

'It's all I have here.'

'You have a wife and children who love you.'

'Who are far away across the bay where I cannot visit.'

'The authorities won't allow you any freedom?'

'I am a dangerous convict, apparently. I mustn't infect the population of Perth with my radical ideas.'

Annie suddenly felt so sorry for her husband. 'It will improve, trust me, life will improve.'

'Will it, Annie? Will it really?'

A final loud blast from the ferry. Annie grabbed the hands of Dominic and Honorah and rushed up the gangway just as a sailor was about to pull it on to the boat.

She turned to wave goodbye to Daniel, but he wasn't there.

He had already left the dockside without waving goodbye.

CHAPTER FORTY-THREE

Thursday, September 17, 2020
Perth, Australia

Jayne stared at her monitor. The States Record Office didn't open for another two hours. It would take her less than thirty minutes to get there by Uber. A shower and getting dressed wouldn't take more than ten minutes. She could do her makeup in the Uber with just about eighty minutes to kill.

She could sit getting antsier and antsier while she was waiting, or she could do some more work. Daniel Sheehan could wait until she reached the record office. Why didn't she see if she could find out more background about Annie's life in Sydney?

Perhaps later in the year, when the lockdown and travel restrictions eased, she could go to Sydney and look at the files there. Until then she would have to make do with what was online.

She logged on to Findmypast and scanned the records for Australian convicts. One stood out for her: *Results for Australia Convict Conditional and Absolute Pardons 1791–1867*. If Annie had only been sentenced to seven years' transportation, it meant she must have received a ticket-of-leave or a pardon at one point.

She entered Annie's name and one result came up.

Number	Name	Ship
879	**Anne Kelly**	**Sir Charles Forbes**

She checked the heading at the top of the record. This was a compendium of all those granted pardons, collected in 1851 by some bureaucrat, no doubt in answer to a request from London. There was more information above Annie's list.

List of seventy-two persons who were convicted in the United Kingdom and recommended by His Excellency, the Governor of New South Wales, to receive the indulgence of Conditional Pardons available everywhere save in the said United Kingdom.

So Annie could never have gone back. The pardon she received was conditional and not valid in the United Kingdom.

But surely she had completed her sentence, so why shouldn't she have been free?

For some reason, she and seventy-one others had been denied that right. What a harsh system convict transportation was. Even when a person had served their sentence, the colonial government still controlled their lives.

Jayne's heart went out to Annie. How strong this woman must have been to have achieved so much despite so many setbacks.

She checked the clock. Time for one more search.

She opened the Trove tab and searched for Sydney newspapers, 1840 to 1860, entering Annie's married name of Sheehan.

Two articles came up.

The first was from the *Sydney Morning Herald*, dated July 1846.

A NEW CURE FOR THE SYDNEY DISEASE?

For many years, Mr Wiggs' Energy Elixir has been produced and sold in our city as a cure for that peculiar lack of energy and debility which seems to plague Sydney people in the summer months.

It is such a common affliction that Mr Wiggs, the renowned proprietor of his eponymous pharmacy, has dubbed it with no little wit, the Parramatta Paralysis.

It affects husbands as they go about their work.

It overwhelms their wives as they face the daily round of washing and housework.

It stuns our legislators into a stupendous turpitude that means no serious legislation is attempted in the

summer months.

It quietens our children as they fall asleep over their school desks in the middle of the afternoon.

It chills judges. It stills our policemen. It troubles our farmers. It makes our dockers dally.

It is the Parramatta Paralysis and it affects everyone in our fair city, to a greater or lesser extent.

Indeed, the only people it doesn't seem to affect are the gentlemen who plague our highways with their imprecations and criminality; the Bushwhackers. Many of our fellow citizens hope it would affect them but, alas, it has yet to take a hold on their hard hearts.

But finally, a cure has been found and this cure is now in a new, stronger, more energetic formula developed by that wizard of herbal cures, Mrs Annie Sheehan, with the creative input and help of Mrs Marjorie Furlong and the redoubtable Mr Wiggs.

Mrs Sheehan, originally from Queen's County, Ireland, developed the Elixir from an old recipe handed down for generations in her family. A clan renowned in Ireland for being the traditional doctors to Irish kings. Indeed, it has come to this correspondent's knowledge, though this is denied as hearsay by Mrs Sheehan, that the Elixir was drunk before the Battle of Clontarf by no less a hero than Brian Boru.

I asked Mrs Sheehan about the ingredients found in the Elixir but she was reluctant to divulge her secrets. I suppose after 800 years the recipe is closely guarded. But despite not knowing what was in it, I can sing its praises after drinking just one bottle every day for a week. It has banished a peculiar affliction which affects all writers and particularly your humble correspondent. I am talking about writer's block, of course. After Mrs Sheehan's Elixir, I no longer stare at white pages. I no longer fear a lack of ideas. I no longer spend time searching for something to do to avoid actually writing.

Instead, I sit down at my desk with a smile on my face and write this correspondence to you as quick as a convict takes his ticket-of-leave.

And there can be no better advertisement than that!!

MRS SHEEHAN'S NEW AND IMPROVED ELIXIR, FORMERLY KNOWN AS MR WIGGS' ENERGY ELIXIR, IS NOW AVAILABLE AT MR WIGGS' PHARMACY OR DIRECTLY FROM THE HONOURABLE MRS FURLONG.

Jayne smiled to herself. Even in Sydney, Annie had been practising her craft. If she was so successful, why did she leave?

She clicked on the second link. A small notice appeared, again from the *Sydney Morning Herald*. This time the date was 1849.

Mr and Mrs Daniel Sheehan wish to thank all those who attended the funeral of their son John at St Mary's Church last Monday.
We know our son is sitting at the side of God in Heaven.
Masses will be said by Father Therry for the next eight Sundays to commemorate his eternal soul.

At least Jayne now knew what had happened to their firstborn son. She could check the death records for 1849 to find out more details.

She glanced at the clock – 8.50. Where had the time gone?

She rushed to her bedroom, threw off her t-shirt and sweatpants and grabbed a quick shower. Throwing on a nice casual outfit, she called an Uber and received a message that it would be there in seven minutes. With a bit of luck and no traffic, she'd arrive just in time for the record office to open.

Before the Uber arrived, she just had time to send a quick email to Ronald in the UK.

Can you check somebody for me? It's a Daniel Sheehan, he was born in Dublin in 1808, transported to Australia in 1836 and lived in Sydney and probably Perth/Fremantle.

I've attached the details from his transportation ship, plus a link to the source if you want to check for yourself. Usual rates. I'd appreciate a reply ASAP.

Yours, Jayne.

Outside the house, she heard the beep of the Uber's horn. She closed her laptop, grabbed her notebook and all the notes she had prepared for Liz off the kitchen counter, took one last sip of coffee and raced for the door.

As she rushed out, she saw Robert's jacket hanging in the hallway, on its own, all alone. A sharp pain pierced her heart. After this client meeting, she would spend more time with her stepfather; she owed him that much.

CHAPTER FORTY-FOUR

October 1849 to April 1852
Perth, Australia

For the next two years, Annie took the ferry ride out to Fremantle on the last Sunday of each month.

Her life at the convent was going well. The children were enjoying their studies, particularly Dominic, who had revealed an unexpected talent for mathematics and had become a favourite of the nuns for his good looks and quick mind.

She had even started making her balms, tinctures and ointments again, revising the recipe for the Elixir, incorporating more herbs that could only be found in the area around the Swan River. The nuns had allowed her the time and resources to make them.

'As long as you keep making my rheumatism drink, you can do want you want, Mrs Kelly. My old bones have never felt so good. I don't mind in the least,' said the Mother Superior.

In the convent, they were always known by the surname Kelly. At first, Honorah had questioned it.

'I thought I was Honorah Sheehan but the Holy Sisters always call me Honorah Kelly. Why, Mother?'

'You're lucky, dear, you have two names. Most girls only have one.'

She seemed satisfied with this answer. Annie had tried to change their names, but the nuns had decided it was impossible. From now on, they would be the Kellys.

For some reason that Annie didn't quite understand, it made her feel better to be known as Mrs Kelly.

On her one day off a month, she became Mrs Sheehan once again, taking the ferry to Fremantle to see Daniel. At first the children had accompanied her, but soon it became difficult to get them to go. Honorah, particularly, seemed to be afraid of her father, flinching or grabbing Annie's skirts as he bent down to kiss his daughter.

'He smells so, Mother. Why does he smell?'

Under the tutelage of the nuns she had become aware of the necessity of cleanliness, perhaps too much so.

'It's because the washing facilities are primitive in the wool warehouse where he lives.'

'The place doesn't have anywhere to bathe?'

'Not really, and many people use it.'

'How awful.'

Dominic was not as bad, but he did not speak to his father unless asked a direct question and even then, the answers were blunt and almost monosyllabic.

'How are your studies?' asked Daniel every time.

'Fine.'

'What's your favourite subject?'

'Arithmetic.'

'Mine was history. I used to love hearing of Irish heroes of old; the battles they fought, the women they loved, the plots they hatched. Do you like history?'

'No.'

A few times Annie had been forced to go alone without the children. After mass, they begged to be allowed to go to the picnic instead of visiting their father. Annie didn't have the heart to force them.

'They didn't come with me this time, I'm sorry,' she explained.

They were sitting in their usual place in Fremantle; a small hut overlooking the bay. It was where Daniel came when he wanted peace and quiet, away from his fellow convicts.

'I understand. It can't be pleasant wasting your Sunday to come to see an old man.'

She placed her hand on his right arm, feeling the scrawny sinews of his flesh beneath the thin shirt. 'You're not old.'

'I am, and getting older by the hour. There are more ships coming with more convicts from England.'

'Yes, I have seen gangs of them in the town, repairing roads and bridges,' Annie replied. 'Some are being farmed out to agriculturalists. They may even be used to build new buildings in the town according to Governor Hampton.'

'They already are. Stone is being cut for the new convict establishment in Fremantle. I've seen the plans; it looks like a giant starfish is taking over the area.'

'You are still clerk to the commissary?'

He nodded. 'He likes my handwriting, apparently. His superiors have complimented the style and the substance of his reports. At least it means I can come and go as I please and there are few restrictions, even though I am a convict.'

'You need to look after yourself more, drink less. Are you writing?'

'I write reports, but nothing else. As for my drinking, it helps to pass the time. You don't know how lonely it gets here.'

'I am working to bring you to Perth and the nuns are helping me, but the government is not listening. Perhaps when more convicts have arrived, they will need you less and you can ask for a pardon.'

He shook his head, the few grey wisps of hair that remained on his head brushing her face.

'As more ships arrive they will only need me more. I will never get away from this place, Annie. I am destined to be buried here, despised by everybody, hated by my children and pitied by my wife.'

'I…'

'Don't you know I can see the look of pity on your face when you see me? I remember when we first met, it was a look of love, and now there is nothing left.'

'You spoilt it all, Daniel, with your love of Ireland, a country that can give you nothing in return but exile, loneliness and death.'

As soon as the words were out of her mouth, she regretted them. 'I'm sorry, I didn't mean…'

He held his hand up to stop her talking. She couldn't help but notice the blue stains on his thumb and forefinger.

'You are right, I spoilt it all. I should have stilled my voice, curbed my writing. But I didn't. What's past is past. It can't be undone. I am condemned to stay in this place for ever.'

* * *

It was on a cold breezy day at the end of June in 1852 that everything changed.

After mass, she prepared herself as usual to visit Daniel. The children had decided to stay in Perth as one of their classmates was having a birthday party.

Annie strode down to the pier, carrying a few gifts for Daniel; a ham hock she had purchased from the market, three bottles of the Elixir she had brewed a week ago, and a jumper to keep him warm that she had knitted herself.

This time, as the ferry docked in Fremantle, he was waiting to greet her, not hanging back in the shadows of the godowns as he normally did.

As she stepped off the gangplank, he grabbed her arm and, looking sharply to left and right, said, 'Quickly, come this way, I have something to tell you.'

His eyes were aflame with passion, the most animated she had seen him in years.

He almost ran to the hut, dragging her with him and looking over his shoulder constantly. In the shed, he sat her down and whispered, 'I have a way out.'

'What?' she asked. 'You have a way out of what?'

He placed his finger across his lips and shushed her.

'In a tavern near the docks I met a whaling captain. He can take us all to America.'

'What? America? What's in America?'

'My freedom. I can be free there.'

Now she understood. She closed her eyes and let his words flow over her.

'He only wants twenty-five gold sovereigns for you and the children. And if I work my passage, he will give me five guineas back when we arrive in San Francisco. It's my chance to get away from this Godforsaken country. He leaves in four weeks' time, we must be ready by then. Can you raise the money? We need to pay him in advance.'

'I suppose I could at a stretch…' she answered doubtfully, 'but, Daniel, what are you saying? You want us all to leave Australia and go on a whaling ship to America? What are we going to do there?'

'We'll be together and we'll be free. We don't have to stay in America, we can go back to Ireland. We can see our own green country again.'

'But there is nothing there for me, Daniel. My parents are dead and none of our relatives know me. The children are Australian, they were born and raised here.'

'They are not Australian,' he shouted. 'They are Irish, the country of their father's birth.'

Annie stood up. 'I can't go on another ship, I am settled here. The children are happy here.'

'I've thought it all through. We can escape on the last Sunday of next month. You bring the children as usual, but instead of taking the ferry back, we simply go aboard the captain's ship and he sails for America on the high tide. We will be miles offshore by the time they notice I am missing and they won't bother coming after me.'

'You are not listening to me, Daniel. The children are settled here. This is their home, not some mystical place they've only heard about in tales from the nuns. This place, this country, is their home.'

'And what about me? How am I supposed to live here as a convict?'

She sat down beside him again. 'But it won't last for ever. The nuns have been talking to the bishop, and he will help you get a pardon. You won't have to wait long, the pardon will come soon.'

'How long is soon, Annie? Two years? Ten years? Twenty years? Look at yourself, they only gave you a conditional pardon. You can never go back to Ireland as Annie Kelly.'

'But don't you see, I don't want to go back.'

He stopped speaking, his mouth open wide.

After five minutes of silence, he bowed his head and stood up.

'Come with me, Annie.'

She shook her head. 'No, not any more. This is my home. This is our children's home.'

CHAPTER FORTY-FIVE

Thursday, September 17, 2020

Perth, Australia

Jayne jumped out of the Uber and rushed into the library just as a security man was opening the doors. She went up to the third floor where the record office was located. An archivist was standing behind a desk, preparing her notes for the day.

'Good morning. I know I haven't booked a seat but I'd love to look at some of the convict records on microfilm.'

Jayne was turning on all the charm she had.

'I'm sorry, all the seats are booked for today. We're operating at reduced capacity because of social distancing.'

'If it's any help, I'll be finished by ten thirty, I promise.'

'Well, Alan has booked his seat from eleven o'clock…'

'I'll be out well before then.'

The archivist thought for a moment, was about to say no, and then saw the look on Jayne's face. 'Okay, what files can I get you?'

Jayne passed across a list of files she had written that morning.

'If you take Seat 3, I'll bring the microfilms to you.'

'Thank you, you're a lifesaver.'

The woman looked at the list and said, 'Actually, the official title is "archivist", but I'll accept lifesaver as well. Seat 3 is over there.'

Jayne took her place in front of the microfilm reader and pulled her notes from her bag. This really was a bit of a long shot, but if she could find out what happened to Daniel – the 'D' of the letter, she was sure – then she could give Liz the complete story at 10.30.

Five minutes later the archivist returned with a bundle of microfilms. 'If you are looking for a particular convict record, I'd start with the Transportation Records, then go on to the others that you requested. I've added two more films that you might find useful. The first has the letters and memoranda books of the Comptroller General. I know this sounds a bit obscure, but a couple of researchers have found this particularly useful for the day-to-day understanding of the convicts' lives. The second is the Superintendent's Order Books for Fremantle from 1850 to 1874. Most convicts passed through the establishment on their way to other locations or towns. This is indexed so you can find what you are looking for pretty easily. Is there anybody special you are looking for?'

'I'm researching a Daniel Sheehan for a client.'

The archivist thought for a moment. 'The name rings a bell but I can't think from where.'

Jayne glanced at the clock. 'No worries, I'll take it from here.'

The archivist went back to her desk. Jayne loaded the first microfilm with the list of convict arrivals on to the machine and began to scroll. The records contained all the convicts sent to Western Australia from the moment it became a convict state, including the first, the *Scindian* with 75 convicts aboard in June 1850, to the last, the *Hougoumont* with 269 convicts in 1868.

As the letter was dated 1852, she decided to just look at the ships that had arrived before then. Halfway through the third ship, the *Mermaid*, she realised how stupid she had been.

'All these ships came from the United Kingdom, but Daniel Sheehan was already in Australia. He wouldn't have been on any of them,' she chastised herself.

She checked the time again. It was 10 a.m. She had wasted half an hour on totally fruitless work. She was just about to start working on the second set of records she had requested, the Convict Registers, when the archivist came rushing across.

'I've just remembered where I've seen that name.'

'Daniel Sheehan?'

'That's him. He's in the Superintendent's Order Book for 1852. He obviously caused a few problems for the authorities of the time.'

'Can you show me?'

The archivist unloaded the microfilm from Jayne's machine, and checked the stack of boxes beside her desk before finally selecting one. 'This should be it.'

With a speed that came from years of practice, she loaded the microfilm and spooled through the records, stopping just once to see where she was. 'The correspondence starts at the end of July 1852.' Another quick spooling of the microfilm. 'There it is.'

Jayne leant forward and began to read a letter to the Perth Magistrates from the Superintendent of the Convict Establishment in Fremantle, a Thomas Howell.

'Bingo,' she said out loud.

CHAPTER FORTY-SIX

July 25, 1852
Perth, Australia

Annie had finished her work for the day and was preparing to go to bed. The children were already asleep; it had been such a busy day for them with the nuns and they were both exhausted. She checked the door of the range was properly closed and reached out to lower the wick on the oil lamp. There was a soft knock on the door.

'Who is it?' she whispered, fearful of waking the children.

'A friend.' The accent was English and the voice male and gruff.

'I have no male friends. You need to go. This is a convent, the Sisters do not appreciate men being on the grounds.'

'I have a letter from Daniel,' the man hissed.

Annie opened the door a little, peering round the edge into the dark night.

A wretched young man stood on the porch of the cottage, his clothes shabby and his teeth missing. A grubby hand thrust a letter at her.

'He said to give you this.'

She took the letter, seeing her name in Daniel's beautiful handwriting on the folded cover.

'He also said you would give me food and something to drink..'

'I only have what's left over from the nuns' meal this evening.'

'Anything will do We don't eat very much over in Fremantle.'

She checked outside to see if any of the nuns were still awake or walking in the gardens of the convent. 'Come in.'

The young man shuffled through the door, taking off his ragged cap.

In the half-light of the oil lamp, he looked even worse than before. Everything about him was threadbare and he wore no shoes on his feet.

'Sit down,' she ordered.

Placing the letter on the kitchen table, she went to the range and ladled a bowl of chicken soup from the pot, placing it in front of the man. She went back to the bin where she kept the bread and found a stale chunk that still remained from this morning.

'You can eat.'

Without hesitation the man grabbed the spoon and began shovelling the soup into his mouth as if he hadn't eaten for decades.

She walked over to the children's bedroom and peered in. Dominic and Honorah were fast asleep, both their mouths open and hair spread all over the pillows.

She closed the door and walked back to the table. The letter was still lying there. She stared for a long time at the copperplate script of her name on the cover, trying to summon up the courage to open it.

Finally, she leant forward and picked up the letter. As she unfolded it something dropped out, rolling under her chair. She bent down and saw an old penny, lying with the old king's head facing towards her. It was the same penny Daniel had taken from her purse all those years ago.

William IV. Still with his broad forehead and curly hair, but now with a polish across his face where a thumb had continuously rubbed it.

Daniel's thumb.

She scooped it up and placed it on the table. The man still continued eating noisily, now attacking the chunk of bread, ignoring her completely.

She read the letter and tears appeared in her eyes.

Should she go to him?

As he said, they had their marriage vows. 'To have and to hold from this day forward. For better, for worse; for richer, for poorer; in sickness and in health, until death do us part.'

Was this one of those 'through better or worse' times?

She glanced across at the closed door to the children's bedroom. What about them? What right did he have to ask them to spend three months on a whaling ship, only to arrive in America with no money and nowhere to live?

They were happy here in Perth.

She was happy here.

The man finished his soup and was looking at her. 'Daniel said there might be a reply.'

'Tell him there is no reply,' she said firmly, her mind made up.

'Do you mind if I take the rest of the bread with me?'

'It's yours. Would you like some more soup?'

He nodded enthusiastically.

'How is Daniel?' she finally asked.

'He's good, happiest I've seen him in a long while.'

'And how do you know him?'

'He's teaching me how to read and write. He decided to teach all of the convicts who arrived on the *Mermaid*. I'm getting quite good now. I can even read your name on the letter. Annie Kelly.'

She found an old earthenware jar and poured the rest of the soup into it, wrapping up the remaining bread in a piece of cheesecloth.

'Take these with you. You look like you could use more food.'

'The superintendent doesn't feed everybody well, but it's still better than Whitechapel Workhouse.'

She handed him the food.

'Are you sure there's no reply? I think Daniel was expecting one.'

'There is no reply.'

She opened the door, checking once more that none of the nuns was in the gardens. 'Go now, and don't make any noise. You shouldn't be in the convent.'

'Thank you for the food. Daniel said you were a good woman.'

And with that, the man vanished into the dark, gone like a thief in the night.

Annie closed the door and walked slowly to the kitchen table. She picked up the penny and grasped it tightly in her small fist.

Then she began to weep.

CHAPTER FORTY-SEVEN

Thursday, September 17, 2020
Perth, Australia

Liz was waiting for her in the café when she arrived.

As she had promised the archivist, Jayne finished exactly at 10.25, packing up her things and paying for the printouts of the microfilm pages she'd ordered.

She rushed over to where Liz was sitting. 'Have you been here long?'

'No, only five minutes. I can't wait to hear what you have to tell me.'

'Just give me a few minutes.'

Jayne arranged her papers and the printouts in the correct order, took a deep breath and began her story.

'I'm afraid to tell you that most of the family history you told me is a myth, probably created by your three-times great-grandmother herself, Annie Kelly.'

'The family history isn't true?'

'I don't think so. I must admit, when I started I thought it would be an easy assignment as I found an obituary for her very quickly.'

Jayne passed over a printout of the obituary, which Liz

read immediately.

'But this backs up the family history. Sure, the dates might be slightly off, but the essential story is the same.'

'That's what I thought… Until I started looking for documentary evidence of your Annie Kelly's life. I checked the shipping records for her arrival – nothing. I looked for her husband's name in the death records. Nothing. I looked for the children's birth records. No records. I could find nothing about her until I saw a street directory for 1893.'

Jayne passed over those printouts.

Liz smiled. 'These are the addresses of our old house and the location of the first Emporium.'

'So that started me thinking. What if her life story was a myth? People often invent myths about themselves when they aren't proud of something in their past or where they came from. I think it's called "brand building" in modern terminology. Then I remembered the bible, where the children's births were recorded as 1840, 1842 and 1845.'

'I remember. You said the bible was Irish.'

'But that gave us another problem. Registration of Irish births didn't start until 1864. There are church records existing before then, but without a place of birth in Ireland, looking for a Kelly would be like looking for a single wave in an ocean.'

'Tell me about it. There are more Kellys than grains of

sand on Leighton Beach.'

'Actually, it's the second most popular name in Ireland and the most popular in Northern Ireland.'

Liz stared at her.

Jayne shrugged her shoulders. 'I looked it up. Anyway, the births would be hard to find. But then a friend of mine said that these bibles were often given as a going-away gift when people left Ireland.'

'Interesting…'

'So then I had an epiphany. What if Annie actually came to Australia a lot earlier? What if the story of her being a "free migrant" wasn't true?'

'What do you mean?'

'What if she came here as a convict?'

Liz clasped her hand to her mouth. 'Really, I have convict ancestors? My brother will be so pleased.'

Jayne then took her through everything she had found about Annie Kelly and her marriage to Daniel Sheehan.

'So she was never married to Peter Brennan? Our surname should be Sheehan?'

'I found the answer in the state's records this morning.' She passed another printout to Liz. 'This is a letter from the Superintendent of the Convict Establishment in Fremantle to the Comptroller General of the colony.' She began reading out loud from her copy.

'"Sir, I have the distressing news to report of the escape of an Irish convict, Daniel Sheehan. He was discovered missing when he did not report to work as a clerk in the Commissary. Further investigations revealed that Sheehan left the colony aboard the Whaling Ship, *Pensevant*, John Robinson, Master, bound for San Francisco on the first tide of July twenty-sixth. He posed as another sailor, Peter Brennan, who had been taken ill the week before. The ship is now long gone and it would be fruitless sending the cutter after it."'

'Is that where the name Peter Brennan comes from?' asked Liz. 'It was the name he used to escape on the ship.'

'I think so.' She carried on reading the letter. '"Daniel Sheehan was sentenced in 1835 to Transportation for Life and served the first part of his sentence in New South Wales. In 1849, he was arrested in that colony for sedition and transported to Perth along with nine other convicts. He leaves behind a wife and two children in Perth. I have ascertained that his wife, one Anne Kelly, also an ex-convict but now with a Certificate of Freedom, is gainfully employed by the Sisters of Mercy as a housekeeper in their convent in Perth.

'"Sir, I apologise for the inconvenience this man's actions have caused you. I have now tightened up security with all men locked up overnight when they finish their work.

'"I remain your obedient servant,

'"Thomas Howell, Superintendent."'

'So this Daniel Sheehan was my three-times great-grandfather?' Liz said.

'He was the father of Dominic Kelly, who continued the family business after the death of Annie in 1904. According to the superintendent, Daniel Sheehan escaped on a whaling ship to San Francisco, leaving his wife and children behind in Perth.'

'So Annie had to bring them up alone. What happened to him?'

'At the moment, I don't know. I've asked my associate in the UK to follow up with the Irish records to see if he returned there. If we can't find him, we will then start looking in the American records.'

'Left his wife and children behind to fend for themselves…' Liz sighed. 'Who could do that?'

'I wouldn't be so quick to condemn him. We don't know what was happening. The letter gives a few clues and it indicates that he did love his wife. My own feeling is that he was transported for life and saw no hope for himself in Australia.'

'But Annie saw hope and she prospered despite his absence.'

'Or maybe because of it…'

Just then, Jayne's phone rang and Vera's name came up on the screen.

'I'm sorry, I must take this.' She turned away slightly. 'Hi Vera, how's Robert?'

'He's just opened his eyes and wants a cup of tea.'

Jayne beamed. 'That's so like him.'

'Harry is here too, he's brought us luck.'

'I'm just finishing up with the client now. I'll come to the hospital in thirty minutes.' A short pause where she remembered to be grateful for everything in her life. 'That's great news, Vera. It's been a good day.'

CHAPTER FORTY-EIGHT

February 25, 1904
Perth, Australia

Annie felt tired. The interview with the young newspaperman had taken more out of her than she thought. He was so young, that journalist.

They were all so young.

She looked around her bedroom. The rich drapes, sumptuous fabrics, soft velvets and shimmering silks, all bought with the money made from the Elixir.

She had repeated the story to the young journalist that she had told so many times over the years: her arrival in Perth as a free migrant, the death of her husband on the ship, bringing up two children, and the foundation of the Emporium.

None of it true, of course, but she had told it so often she had almost begun to believe it was what had happened. Still, she had to keep up the facade of respectability; the family of her granddaughter's husband expected it. After all, one of their ancestors had been a governor of New South Wales.

She smiled to herself.

Little did they know that he was the man who had actually signed her Certificate of Freedom all those years ago. So they were related, but in a very roundabout way.

She raised herself slowly from the armchair. Her bones hurt more and more these days, even the slightest effort left her out of breath. She would take a bottle of the Elixir tomorrow morning, but it wasn't the same any more. They skimped on the ingredients and the time spent boiling the bones.

As her grandson said, 'Two hours is enough, Grandma. If we boil them for twelve as you are suggesting, we will produce far less of the Elixir and our profit margins will decrease.'

Profit margins! That's all the young people talked about. As if medicine was about making money.

'Make a good product that works and people will buy it,' she said out loud to nobody.

But nobody listened to her any more. All they cared about was their new-fangled marketing ideas and better ways to distribute goods to the small setttlements and towns of Western Australia.

'Pah, just make a good product. I keep telling them, but nobody listens.'

She took one step towards her bureau and stopped, swaying slightly. Ever since the old queen had died, Annie had lost all her energy. It was as if the death of Victoria – a woman who had ruled over them for so many years, building a great empire that stretched out from that small country off the coast of Europe across Asia and the Far East, reaching all the way to Perth, Sydney, and even down to Auckland – had closed a chapter on her life.

She hardly remembered Ireland any more. A few hazy details of her father and mother, bless their souls, and a small town of just two streets dominated by an English landlord and English laws.

What had happened to Honorah?

Not her daughter, but the woman she had met all those years ago in Grangegorman. So full of life and energy. Annie hoped she had lived a good life, getting out of the slums.

She took a few more steps forward, finally grasping the bureau and using it to steady herself.

She knew she didn't have long left to live. The doctors lied to her, telling her how fit and well she was.

But she knew the truth. She knew she didn't have long left in this world.

It would soon be time to meet Daniel again.

She reached forward and opened the top drawer of the bureau, taking out the bible and the penny he had given to her.

She opened the front page of the book, seeing his handwriting with the names of her children written in his beautiful copperplate script. Beneath them she had written the names of Dominic's children herself, in her more functional hand.

She would give the bible to Dominic; he should continue the tradition of writing the names of the family members in it as they were born.

He wouldn't enjoy doing it, though. He never talked about the past or their father.

She remembered the morning after Daniel's friend had appeared at the convent with the letter. She had explained to them that their father was going away.

'Will we ever see him again?' Dominic had asked.

'I'm not sure. I don't know,' she had answered.

He had nodded, collected his schoolbooks and walked out of the door to join his classes. From that day to this, he had never mentioned his father once.

Annie felt he almost believed that their father had died on the ship they took to come to Perth. He had told the story so many times, it had become his truth.

Even when she found out about Daniel's death in the Dublin Workhouse in 1864, Dominic had barely listened, simply saying, 'He died?' Then he'd shrugged his shoulders and carried on reading his book.

She picked up the penny. The old king's head was still there, his cheeks polished by Daniel's thumb. Memories of her husband flooded back to her.

The curl of ginger hair that sat just above his left eye.

The beauty of his hands and the way they held a pen.

The softness of his voice as he spoke Irish with a man who'd just come off the boat from Dublin.

The passion with which he loved her and Ireland, the two women who conquered his heart.

She grasped the coin tighter in her small, wrinkled fist as the memories flooded back, becoming stronger with every second.

She didn't regret staying in Australia. On the contrary, it had been the right choice for her and their family.

It was just a shame that Daniel could not love the country, or her, as much as he loved Ireland.

She had lost the love of her life to another woman.

One with green hair and a gold, green and white tri-colour draped across her shoulders.

A solitary tear escaped from Annie's eyes. She put the bible and the penny back in their place in the top drawer of the bureau, shuffling back to her armchair in her bedroom.

She hadn't long to go, she was sure.

Then it would be time to meet Daniel again.

CHAPTER FORTY-NINE

Monday, October 12, 2020
Perth, Australia

Jayne placed both her pieces of hand baggage carefully in the overhead locker of the plane. Next to her, Vera was already tucking Robert into his business-class seat.

'It's going to be a long flight home, Vera, do you want anything from the bag?'

'Thank you, Jayne, I have all I need.' She held up two needles, a large ball of yellow wool and a half-finished child's sweater. 'I'll be able to finish a lot of this on the flight.'

Jayne sat down next to her and looked out of the window. The flat landscape of Western Australia stretched out into the distance. The stewardess from Singapore Airlines came round to check their seat belts were firmly fastened.

'We'll be taking off soon,' said Jayne, glancing up at the locker above her head.

'I hope Harry drives home safely.'

Harry Duckworth had taken them to the airport that morning, promising to visit his half-sister in England the following year. 'I'm looking forward to going to Pendle Hill again. You'll need to go up with me, Robert.'

'I think my days of climbing the hill are over. But I'll watch you do it from the bottom, a pint in my hand.'

After giving them the scare with his heart attack, Robert had been ordered to take life easy by the doctors. A stent had been placed in one of his arteries during a coronary angioplasty and he had finally been cleared to fly by the cardiologist.

Since then he had been looked after by Vera, mothered so much he was actually complaining about it.

'Don't fuss so, Vera, you'll have me ill again with all your mithering.'

'That's a horrid thing to say, Robert Cartwright, after what happened.'

Robert looked apologetic but it didn't stop his complaining.

Vera had arranged for a golf buggy to take him to the plane so he wouldn't have to walk through the airport.

'I'm not an invalid. Thousands of people have had heart attacks and thousands will in the future.'

'You are going to sit in that buggy and be looked after, not straining yourself walking through a crowded airport. And if you don't, I'm not going back with you to England. Understand?'

He understood.

But as with many people who'd had heart attacks, he

was slowly coming to terms with the new reality of his condition.

Despite everything that was happening in England, he announced one day that he wanted to go back.

'I'm missing home. It's time to go back.'

'But the situation is not looking great, Robert. A couple of weeks ago Boris Johnson announced that the UK was at a critical moment and he wouldn't hesitate to impose further restrictions.'

'I still want to go back, Jayne. After the heart attack, I want to see Lancashire again.'

So they had booked the flights and were about to leave.

'Did you see Duncan before you left?' asked Vera from her seat across the aisle.

'Just for a few minutes. He is now handling Liz's family history, with Ronald doing the legwork in England and Ireland. Last week, Ronald found Daniel Sheehan's grave in Glasnevin cemetery in Dublin.'

'Really? That's amazing.'

'What is even better was the inscription on the tombstone. It said "This memorial is dedicated to a true patriot of Ireland, Daniel Sheehan (1808 to 1864) from his loving wife, Anne Sheehan, nee Kelly. Love is an affliction no herb can heal."'

'The last part is beautiful.' Vera glanced across at Robert. 'I know exactly how she felt.'

Jayne reached out and held her hand.

'Don't you miss not finishing your research for your client?'

'Not really. I solved the answer to the two questions that Liz asked me. We found out where Annie Kelly came from and who had written the letter. Duncan and Ronald can find out the rest if Liz wants to know.' She thought for a moment. 'I also realised that I can be so obsessed with my work, I forget to be grateful for the people in my life, like you and Robert. I want to spend more time with the both of you. So if they announce another lockdown, why don't you come to live with me instead of staying at the Residential Home? I'd love to have you.'

Vera glanced across at Robert, who was trying to work out the controls on his seat. 'Even Mr Grumpy over there?'

'Even Mr Grumpy.'

'Well, we'd be delighted to come and stay. It's a worry for me going back into the Home during another lockdown. After the operation, he's still vulnerable.'

'We can both look after him, can't we?'

'Whether he wants us to or not.'

They both laughed as the engine sound grew louder and the plane rolled forward. Over the tannoy, the captain announced, 'Cabin crew, prepare for take-off.'

Robert turned to them and said, 'What's so funny? I can't work out the controls of the television.'

They both laughed again, louder this time.

He turned back in his seat and said grumpily, 'Women. Can't live with 'em and can't live without 'em.'

Jayne and Vera stopped laughing and looked at each other for a moment, before collapsing with laughter yet again.

It was good to be going home.

HISTORICAL NOTE

Between 1788 and 1868, about 162,000 convicts were transported from Great Britain and Ireland to various penal colonies in Australia.

In 1787, the First Fleet of eleven convict ships set sail for Botany Bay, arriving on 20 January 1788 to found Sydney, New South Wales, the first European settlement on the continent. Other penal colonies were later established in Van Diemen's Land (Tasmania) in 1803 and Queensland in 1824. Western Australia – established as Swan River Colony in 1829 – initially was intended solely for free settlers, but commenced receiving convicts in 1850. South Australia and Victoria, established in 1836 and 1850 respectively, officially remained free colonies.

Obviously, Annie and Daniel's story is fictional but I have drawn on contemporary sources and genealogical documents to give background to their lives. For genealogists, most of the usual Census documents do not exist as many were destroyed by fire. However, census substitutes, particularly muster roles, are still available for research.

As befitting the bureaucratic nature of the convict system, records are very good and readily available at State libraries and online. As described in the novel, the records go into remarkable detail of the physical description of each and every convict, male or female. This was for one simple reason - if they ran away, they had to be readily identified and returned to their Masters or sent to gaol.

Such documents are a god-send for anybody looking for convict ancestors.

Between 1791 and 1867 about 40,000 Irish convicts were sent to the Australian colonies. Roughly a quarter of them were women. The bulk of those transported had been convicted of larceny. Less common offences were forgery, embezzlement, fraud, highway robbery, assault, housebreaking and arson. About 600 of the transported convicts were political prisoners mainly involved in, but not limited to , the Irish uprisings again British colonial rule of the island in the nineteenth century.

The convicts were usually transported for seven or fourteen years, or for life. Serious crimes, such as rape and murder, became transportable offences in the 1830s, but since they were also punishable by death, comparatively few convicts were transported for such crimes.

Life was harsh and draconian. On arrival in Australian, convicts were assigned to a Master (or Mistress) who effectively wielded the power of life or death over them. The only escape was to run away or to obtain a ticket of leave which allowed convicts to work for themselves provided that they remained in a specified area, reported regularly to local authorities and attended divine worship every Sunday.

A certificate of freedom was issued at the completion of a convict's sentence, as proof he/she was a free person. Often, as in Annie's case, these certificates were conditional, allowing freedom in the colony but banning any return to the United Kingdom.

Some convicts, particularly political prisoners, did escape from the colony. The best known example is Thomas Meagher, who went on to lead a brigade of Irishmen fighting on the Union side in the American Civil War.

Once emancipated, most ex-convicts stayed in Australia and joined the free settlers, with some rising to prominent positions in Australian society. However, convictism carried a social stigma and, for some later Australians, being of convict descent instilled a sense of shame and cultural cringe.

Attitudes to the Irish in Australia were no less problematic. The Irish in the country were negatively stereotyped both explicitly and implicitly in the 19th and early 20th century.

Sir Edward Scott, professor of history at the University of Melbourne from 1913 to 1936, described Irish prisoners transported in the wake of the United Irishmen rebellion as 'rebels of life-long disposition, bitter enemies of …authority.' Scott made no attempt to understand the causes of Irish disaffection, merely portraying them as an 'innately turbulent and seditious people' whose 'restless and diabolical spirit had to be stamped out by vigorously exemplary means', that is, Scott wrote by 'the cat and the gallows.'

Attitudes became more accepting as the 20th century developed and people of Convict or Irish descent rose to positions of power and authority in Australian society. It is now considered by many Australians to be a cause for celebration to discover a convict in one's lineage. Almost 20% of modern Australians, in addition to 2 million Britons, have some convict ancestry.

St Patrick's Day on March 17th has become a celebration of not only Irishness but also what it means to be Irish in Australia.

The last word should be left to Paul Keating, former Australian Prime Minister whose maternal grandfather, Fred Chapman, was the son of two convicts, John Chapman and Sarah Gallagher, both of whom had been transported for theft in the 1830s.

'Australia without the Irish would be unthinkable… unimaginable…unspeakable.'

AUTHOR'S NOTE

If you enjoyed reading this Jayne Sinclair Genealogical Mystery, please consider leaving a short review on Amazon. It will help other readers know how much you enjoyed the book.

If you would like to get in touch, I can be reached at www.writermjlee.com. I look forward to hearing from you.

OTHER BOOKS IN THE JAYNE SINCLAIR SERIES:

The Irish Inheritance

When an adopted American businessman who is dying of cancer asks her to investigate his background, it opens up a world of intrigue and forgotten secrets for Jayne Sinclair, genealogical investigator.

She only has two clues: a book and an old photograph. Can she find out the truth before her client dies?

The Somme Legacy

Who is the real heir to the Lappiter millions? This is the problem facing genealogical investigator Jayne Sinclair.

Her quest leads to a secret that has been buried in the trenches of World War One for over a hundred years — and a race against time to discover the truth of the Somme Legacy.

The American Candidate

Jayne Sinclair, genealogical investigator, is tasked to research the family history of a potential candidate for the Presidency of the United States of America. A man whose grandfather had emigrated to the country seventy years before.

When the politician who commissioned the genealogical research is shot dead in front of her, Jayne is forced to flee for her life. Why was he killed? And who is trying to stop the details of the American Candidate's family past from being revealed?

The Vanished Child

What would you do if you discovered you had a brother you never knew existed?

On her deathbed, Freda Duckworth confesses to giving birth to an illegitimate child in 1944 and placing him in a children's home. Seven years later she returned for him, but he had vanished. What happened to the child? Why did he disappear? Where did he go?

Jayne Sinclair, genealogical investigator, is faced with lies, secrets and one of the most shameful episodes in recent history as she attempts to uncover the truth.

Can she find the Vanished Child?

The Silent Christmas

In a time of war, they discovered peace.

When David Wright finds a label, a silver button and a lump of old leather in a chest in the attic, it opens up a window on to the true joy of Christmas.

Jayne Sinclair, genealogical investigator, has just a few days to unravel the mystery and discover the truth of what happened on December 25, 1914.

Why did her client's great-grandfather keep these objects hidden for so long? What did they mean to him? And will they help bring the joy of Christmas to a young boy stuck in hospital?

The Sinclair Betrayal

In the middle of a war, the first casualty is truth.

Jayne Sinclair is back and this time she's investigating her own family history.

For years, Jayne has avoided researching the past of her own family.

There are just too many secrets she would prefer to stay hidden. Then she is forced to face up to the biggest secret of all: her father is still alive. Even worse, he is in prison for the cold-blooded killing of an old civil servant. A killing supposedly motivated by the betrayal and death of his mother decades before.

>Was he guilty or innocent?
>Was her grandmother really a spy?
>And who betrayed her to the Germans?

Jayne uses all her genealogical and police skills to investigate the world of the SOE and of secrets hidden in the dark days of World War Two.

A world that leads her into a battle with herself, her conscience and her own family.

The Merchant's Daughter

After a DNA test, Rachel Marlowe, an actress from an aristocratic family, learns she has an African ancestor.

She has always been told her family had been in England since 1066, the time of William the Conqueror, and they have a family tree showing an unbroken line of male descendants.

Unable to discover the truth herself, she turns to Jayne Sinclair to research her past.

Which one of her forebears is Rachel's African ancestor? And who is desperate to stop Jayne Sinclair uncovering the truth?

Jayne digs deep into the secrets of the family, buried in the slave trade and the great sugar estates of the Caribbean.

Can she discover the truth hidden in time?

The Christmas Carol

When an antique dealer asks Jayne Sinclair, genealogical investigator, to discover the provenance of a first edition of Charles Dickens', A Christmas Carol, she is faced with one of the most difficult challenges of her career.

How does she find the family of the mysterious man in the hand-written dedication, when all she has is a name, a place, Victorian Manchester, and a date, December 19, 1843?

She has just three days to uncover the truth before the auction. Even worse, she faces spending her own Christmas alone; her family having decided to visit relatives in Scotland.

Jayne is in a race against time to find the family of the man and the reason why Dickens wrote the dedication. Even more, she has to dig deep within herself to find the true joy of Christmas. A secret discovered by Charles Dickens many years ago.

Can she find the truth behind a Christmas past to deliver a Christmas present?

The Missing Father

Alice Taylor was adopted in 1942 when she was three years old. Her adoptive parents never told her about her birth family and even changed her Christian name. Now, seventy-seven years later, she wants to know the truth.

Who were her birth parents?

How did her mother die?

What happened to her missing father?

Jayne Sinclair, genealogical investigator, has just a few days to discover the truth before she goes for a well-earned break in Australia.

Can she discover the truth hidden in the chaos of the war?

Printed in Great Britain
by Amazon